CW00932928

A STRIKE PAST TIME

A Censored Time Novel

Corinne Arrowood

Copyright © 2021 Corinne Arrowood All rights reserved.

No part of this publication may be reproduced, stored or transmitted in any form or by any means, electronic, mechanical, photocopying, recording, scanning, or otherwise without written permission from the publisher. It is illegal to copy this book, post it to a website, or distribute it by any other means without permission.

This is a work of fiction. Names, characters, places, and incidents, either are the product of the author's imagination or are used fictitiously. Any resemblance to actual persons, living or dead, events, or locales, is entirely coincidental.

First Paperback Edition, 2021

Published by Corinne Arrowood
United States of America
www.corinnearrowood.com

ISBN: 978-1-7368189-9-2 (paperback)
ISBN: 978-1-7368189-8-5 (ebook)
ISBN: 979-8-9851087-0-5 (Hardcover)

Cover and Interior Design by Gene Mollica Studio, LLC

Contents

MY GIRL

Michael's heart thumped hard with excitement, like a kid waiting for Christmas morning. "Relax and breathe, Rainie. You know what to do." His gaze shifted to her ice-blue eyes. Her pupils, already big as saucers, were always one of her tell-tale signs of excitement. The sight before him quickened his pulse. "You're not breathing, my love." His voice was gentle.

There was no controlling the trembling, hard as she tried. The room, once dim, was now blindingly bright, like a floodlight-illuminated ball field.

"For the love of God, Michael, enjoy, but I don't need a blow-by-blow, you know how I am. You forget you got the good end of this deal. It's your favorite view," she said wryly. He blushed, and he knew she saw it. "Blushing Michael, unusual for you."

"If you could only see what I see." His breathing started to quicken; the excitement was almost unbearable. "Oh my God, it's time you give it all you got." His voice quivered as the sweat beaded on his brow and upper lip.

"Jesus, the pressure is insane." He knew she had performed as well as she could with all that she had to give. The moment had come. "Ah! Ah! Oh, sweet Jesus!" Everything tightened with great force, but the release was divine. Michael's eyes filled with tears. It was the most glorious experience he had ever had.

"Michael, you need to breathe."

"I am." He took her in his arms. He beamed, a look of love on his face. "Michaela, time to meet Mommy. She's beautiful, Rainie. Oh my God, she's beautiful. So perfect." He put their baby girl on Rainie's chest. "We did it, Rai. Isn't she the most beautiful—"

"Now, you need to breathe, Michael." Tears trailed down the sides of Rainie's face. "Oh, my sweet girl." Rainie gently ran her fingers along the baby's back. It was still sticky, and she had bits of light film on her skin, but she seemed peaceful. Thankfully she wasn't the squalling ball of energy Thomas had been. Henry, while quieter, had still twitched and moved when he'd been put on her chest. Michaela was calm, content being skin-to-skin with Rainie. The moment was tender. She could have laid there with Michaela forever, but it was time for the nurse to take her.

"I won't have her long, I promise." The nurse smiled.

Michael kissed Rainie over and over. He dutifully followed the nurse, observing as she put the baby in the incubator and began to gently swab her mouth and suction her nose. He marveled at the tiny hands and fingers, complete with the smallest of fingernails. He looked over at Rainie. "I ask you; how can anyone not believe in God? One look at this baby, and wow. It wasn't just two cells merging and dividing; God was right there at the point of conception."

While it may have seemed an eternity to the awaiting grandparents, the whole birthing experience was maybe four hours from admitting to sutures. Along with the nurse, Michael rolled the baby out so the family could have a quick peek and photo before taking her into the nursery to get washed, weighed, and an overall check from head to toe. He stood next to his dad and John as the three marveled over the tiny princess. Rainie's and Michael's moms were watching Rainie's two boys as they observed their new sister. Both boys, while usually rowdy, were quiet. They didn't miss a thing.

"Mike, how's Rainie?" Her dad, while excited, held apprehension in his eyes.

"Your girl is outstanding, absolutely amazing. Even though I've seen my fair share of babies being born, it's a different ballgame when it's your own." Michael's eyes misted as he swallowed hard. It was hard to hold back the tears; the experience made his heart bound. The whole thing was surreal and felt like a dream, like an out-of-body experience. "You'll be able to see her very soon. I know she wants to freshen up before seeing everyone, but she knows you're anxious."

The family went to the nursery viewing window when the nurse rolled the baby away.

Thomas looked at Henry. "I'm gonna call her Mickey. Michaela Lorraine is a long name for such a little baby."

Henry scrunched his forehead in disapproval. "What, like Mickey Mouse? No way! I'm gonna call her McKay, maybe." Faces pressed against the window produced small patches of fog, waxing and waning with their excited breaths. Henry watched as the nurse moved his tiny sister like a doll or a stuffed toy. Not gently, like when they held Auntie M's twins. He scowled at her. Looking back at his grandmothers, he said, "Mimi, MaMiss, what are they doing to her? You have to be careful with babies, and they're not being careful." Both boys carefully scrutinized the actions of the nurse.

"Not to worry, Henry, these gals have been taking care of babies a long time and know exactly what they're doing." Missy moved close behind him, resting her hands on his shoulders. "I can tell you're gonna be a great big brother. They're getting her ready for all of us to admire."

The nurses swaddled Michaela up and put a pink cap on her head. They put her back in the cart, all bundled up, and pushed the cart up close to the window so everyone could gaze at the new little miracle. The boys pressed their faces on the window again. Their silence spoke to their awe over their baby sister.

Michaela was perfect, weighing in at eight pounds, one ounce, and twenty-two inches long. Her face was pastel pink, and her tiny lips ruby red.

The whole revolting situation with Rainie's ex, Tom, the murder, and then Rainie being kidnapped, man-handled, and nearly killed, Michael had worried about the consequences, and had had concerns for Rainie, the pregnancy, and the baby. Both she and the doctor had tried to ease his apprehension, but now seeing his beautiful, healthy bundle of love and happy wife for himself, all was right in the world.

Word came out that Rainie was ready for company. The rush to the door was like a tidal wave coming ashore. Michael went in with the group, stayed long enough to know she was back in control, then left to go home to pick up a few things, grab a quick bite, and shower. It had been a whirlwind, and the impact of the birth had not settled in by a long shot. The first contractions had begun close to midnight and had lasted throughout the night, so neither of them had gotten an ounce of sleep. It wasn't until well after lunch the next day, when her contractions had picked up speed and intensity, that Rainie and Michael had left for the hospital. Her parents were soon to follow, as were his, and then Allie, the nanny for Rainie's two boys, brought them when it was near go-time, and now Michaela had made her entrance.

⁊\⁊

As Michael pulled into the driveway, he could see the dog's, Bonnie and Clyde, nose fog on the back windowpanes. They had known something was up the night before and stayed glued to Rainie's side, prancing around tediously, unable to remain still. Wherever she went, they were right there.

"Stella, I'm home," Michael sang out. The words had become a ritual when he or Rainie walked into the house by themselves.

It didn't feel like home to him. His heart sunk into his gut. Usually, there was a plethora of noise; the current silence was deafening. Once in their bedroom, he checked himself out in the mirror. He looked rough, beat, and exhausted. He couldn't even fathom how Rainie felt. She had been right; he had gotten the good end of the deal. Pushing an eight-pound person out of one's body was hard to digest, but he had seen it all. He had watched as the top of Michaela's head crowned, her shoulders manipulated out, and then the rest with that final push. He sat on the bed and looked at her nightstand with a picture of him and Rainie, which stirred his memory.

Thinking back to the weekend they thought Michaela had been conceived, a wry smile formed on his face. He remembered how Rainie had pulled a surprise dominatrix role on him. He laughed to himself. While he had dabbled in the lifestyle for a short time in his life, he loved the way they played. It wasn't the punishing and disciplined days of his past, when he'd needed someone to take charge of his pent-up heartache. Theirs was a mere adventure, with the woman he truly wanted and needed. The club had been perfect for extracting the rage out of him, but he was master of Pandora, the private den of delight in their French Quarter carriage house, unless on a whim Rainie chose the lead role. The few women he'd invited to Pandora in his dark past were the kind that demanded a heavy hand, and the more controlling he was, the greater the pleasure, but it was purely physical. On the other hand, Rainie had taken lovemaking to a deeper and much higher level, one charged with love and undying passion. Her ravenous sexual appetite was toe-curling, and just the thought of her made his fire burn.

They flip-flopped between the dominant and submissive roles as an addition to their boudoir fun, but it was only on the rare occasion. That particular evening, Rainie had worn a black leather bustier with zippered panels. He remembered how she'd made him unzip the panels that exposed her perfectly round breasts, but she hadn't let him touch her at first, only look and build his desire. Her leather mini hit right below her ass, so when she'd ordered him to his knees, everything under her skirt was but a peek. She'd stood over him in high-heeled black boots that had the look of fuck-me-hard, but she'd been in control, and he'd been at her mercy for the night. She'd even gone as far as to wear a mask that covered the top part of her face, leaving her full red lips exposed to tantalize him. The more he thought about that night, the harder his cock got. He could feel the race of his pulse from the base, up the shaft, to the very tip.

He pushed the image from his mind and jumped in the shower. Time was of the essence, and he desperately wanted to get back to his two girls. Thoughts of playtimes were better suited for a more appropriate occasion. The spray of water on his body sent his blood coursing, and with it, brought renewed energy with thoughts of his wife and daughter. The shower was brief. He looked in the mirror and had to admit he looked a hundred percent better. "Michaela Landry. Thank you, God, for such a perfect little girl and a most amazing wife." The words stuck in his throat with an overwhelming feeling of thankfulness and the need to swallow the balled-up emotion. Padding around the bedroom, he grabbed his phone and called Rainie.

"It's me," he said into the phone.

"Yes, I know Michael. Who else would it be?" She paused, waiting for him to say why he'd called. She could be ever so feisty and thick with sarcasm.

"Everything still okay there? Need me to bring you anything?"

"My love," she instructed, "you need to get a grip. Women have babies all the time. I'm fine, and Michaela is as well. The whole family is loving on her. Take your time, and don't forget to grab your bag. Allie will be with the boys."

"You are making everyone put masks on? And remember, no kissing on her face, only feet."

"Pour yourself a glass of wine. Relax. No one is wearing masks, and Michaela is getting plenty of love. Breathe, please. If I saw you right now, I wouldn't have guessed you were a doctor, let alone a surgeon. Too bad I can't be with you to settle your nerves. What was it you told me the first time your parents came to our house? Hm. Remember?" Her voice drifted as if in thought.

"I'll be there soon. I love you." He quickly hung up. There it was again, hard as a rock and throbbing. Back in the shower he went. He let his mind go back to that night in Pandora, before his parents had come to town to see the new house. He had her restrained and could clearly remember the vision of her full-frontal view, her hard little pearl begging for a kiss. It wasn't the roughest sex they'd had, but with the scarf covering her eyes, Rainie had become unglued. He gripped himself tightly. Her lips had been like soft butter, and his cock like a hot knife. Just the memory made a heat wave pulse through his body, and he exploded like a young boy jacking off for the first time. He sat on the bench and let the water beat down on him.

Getting out of the shower, he quickly dressed, grabbed everything he needed, and bolted to the car. What the hell is wrong with me? My wife is recovering from birthing my daughter, and my fine how-do-you-do is bopping my baloney. Fine dad I am. Dang Rainie, she knew what she was doing. Shit.

By the time he arrived at the hospital, the calamity of visitors was over, Allie had taken the boys, and it was only Rainie, Michaela, and the grandparents. Dropping his bag, he went to the bed, kissed Rainie, and kissed the top of the baby's cap. Rainie gave him a smirk with laughter behind her eyes. He kissed her on the lips again with a huge smile. "You did that on purpose." She laughed with a sharp tone at his comment.

"Maybe," she whispered back seductively.

"Michael," his mom said, waiting for a hug from him, "Michaela is the calmest baby I think I've ever seen. She's content in anyone's arms" She patted his face, "Darling, you look so much better. I have to say you were looking a bit rough, like you had given birth." To think of it, he had looked pretty bad. When he had checked his reflection back at the house, his face was red and eyes puffy, whereas Rainie, through all the sweating, breathing, and pushing, seemed to glow.

Jack stood and gave Michael one of his bear hugs. "Mike, we're gonna have our work cut out for us. She's a beauty with your hair and, dollars to donuts, her momma's eyes. Son, she's gonna be one beautiful girl." Her mom and dad kissed Rainie goodbye, and the grands all left together.

Edging on the bed, Michael asked, "How are you feeling?" He kissed them both again.

"Sore, but not too bad. The question is, how are you feeling?" She laughed with a quick outburst. "Michael, you needed to, as you have elegantly put it so many times, calm the fuck down. You were out of control. More relaxed now, I hope."

He gazed into her devilishly beautiful ice-blue eyes. "You're off-limits for what, six weeks? It's gonna be a long six weeks. What you deserve is a spanking and a good one at that. You realize it could've been most frustrating." He stroked her hair from her face.

"Michael, I know you well, and your mind can recall every minute detail. I had a feeling our shower was gonna get a spray of its own. You seem far more rational and relaxed now. My love, you were great in labor and delivery, but after Michaela entered the world, you went out of control. Head's up, she's gonna skin her knee, fall on the steps, stick something either up her nose or in her ear. You can't keep her in a bubble." Her eyes emanated love as she spoke to him. "I love you, Michael, for the crazy over-protective person you are. You always make me feel safe and secure, and she's gonna appreciate it one day, but Daddy, you got one rough road ahead of you if you don't stop and breathe." She exhaled with a laugh.

There was a knock on the door. "Delivery for Mrs. Landry."

"Come in," Rainie called out.

It was two delivery men. One had a giant teddy bear, and the other had an arrangement of at least two dozen, if not three dozen, perfectly pink roses. Michael and Rainie looked at each other in question, both shrugging. Michael got up to tip them and grab the card.

"Welcome to the world, Michaela Landry." It was signed M.

"M?" Rainie asked Michael. It had to be Mer, but she wouldn't have just put an M; it would've said Love, Auntie M and Paul. "If this is Mer's idea of funny, she's gonna hear about it. What the hell are we going to do with a six-foot teddy bear? That's the biggest dang bear I've ever seen."

There was another tap on the door; this time, Michael said, "Yes?"

Three nurses walked in with huge smiles. "Dr. and Mrs. Landry?" They nodded. "They weren't kidding. Sorry, y'all, but the buzz is there's a giant stuffed bear, and we had to see it." The nurses were all in their mid-twenties, dressed in nursery print scrubs. The giggles and bubbly ear-to-ear smiles showed how awestruck they were by the humongous cushy bear.

Rainie, in laughter, said to the nurses, "It's the biggest freakin' bear I've ever seen, and I think my dearest friend sent it. I'm gonna kill her. Who buys a six-foot bear? And what does one do with a six-foot bear?"

One of them snickered a response. "Girl, I don't know, but I hope y'all got a big car." They spent a few minutes feeling the softness of the stuffed animal, cooing over the baby, and taking selfies hugging the giant bear.

After things settled down, Rainie called Mer. "What the hell is wrong with you? Is this a joke? The flowers are gorgeous, but really, a six-foot teddy?"

"Rainie, are you okay?" She sounded concerned. "Sorry, but the twins have kept me busy to the point I haven't been able to order flowers yet. I'm coming to see the little princess before you leave the hospital tomorrow morning if these two aren't grouchy. Somebody else sent the flowers and a six-foot bear. What the hell you gonna do with that?"

"Shit, if not you, then who? It was signed M. If it were Missy, she would've mentioned it or waited until it arrived. I have no idea; if you think of anyone, let me know." Mer mentioned she had talked to Rainie's mom and had all the particulars on little Michaela.

Michael and Rainie questioned the mystery of the bear for the next thirty minutes. Michael insisted on holding the baby and not putting her down at all. He kept looking at her, then back at Rainie.

"Amazing, we came to the hospital as two people, and we'll leave as three. It's truly unbelievable when you stop and think of it." The baby lay on his chest, and with every word, he'd lightly kiss the top of her baby beanie. "Rai, she's perfect. I don't believe there's ever been a prettier baby." Rainie smiled and nodded her head, like, 'Okay, crazy man.' "It was love at first sight, a bit like how I fell in love with you. Stop and think about that one." He didn't take his eyes off Michaela.

"Put her in the bassinet, Michael, and come sit by me. I'm gonna have to nurse her in the next half hour, and I want time with you."

"As you wish." He put the baby down and sat on the edge of the bed. Just as he was going to say something, his phone rang. Looking harassed with a frown on his face, he answered, "Mike Landry."

The voice on the phone was one he'd heard only one other time, right after he'd rescued Rainie from Randy Tolbert, who he'd killed and left dead on the floor of a condemned fishing camp.

HELLO

"Dr. Landry, congratulations to you and Mrs. Landry on the birth of Michaela. I hope you received my gift for both baby and Mom. I will not keep you long as this is an extraordinary time for your family, but we need to talk. When will you return to work? Perhaps I could pick you up before office hours?" Michael was silent. "I wish you no harm, Dr. Landry. I need to arrange for your services."

"Day after tomorrow. I'll be there at eight; we open at nine. Is an hour enough time? I'm booked the rest of the day."

"An hour will be more than enough. Thursday at eight. Good evening and again, congratulations." The call ended. The accent was noticeable, but his English eloquent.

Michael's stomach knotted, and he could feel the apprehension as every muscle in his body tightened; his heart began wildly beating in fear, but he also felt the blood drain from his face with dread.

Rainie watched him. "Michael, are you okay? Who was that? What'd they want?" Her eyebrows drew close with concern. "Something's wrong. I can tell, so don't say nothing's wrong."

He could hear his own voice in an internal debate. To tell or not? How would he feel if the call came to Rainie, and she didn't tell? "It was a voice I've heard once before." A shiver ran up his body, like the biting cold wind on the streets of Manhattan during December. "The M on the card of our baby's giant bear was Mateo Moreno. It's only been, what, six hours since she was born, and he already knows Michaela's name? He wants to meet with me, but not in the office."

Rainie's soft, euphoric smile had transformed to a look of terror. Her jaw slightly dropped, the sweet upward curl of her lips was gone, her expression drastically changed, and as if in slow motion, she turned her head toward the bassinet. The silent tension created an icy feel to the room. "Why, Michael? Why does he want to meet with you?" Her voice started to take on a growl, like a momma bear with her young. "It's regarding Randy, right?"

He sat on the edge of her bed again and took her hands in his. "Nothing is going to happen to our family. Listen. He wants to utilize my services. Why and how, I have no clue. He assured me before anything that he wished us no harm. Whatever I need to do to keep our family safe, I'm prepared to do it."

Michael reflected on all the calls he'd received from Detective Marse after Tolbert's disappearance. Both Marse and the Jefferson Parish sheriff's investigative unit had tag-teamed him and Rainie with questions. She had handled it all well, and the calls had subsided. Maybe Marse called it off because of the progressing pregnancy. Who knew?

Rainie's demeanor changed decidedly, and she was all business with her normal ball-bustin' attitude. She stared into his eyes. "Michael, let him know this is the one and only time you'll help him, and then our debt will have been paid in full. And, I want to know everything, got it?"

He took her face in his hands. "All the way, I promise." He then planted his lips on her soft, succulent puckers. "I love your lips; they're perfectly plump and so wonderful to kiss."

"Read these plump lips, my friend; he better not threaten or insinuate anything regarding Michaela. He may be all big badass cartel man, but I'll rip his balls off with my bare hands if he so much as implies anything. Do you hear me, Michael?" He started to plant another kiss on her, but she turned her head, then looked back at him. "I mean it, Michael." She looked him dead in the eyes and calmly said, "It's that time, hand the little princess over to me. Believe it or not, I am breathing and have calmed my heart. The last thing I want is a colicky baby, and if she feels me or you, for that matter, fearful, angry, or upset when holding her, she'll pick up on it, and then we've got colic. No thank you."

It felt right for him to hold his baby girl. "Michaela, we have to let Mommy know. There will be no stress. Remind her I've got great stress-relieving skills." As he placed her in Rainie's arms, he kissed her forehead.

Nursing came naturally for Rainie with Michaela. Michael smiled, watching them. "What now, Dr. Feelgood? I can see your mind wandering," she taunted.

"Getting your beautiful perfect nipples toughened up for nursing has been my pleasure." He watched as she blushed. "I love that I still make you blush. I won't take a picture as that might be in poor taste, but you are even beautiful and sexy with a baby on your breast." He sat quietly on the edge of the bed and watched as warm flushes of joy fluttered in his stomach like a dance of two butterflies. Nothing was going to ruin the moment, not even a call from a cold-blooded murderer.

During the night, every time Rainie would wake to nurse, he'd wake. "Michael, you need to sleep. We go home tomorrow, and I'll need you at the top of your game. For the next couple of weeks, it's gonna be a zoo in our house trying to establish a routine. It would help if you stayed on your schedule, and the boys on theirs and Michaela and I will adjust. It'll all come together. It's not my first rodeo, cowboy." Her eyes glistened as she smiled at him.

Rainie's new ride, a black Lexus with three rows, was perfect for transporting Michaela home from the hospital. Proud brothers, Thomas and Henry, sat in the far back, peering over at their new baby sister. Michael watched the boys as they kept an eye on her every movement. "Guys, she doing okay back there?"

Two eager voices chimed, "Yes."

"Seems like all she does is sleep," Henry was quick to add.

Thomas guffawed, "Oh, no, she eats Mom's boobies and poops."

Rainie turned around. "Boobies? Eats my boobies? It's called nursing."

Thomas cocked his head, looking into Rainie's eyes. "Okay then,

Henry, she poops after she's nursing." He rolled his eyes, and both boys snickered. "Mom, did we poop gold?"

"What?"

"Her poop is gold, Mom. Like the goose that laid the golden egg or Rumpelstiltskin in Once Upon a Time. He turned straw into gold. Michaela poops gold." The two boys broke out in hysterical laughter.

"It's a color people refer to as baby poop brown when describing a certain brown color. And, yes, all babies, including you two!" Michael looked at Rainie, fighting back laughter.

"Michael, you better hold it in. All I need is you furthering this line of conversation."

Allie and the grandparents were all at the house when they arrived. The boys went straight into the yard. It was like a swarm of bees around a honey pot, everyone offering to carry the baby inside. In the long run, Jack won, and Michael was reduced to carrying bags and vases of flowers.

"What on earth is on the roof of your car?" Rainie's mom asked her.

"It's the biggest freakin' teddy bear in the world, I think. A client sent it along with the three dozen pink roses. A bit over the top, and I'm not sure where it'll go. We probably should've left it for the pediatric unit." Rainie sounded exhausted. "Dad, can you put it in my office for now?"

The moms helped Rainie upstairs while Jack brought the sleeping princess into their room. Rainie quickly swaddled the baby and put her in the cradle by their bed. "Starting this game off right. That's her bed; this is our bed. Dang, it's almost feeding time again." Jack excused himself posthaste.

It took a while, but everyone left, and it was just them, Allie, and the kids. The grands had fed, cleaned, and made enough food for the rest of the week. The novelty would soon wear off, and they would establish a routine. Michael kept thinking how good it was to sleep in their own bed. The hospital hide-a-bed had been miserably uncomfortable. The next morning came quickly, and the day passed in a fast blur. Thursday morning arrived with a 6 a.m. feeding and too many nerves for him to stay in bed.

"I don't want to go to work today. I want to stay and be with y'all." He almost pouted.

Watching Michael buckling his belt from the bed, Rainie said with determination, "It's Botox Thursday and meeting with the big M. Call me as soon as you're back in the office. Firstly, I want to know you're safe, but I also wanna know what he said. You can tell him what I said—I'll tear his balls off." She stood, placing the baby in the bassinette.

Michael finished his coif and turned to her. "I remember, and I have no plans of getting into any pissing contests. A Colombian cartel boss is no one to fuck around with, period, but someone as powerful as Mateo Moreno, I'm not even gonna joke in such a vein. I'm gonna listen and go from there." He pulled her close. Through their clothes, he could feel the heat from her breasts. He stood back, casting his eyes on her breasts. "Rai, they're so hot. Do you need ice packs or something? I think your milk is getting ready to come in. Jesus, they're huge." He gently opened her peignoir, unfastened the cups of her bra, and delicately ran his fingers over her engorged breasts. "Do I need to get you something? They're extremely warm to the touch, gotta be uncomfortable. Anything at all that I can do for you?" Her breasts were hard and more than warm.

Kiss me goodbye, drive carefully to work, and please give me Michaela. She's the only one who can help at this point. Unless you—"

As he handed her the baby, "Um, that's a big N-O." She had to laugh. His facial expression was hilarious. His eyes widened twice their size, and he looked like he'd just eaten a shit sandwich. His nose and lips puckered. He kissed both his ladies as he left. "Promise I'll call, no worries."

☜☞

Arriving at the office a little before eight, Michael couldn't help but notice the big black stretch limo parked in front. He slipped into his parking spot and walked to the limo. The driver got out and opened the door for him to get in. As soon as he was in, the car pulled off. Mateo was seated directly in front of him, back against the front seat.

He signaled the driver and a window glided closed, separating the driver from the back of the limousine.

"Dr. Landry, it is good to meet you in person. Sorry for the inconvenience, but I am an exceptionally cautious man. In my position, one needs to be. I will get right to the point. I need to alter my appearance." He handed Michael a picture. The picture was of an Anglo male with a high brow, slightly turned-up nose, fleshy cheeks without definition of cheekbones, roundish caramel-colored eyes, broad lips, and a less-defined jaw-line than Mateo had. Not a bad-looking man, but certainly nowhere near as handsome a man as Mateo. Michael knew his face revealed a perplexed look; he looked back and forth between the picture and Mateo. "Dr. Landry, sir, can you use your skills to create this man?" Mateo was a handsome man. He had beautiful dark skin with few lines, just those on his forehead and a few fine lines by his eyes. His hair was jet black with some slight silvering at the temples. He had extremely dark almond-shaped eyes, a perfectly straight nose, chiseled cheekbones, and a squared jawline—almost the polar opposite of the man in the picture.

Michael adjusted in the seat. "Yes, I can, but it can't be done in one surgery—maybe two, three. You're looking for a total transformation? This man has a light complexion, and yours is much darker. There are bleaching techniques to lighten skin, but you would have to do it over time. I can see you want to be unrecognizable. Does it have to be this man? I'm not sure you'll be happy with this face. I could do something equally as transformative, but maybe a look you might like better. But to answer your question. Can I do it? Certainly." Michael stretched his legs out. "What is your time frame? As I said, I will require multiple dates. I work out of—"

Mateo cut him off. "I will build a surgical suite to your specifications, bring on a full staff for my medical care and convalescence. I will build it on an island in the North Atlantic still owned by the French. I know you are fluent in French, as am I. You will have everything you need. Come and go between surgeries. Away from your family three days at a time. A day for travel, a day for the surgery, and then travel back home. I know what I ask is much."

"Do I have a choice in the matter?" Michael sat with his hands clasped in his lap.

"Absolutely. I had hoped our history together might create a better bond, but as you have a new baby, I can see where you might not want to leave home." Mateo's mannerisms were calm and gentle. When Michael thought of Latino men, the image he saw was usually wild, animated gesturing and louder voices. This man was anything but wild or loud. In fact, Mateo spoke in a clear, controlled tone—his words felt carefully chosen.

Michael explained, "I usually require a meeting with my psychiatrist to determine the stability and reason behind the request for altering one's appearance. I have to imagine this would be unacceptable in your case." Mateo nodded in confirmation. "I'll need some fast, straight answers from you to even consider your request." He nodded again. "What is it you're hoping to achieve by making these changes you're requesting? A better self-image, pleasing your partner? Or why? There are many reasons people want to alter something in their appearance. I ask because it is irreversible, like rhinoplasty but as opposed to breast augmentation, which is reversible. Your change would be permanent."

With a calm smile, Mateo responded, "The question is simple to answer, Dr. Landry. I want to stay alive. A hefty prize has been offered for my assassination by a rivaling adversary. They will stop at nothing until I am dead. They will kill my family, my wife, my children, my lover to flush me out in the open. The quicker I die, the better for all my loved ones. I do not want to die, but I can no longer live as Mateo Moreno. I need to be a, as you say, John Doe."

Michael stared at the man; eyes squinted with an expression as though he were trying to read Mateo's soul. "How can I be assured, Mr. Moreno, that, once the surgeries are complete, my life or the lives of my family won't be in jeopardy? I will know, as will the team you hire to assist me. That's a problem I can foresee. From what you have said, I imagine time is of the essence?"

Still, with complete composure, Mateo answered, "Yes. The only assurance you will have is my word. I have thought this through, and it is a matter of many lives and potential deaths. Once done, you will never hear from me again unless you so choose. There will not be any links to me. Only the initial surgical team could identify me if they were so inclined, but I doubt it to be the case. I can disappear, no problem, but if I do not die, everyone I love will."

"Are you a religious man, Mateo? Do you believe in God?" Michael looked him directly in the eyes, studying any slight shift indicative of dishonesty.

"Yes, yes I do. You are looking at me, thinking I am a bad man. I run a successful business. I am a businessman. Have I killed people? Yes, I have—people who have hurt my family, my friends, and ones that have tried to kill me—to kill for the sake of killing, no sir. That I have not done. I will pay you handsomely even though I know money is not your motivator. Your time away from your business and family is valuable. You will be well-compensated, and in cash; I am talking seven figures, Dr. Landry. I will call you tomorrow for your answer. If it is yes, I will need all your requirements for a complete surgery suite within twenty-four hours. The suite will be completed in no longer than four weeks, at which time I will send you everything you will need. Thank you for meeting with me. I will expect your answer tomorrow." Mateo put his hand out. Michael clasped it, locked eyes with him as though trying to get a clear read. Was he about to dance with the devil or prevent innocent deaths?

He ticked it over and over in his mind, but he already knew the answer. Even though Mateo was a brutally dangerous man and possessed a wealth of power, he saw a softness in his soul. This craziness was all born from the twisted law firm held on retainer by Mateo, then Tom, Rainie's ex linking to her and suspicions of her knowledge of the situation, and voila, here he was sitting across from the most notorious man in all of Colombia. He pondered Mateo's story and what kind of circumstances had led him to become the most powerful and feared man in Colombia.

☙❧

It was Botox Thursday, and like every Thursday, it ran without a hitch. Similar to the buzz in the office after the engagement and the wedding, the birth of Michael's daughter had everyone talking, wanting to see pictures, and sharing tons of oohs and ahhs.

Before the first round of patients, he called Rainie. "Gotta be quick, lots to tell tonight, but I feel okay about the whole thing. I didn't say yes until I could talk to you. I love you. How's my princess?"

"Oh, I see how it is. I'm chopped liver now that the princess is here." She sounded amused.

"Chopped liver, never! Every day, my wife, I love you more and more. Our princess is amazing, no denying, but so are our two boys. Rainie, we are blessed beyond words."

"Michael, you get so serious. I'm pulling your chain, and it looks like it worked. She's doing well and has taken to nursing like a hummingbird to nectar. Two hours pass too fast. I feel like I'm constantly feeding but can't beat the closeness—it's awesome. We'll talk tonight. I'm most intrigued and can't wait to hear. Love you, bye."

"Love you. Later."

Thursdays always seemed to fly by like a blur, and with this new situation simmering in the back of his mind, it flew by even faster. His mom had dinner on the table and was already feeding the boys by the time he got home. With Michaela in the crook of her arm, Rainie buzzed around, trying to help. The boys were adjusting to their new sister.

Michael briefly went over the meeting with Mateo. He told her he felt for the man and was prepared to commit his services if she was okay with it. Before he'd even told her, she already knew the answer just by the tone of his voice and his peace-filled heart.

WHAT'S NEXT

Four weeks flew by, and life got into a groove quickly. Rainie was like a sergeant major, and everything went by her timeline. The routine she had established throughout the years was in place, and Michaela would have to adjust. Since she had practical experience, Michael danced to her tune, even though he wanted to hold his baby girl more. "Michael, you're bonding with her beautifully, but if you hold her too much, the baby will develop arm-itis, and you'll create an attention-seeking individual, basically a whiny crybaby. She is content in her Mamaroo once she's fed and changed. Maybe it's all that 'Breathe, Rainie.'" She mimicked his voice as she took on a smooth, deep tone, then laughed. "As you relieved my stress, you made her content; consequently, we have one chillaxed baby!"

The doorbell rang. As promised, Michael received a special delivery. The instructions were precise. He was to be picked up from his house at five in the morning, taken to a private jet at the Lakefront Airport to a small airfield somewhere in Newfoundland, then via helicopter to a private island. His passport was for Francois Marchand from Quebec. His business was international finance, at least for the travel part. Included in the directions was a complete dossier, which he was to study during his flight. He had one day to re-arrange his schedule.

Michael went straight upstairs to their bedroom. Rainie was right on his heels. As planned, it had been a day shy of four weeks. He'd be in the office for Botox Thursday, jet out the next morning, before the crack of dawn, and be home Sunday evening in time for dinner. As he read the words over and over, his stomach churned and knotted. He could feel the burn and taste the bitterness of bile coming up the back of his throat. A cold sweat began to form on his skin, and his hands felt clammy.

Rainie took one look at him. "Okay, Michael, we haven't spoken one word of this since the meeting with him. Spill it, and I mean all of it."

"Rai, the less you know, the better." He ran his hand through his hair, looking down to the floor where he had dropped the dossier.

"Bullshit! We've been in it together since Marco's murder. We'll be in it together and see this through. I don't need specifics, like top secret crap, but I'd like to know when you're leaving and when to expect you back. What do I say if someone calls for you? It'll be my luck to have Marse show up. What do I say?" She faced him with squared shoulders, a set jaw, and eyes that punctuated withholding information was not an option.

"I've gone deep-sea fishing and can't be reached. I'll be back Sunday evening for dinner, but nobody's gonna be looking for me." She picked up the papers, kept eye contact with him, and placed them down on the bed.

"Lay back," she commanded.

"Not now, baby." He sounded weary to her.

"Lay back, Michael. Everything is gonna be alright. Now, lay back!" She demanded. He laid back on the bed and watched as she unfastened his belt, unzipped his trousers, and tugged his pants and boxers open. While his mind was consumed, things took a little longer, but in the long run, his body cooperated, and the pensiveness subsided.

She pulled away from him and placed his throbbing rod between her breasts as she pushed them inward, forming a tight crevice. He turned and pinned her on the bed, sliding his body up and down hers. "Your body is so hot. I can't hold back much longer. I want you, Rai." He started moving down her body, but she stopped him.

"Not yet, my love. Not yet. It's my turn for due diligence. Pretend we're in the stable. What'd that girl say? Oh yeah, baby, put one knee over my right shoulder and then the other—"

He kneeled as instructed. Rainie had never been one for much foreplay; she liked it raw and purposeful, pursuing the matter until the desired outcome. Each expulsion flashed like bolts of lightning from his loins. He rolled off of her onto his back. She tickled his stomach as her hand lightly traced the formation of his defined muscles. "Three more weeks to go?" he asked.

"Maybe sooner. Waiting for my first monthly reminder, and then we're good to go, but yes, doc appointment is three weeks exactly, and have I got plans for you!" She gave him a sinister laugh as her eyes took on a laser-like intensity.

He rolled on top of her again, holding both her hands over her head, "No, my beautiful wife, it is I who have plans for you, and it includes a few hours visiting Pandora." Shivers ran through his body as steamy memories lingered in his imagination. He was going to have her, and he'd make sure he was at the top of his game. He pressed his lips against hers with just the perfect pressure to explore her mouth, and then once the sizzle was on, he calmly eased back the passion, turning it to an amazingly tender moment. All those experiences growing up with the wild girls from River Road taught him how to deliver a clit-tingling kiss. He felt her body rock into him, entrapping his legs with her ankles, pulling him closer.

She let go of him, realizing her milk was all over, and her top was soaking wet. "Oops."

"Oops?" He took one look at her, "Yeah, I'd say oops. I think we both need a shower."

❧

Michael's crack-of-dawn ride arrived on time. He loped to the car with the gym bag in hand. The ride to the airport was silent. Thoughts randomly passed through his mind, and he questioned the wisdom of his decision. There was definitely something meaningful in the look of Mateo's eyes. The man cared and was scared for those he loved, to the point where he was giving up everything to protect them. If he were the horrible monster portrayed on the news or in articles, he wouldn't have cared who or what the collateral damage might be, but he cared and deeply. Michael knew the power Mateo wielded was great and that he was a brutal man when it came to his business dealings. He was sure the ramifications from screwing with Mateo's dealings involved torture and gruesome slayings at his command.

The thoughts of cartel business flashed him back to the lunacy in the abandoned fishing camp. Just the mere sound of Randy Tolbert smacking Rainie had brought him to act on instinct, and he hadn't thought twice about crushing the man's windpipe or shooting him point-blank. It was a matter of protecting his family, and nothing else had mattered. Yes, Rainie had initiated the situation by riding in the car with Marco, and it could be argued she'd naively walked into a cartel drug house. Still, she'd been so messed up at the time; incapable of making a prudent decision. She had turned her life around and being her knight in shining armor had won his way into her heart. His burning love for her had been ignited the first time he'd seen her at the frat house, and there was nothing he wouldn't do for her, his boys, and now his princess. While sophisticated to the eyes of the world and held in high esteem of many, he was at the core a most primal being.

The flight was long; Michael lounged back in the seat. A broad smile came across his face as he closed his eyes, remembering the beginning of their honeymoon, when they'd joined the mile-high club, fondly. Damn, his wife was sexy, and just the thought of her created a tingle in his body. He better start looking at the dossier again and taking on the persona of Francois Marchand. He rehearsed saying the name, getting it to roll easily off his tongue. It had to be second nature, and his loving character had to be replaced with an attitude of all-outta-give-a-fucks.

Private jets were a class unto themselves. One thing was for sure— Mateo had his plans smooth as silk, not a ripple or hiccup along the way. As they started the descent, Michael slugged back a three-finger pour of fine whiskey. With a quick prayer, he prepared himself for the endeavor ahead.

Waiting on the airfield was a helicopter, blades at the ready. Michael grabbed his bag and quickly boarded the copter. Once strapped in, they were up and out. The view was spectacular.

"Bon vol, Monsieur Marchand?" (Good flight, Mr. Marchand?) The pilot rendered a pensive smile.

"Oui." (Yes.) Michael kept his answers concise. While he would have loved to expound on the beauty of the view, Monsieur Marchand was aloof and a man of few words with a demeanor of arrogance. He could read the intimidation on the pilot's face. The rest of the journey was without conversation. Michael wondered if the entire episode would be with little dialogue. Obviously, there had to be free and direct speaking with those assisting in surgery. Was Marchand only for travel purposes, or was he claiming the name Docteur Marchand, or was there going to be another identity? He felt like Alice through the looking glass.

One thing about a whirlybird was it could land directly on a target. The pilot handled it with precision and, after landing, shouted out, "Au revoir" (Goodbye) as Michael climbed out.

Michael, as Monsieur Marchand, walked straight to the car, yielding, at best, a half-wave to the pilot at his back. Michael wanted to thank him and express his admiration for his precise landing, but he wasn't himself, so he continued with the aloof asshole persona.

The driver stood with the door open, closed the door as he got in the car, then took his bag to the trunk. No hello or fuck you. Indeed, there was an envelope on the seat. It contained an ID tag with a scan strip. All it said was Marchand.

The car sped along winding roads. In the distance, Michael saw a white, windowless building. He speculated it was somewhere around ten thousand square feet. The closer they got, the bigger it got. His speculation was way off. The driver got out of the car, collected his bag, and swiped his ID to unlock the door. He walked him through what seemed a maze of hallways. He stopped, told Michael to scan his card, and opened the door.

It was like a large hotel room. "Laisse ton sac. Il vous attend." (Leave your bag. He is waiting for you.)

Michael dropped his bag on the bed. Okay, he thought, he's waiting for me, and of course, he would follow the driver. "Bon." (Good.) The driver's ID said Noir. He was all in black, so his name was befitting. The man was every bit of six-feet-six, topping the scale at roughly 250, he speculated. His arms were nothing but muscle. Michael imagined he played double duty as a driver and bodyguard. If Michael were a betting man, he'd say Noir had a gun strapped somewhere—but he didn't see it. They entered the room. Mateo thanked the driver and sent him on his way.

Mateo put his hand out for Michael to shake. "C'est bon de te voir. J'espere que vos voyages ont ete satisfaisants." (It is good to see you. I trust your trip was to your satisfaction.)

"Parfait." (Perfect.) Michael's travel and everything thus far had been perfect. He noticed that Mateo's skin was noticeably lighter. "Beaucoup plus leger." (Very much lighter.) Michael took Mateo's, now known as William LaSalle, face in his hand. "Je voudrais voir la suite de chrurgie maintenant alors mange. Je suis faim." (I would like to see the surgery suite and eat. I am starving.)

Mateo led him out of the door, explaining that besides the surgery suite, there were ten bedrooms, twelve baths, two kitchens, a chef, a staffed dining area, and an indoor heated pool. He opened the door to the surgery suite. It was everything Michael had required and quite impressive. As he acquainted himself with the surgical suite, his stomach churned with excitement, and his pulse raced like a little boy getting his training wheels taken off his bike. It was exhilarating while scary as shit. He could feel the rush of fight or flight. But he totally dug the adrenalin high of living on the edge.

Everything was to perfection. Michael smiled at Mateo. "Parfait, monsieur." (Perfect, sir.) The light over the examination table was bright. Mateo's diligence with the skin treatment was evident, and it was time Michael explained the order of the procedures. The bone re-shaping— basically breaking bones and putting them back together along with some shaving—then adding bone material for grafting, would be first. The reconstruction was going to be intense, but with the intensity came a thrill. Blood coursed through his veins as his heart pumped like the drum in a marching band—a boy with a new toy. The healing of bone would take much longer than soft tissue work. Consequently, the cosmetic work would come sometime after reconstruction.

Mateo led the way to the dining room. They chatted the whole way. It had been a long time since Michael had spoken only French or any language other than English. While his mom had taught them, whatever the language, it was the only language spoken in the house unless his dad was home. He was most definitely fluent but had never had reason to learn surgical instruments and terminologies in French. Even though he'd memorized the names for all of the relevant surgical instruments and phrases, Michael wondered if he would slip into English under pressure, and then he'd be shit-out-of-luck, because the team was French. He suspected bilingual but couldn't count on it.

Mateo had spared no expense and the thought that he'd made it all come together in a matter of a four weeks was astounding. The dining room was lovely, like a quaint bed and breakfast on the east coast. Michael no longer felt on guard in the setting. His nerves were calm, and his stomach was growling from hunger and anticipation. As there was no warmth from natural light, Mateo's décor provided the feel. The two men talked about sporting events, global politics and even touched on religion. There was nothing regarding their families or their lives at home. Before sunrise the following day, they'd meet again, only this time for surgery.

☜☞

Emmanuel Lopez was a greedy, egotistical tyrant with a dark masochistic streak. He held a deep disdain, born from intense envy, for Mateo Moreno. It went far deeper than business; it was personal. His father had chosen to bring the poor cabana boy, Mateo, into the family business, bolstering him through the ranks, but had left Manny behind. Young Mateo had been a hard and faithful worker, never expecting anything in return, while Emmanuel was spoiled and whined about everything his father asked of him. His father, Alejandro Lopez, had run a tight organization with an army of loyal soldiers, and was one of the most powerful men in all of Colombia. Unfortunately, Emmanuel's flawed personality had significantly reduced the business in the five short years following his father's death.

Wiser and more astute, Mateo had kept a close eye and an ear to the ground regarding Manny. He'd learned the childish man had planned to assassinate Mateo, and thus he branched off, forming his own business. The once-loyal soldiers of Alejandro followed Mateo, a far more reasonable and savvier businessman. The embitterment ran deep, and Manny was obsessed with the desire to exact revenge. For years, Mateo had side-stepped Manny like a bothersome gnat. It wasn't until Manny had offered allegiance to a group of bandas criminales that Mateo saw where the older business ways were changing. While his organization was more into the drug trade, Mateo stayed away from human trafficking. It disgusted him. He'd quickly tired of the constant game of cat and mouse. He was always fighting to keep his family out of the line of fire, and it was becoming more and more difficult.

Mateo had orchestrated and staged his own assassination, and it was executed with precision and enough theatrics for perfection. He figured Manny would start a rumor that he'd been the mastermind behind the massive explosion. The truth was anyone with half a brain knew Manny didn't have the intellect or balls to organize the deed. Once all the pieces were in place, what appeared to be a sloppy miscalculation on Mateo's part was the finishing touch, completing his plan for retirement and beginning a fresh new start on life.

Mateo had his new identity and life. His wife, the grieving widow, could now formally join her lover of many years, his children had their own lives, and his lover, Marguerite, could return to the United States forever. In one fell swoop, he'd freed everyone that meant anything to him, and life would go on.

ᗣᗆ

It was a task Rick Marse procrastinated on completing because he thought it ridiculous and a waste of time, but it had been a few months since he had spoken to Doctor and Mrs. Landry. While he'd thought the case had been put to bed, an inquiry came down from the powers that be regarding the progress being made locating Randolph Tolbert or his remains. As far as Marse was concerned, they'd all gotten what they'd deserved. Grayson Smith and Randy Tolbert had murdered their partner Tom Todd and his young wife, Diane, so they could rot in hell as far as he was concerned. Somewhere inside, he felt sorry for the other partner in their business, Bob Thibeaux. When Marse had interviewed him, it had been crystal clear his crime was poor judgment. He should've kept his johnson off the playing field and at home solely with his wife.

The level of debauchery at Tolbert, Thibeaux, Smith, and Todd was hard to grasp. The worst thing the firm ever did was bring on Grayson Smith as a partner. With him came the Cartagena cartel and cash pay-offs. Tom Todd had merely been at the wrong place at the wrong time and had seen Grayson stashing cash from a pay-off, which had cost him his life and the life of Diane. The wrong place, wrong time mistake trickled down as Diane saw Tom stashing cash, and that mistake jumped to another when she forced his hand in marriage. Grayson was guilty of a plethora of sins, but there was no doubt he'd arranged the double homicide.

Why Randy Tolbert had kidnapped Rainie Landry was a question Marse asked himself over and over. Was it because she knew about all the hanky-panky, or was it that she knew about the cash involvement with the cartel? He could postulate all he wanted, but Rick doubted he would get the truthful reason for Tolbert's actions.

He rang the doorbell of the Landry's home. One of the boys answered the door, and he could hear Rainie telling him not to open the door. Babe in arms, she came to the front. "Hi Detective Marse, please come in." She turned to the boy. "Thomas, wait for me in your room."

"What a pretty baby. A girl, I see. What did y'all name her?"

"Michaela, but I know you didn't come to see the baby." Rainie wasn't about to mince words with him.

"It's lagniappe for me. I'm a sucker for babies; what can I say? I need to speak with Doctor Landry and figured he'd be home since it was Saturday." Rainie made no further move to ask him to stay and stood resolute.

"I'm sorry, he's not. Believe me, am I sorry." She nodded with affirmation and what looked to be aggravation.

"When do you expect him?" Marse politely asked with a crooked, cocky half-smile. He was amused and could see Rainie clearly was not.

Marse could see she was uncomfortable, but after a prolonged pause, she answered while fiddling with the baby's clothes, trying to avoid eye contact. "He's deep-sea fishing out in the Gulf." She looked up at him, and he saw the confidence return as she looked him directly in the eyes. "He'll be back for dinner Sunday." Marse could read that the fishing trip was a lie but also knew, sure as shit, Dr. Landry would be home Sunday evening.

"Sorry to disturb you. Congratulations, so it's two boys and a girl now? There's gonna be a lot of action in your house over the next few years, Mrs. Landry." Marse smiled. He genuinely liked her and her husband and knew beyond a shadow of a doubt that something had happened the day Rainie was abducted by Randy Tolbert. Doctor Landry was always composed and mild-mannered, but that day, Marse had heard a hardened edge. An edge that said he was not a man to be toyed with, especially when it came to his wife. Marse didn't blame him; God help the son-of-a-bitch who tried any funny business with his family. He knew how to dispose of a body so it would never be found, and evidently, so did Mike Landry.

❧

Michael met his team before going into surgery, explained his expectations, and made sure they were all on the same page. They gelled from the onset, which made him even more confident. Considering a good seventy percent of his practice was reconstruction, he knew he was perfectly capable of the surgery; perhaps the uneasiness had to do with the hush-hush on the down-low situation. But the interaction between him and Mateo had quelled any feelings of intimidation or trepidation regarding his safety and that of his family.

As he walked into the pre-op/recovery room, Mateo greeted him. "Bonjour, Docteur Marchand." He had established a good rapport with his patient from their two meetings; the meeting of proposition and then, when he'd arrived, toured and dined the previous evening.

Michael smiled, "Bonjour, monsieur. Nerveux?" (Hello, sir. Nervous?)

With a slightly sad but determined countenance, Mateo shook his head. "Non. Mon reflet dans le miroir me manquera." (I will miss my reflection in the mirror). He turned his palms up, like he was saying it is what it is. Michael understood. He'd miss his own reflection if it were to change. It was a thought that might follow him, and the accuracy of Mateo's statement rang true. It was indeed the reflection in a mirror or windowpane that exacted human identity—not spiritual, that was the soul, but most definitely human.

Michael marked Mateo's face with his pen, carefully studying to make certain he was 100 percent pleased with the map he'd created. He winked at Mateo and smiled. "Pas de soucis j'ai ce." (No worries, I have this.) It was easy for Michael to say no worries; he wasn't the one saying goodbye to his old self. There had to be grief, but the lengths a man would go for the safety of his family stretched beyond any measure. He, himself, was the proof in the pudding. "Veus un miroir pour un dernier regard?" (Want a mirror for a last look?)

Mateo shook his head no. "Merci."

Michael went to scrub in, and he could see the surgical team was making last adjustments—it all looked to be in order. His music was on, and the team bopped their heads to the beat. It met with approval. Even though masked, he could see smiles in their eyes. Two of the techs walked out as the anesthesiologist checked and rechecked his monitors, then they rolled Mateo into the suite. He was alert and wide-eyed in anticipation. Michael watched while he scrubbed as they transferred his patient to the table and started the sedation. Everything was ready when he made his entrance. One of the nurses gowned him. It was go-time.

☙

"Get a loada the tube," one of the younger detectives expounded. Marse looked up from his desk. He watched the same footage loop around and around. Anyone with a cell phone could record anything and everything at any time, and this was the result. A car passing had caught the destruction as it happened, and the full effects of the incident had gone viral and been snatched up by all the news networks. There had been a massive explosion on the Moreno compound; although it was not confirmed, the media insinuated Mateo Moreno, the most powerful man in Colombia, had been assassinated. Speculation about collateral damage could be as many as fifty other people.

"And we thought we had it bad here. There's not enough money in the world to pay me to work in Colombia. I doubt the head cartel guy got taken out; he's way too guarded, unless someone from his payroll did a turn-coat with another cartel. You never know who's true blue and who's a mole. It's all about the money and power." The young detective sat with his mouth agape.

Marse's mind drummed back to the symphony of thoughts swirling in his head.

Since the whole ordeal with Grayson Smith, the abduction of Rainie Landry, and the suspicious disappearance of Randy Tolbert, cartel discussions were more prevalent. The evidence confirming the Moreno-Smith connection mounted. Violent crime among criminals would surge as other organizations vied for the New Orleans monopoly once owned by Moreno. Marse wondered just how high up the payoffs went—mayor, governor, hell, there was no telling. One thing for sure, the city was already ripe with corruption, and there for the taking.

Marse was a gut or on-a-hunch kind of detective, and he'd always had a cold, nauseous, and uncomfortable feeling around Russ Tobin, one of the other detectives in the department. Tobin was too casual talking about drug and human trafficking rings, and he never seemed surprised when one got popped, like somehow he was in the know all along. It sure as shit wasn't because he was a super-stud detective; Marse was pretty sure it was more about the company he kept.

Moreno and Smith's connection blew Marse away when he first learned about it, and no matter how he stacked the cards, it just didn't add up. No one was able to figure out the mystery link. Despite having a highly tuned instinct for impropriety, international and fed issues were off his radar. Those were a worry for the FBI, a route he had purposely not taken; city cop was rife enough. Law enforcement was in his blood, going back to his dad, his dad's dad, uncles, nephews. One could call it the family business.

In his gut, he knew they'd never find Randy Tolbert's body, but the subject kept coming up. It was usually Russ who brought it up, just after Marse had received another request for an update. Did they really want to find Tolbert, or did they wonder, like he had, why Tolbert had abducted Rainie Landry in the first place? Was he the only one to find it hinky that Mike Landry had found Rainie before anyone else? He got Mike's position and why he'd probably killed Tolbert, but how could he have better intel than the police? Was there a connection to Mike in all the sleazy dealings? It didn't ring true, but he couldn't connect the dots. Hopefully, one day Mike Landry would feel comfortable enough to confide in him. It'd be their secret.

Way Less Sad

Every joint in his body was sore. Michael waited until Mateo was awake enough for ice chips. He hadn't veered from the photo. It had been a long surgery, and Michael's stomach growled loudly. He made his way to the dining room. One of the techs, a blonde female somewhere in her mid-twenties, sat at his table. Her shoulder-length hair was pin-straight, and in some way, she reminded him of John, his brother's, crooked fed plaything. Dirty or not, her intel had led to him finding his abducted wife, and he'd be forever grateful. The young tech attempted to make conversation. He was too tired to talk.

"Une baignade pourrait vous aider a vous detendre." She smiled.

A quick dip in the pool actually sounded appealing, but he didn't have a swimsuit, nor did he fancy doing it in the nude. As it was, he felt guilty for leaving Rainie, Michaela, and the boys, and this was the first of a possible three, maybe four, surgery deal. All he needed was for the blonde tech to walk in while he was swimming in the buff.

He quickly finished his meal and went straight to his room. After experiencing the nurses, techs, and anesthesiologist's quality, Michael felt he was leaving Mateo in capable hands. He quickly fell asleep. Morning came, and it was balls to the wall getting out of there in time to make it home for Sunday dinner. Michael's adrenalin was rushing, knotting his stomach and tensing his sore body again. He felt like Dorothy from the Wizard of Oz; all he wanted to do was get home. His heart thumped with anticipation and eagerness to have it all done and over. The whole itinerary was the same, just in reverse.

Being the surgeon to a man of such power and position could've been daunting, yet it wasn't. Mateo had ensured everything was as required. Transferring from the copter to the jet went even smoother than it had before. Once onboard, he had a glass of wine waiting for him with crackers and cheese to complete the snack. The role of Francois Marchand was no longer awkward. He could rest in his mind without being disturbed or spoken to—that was the life of a pompous asshole.

His mind drifted as he gazed out the window. His pulse was slower, his gestures less rigid, even his body relaxed. There was teasing anticipation of returning home like bubbles rising in a champagne flute, but it was pleasant, unlike the uncomfortable churn of the unknown on the arriving journey. He remembered his and Rainie's last kiss. Recalling the feel of her lips on his created a twitch to his mouth like an effervescent candy, sweet and tingling all at the same time. With eyes still closed, he felt an uncontrollable smile form. His mouth slightly upturned with thoughts of her.

Sleep overtook him as he stretched his body out. Time passed much faster on the journey home. A slight rumble in his stomach woke him as a pleasant aroma aroused his taste buds. Food, yes, a tasty meal, tempted his eyes to open. The filet mignon was delicious, accompanied by a crispy cold salad, potatoes au gratin, and perfectly crusted baguettes. He compared the meal to a tiny bag of pretzels and a miniature bottle of water he could expect on commercial flights. Michael decided no more commercial; they had the money to charter a private jet for any and all vacations. These thoughts cascaded to the conclusion: it was time to bring on a partner, as Rainie had pleaded. It would have to be someone who had the same values: a family man, a church-going man, a surgeon more interested in reconstruction than obsessions of beauty. Definitely not a woman surgeon; he wanted to keep an air of propriety, and gossip might conjure infidelity tales. He had his perfect mate, and if it bothered patients that he didn't want a female surgeon, fuck them, it was his practice.

After his meal, he freshened up, and in no time, they began their descent. He couldn't wait to feel Rainie's arms tightly around him, the seduction of her throaty whispers on his neck, and the crazy excitement from the boys on his return home. They made him feel like a rock star. Oh, to be loved with such intensity.

☙❧

He felt like he'd scored the winning goal as the car pulled up to his home, and the boys came barreling out, screaming his name in exuberance. Their precious faces were filled with love and adoration, and then Rainie stepped out of the front door, holding his little princess. There were no words to successfully describe her beauty. Even in his favorite well-worn scrubs with babe in arms, she had a force of magnetic attraction, and it pulled him from the very base of his being.

Acting like she was checking her non-existent watch, she smiled up at him. "Michael Landry, you are a man of your word. Dinner's damn near on the table, perfect timing." In the crook of one arm, she held Michaela, and the other she opened wide for his hug. She watched as the black car pulled away and her hubs walked to greet her. Just the presence of the vehicle felt ominous.

"God, I've missed you!" he said as he moved in close and inhaled deeply into her hair. A wave of emotion rose in his body, rolling from his toes to his heart. "One down," he told her. She leaned up, gave him a tender kiss on his lips. "Inside, boys," she called out to them. "And as predicted, Michael, I had a visitor this weekend. So, your ass has been fishing in the Gulf, got it? Don't be surprised if Marse ends up at our door tonight; you better put some of my blush on your cheeks because you certainly don't look like someone who's been fishing."

They went in and closed the door. "Maybe I better jump in a steamy hot shower in case Marse does stop by. I'll be sweaty from the shower if I stay in long enough."

☙❧

Down the street, Marse had the perfect angle to observe as the dark car pulled in front of the Landry's home. He watched as the family excitedly emerged from the house. Doctor Landry didn't have a sun-tired, dried sweat, grungy-from-fishing kind of look. Why a car service?

He had already called in the plate. It was a rental. No surprise there. It was perplexing how the puzzle came together. Usually, he had an idea of the players in a cat-and-mouse game, and maybe not the specifics, but at least the broad strokes. The nagging in the pit of his stomach created a heaviness in his whole body. Under normal circumstances, his creep-o-meter was pretty spot-on, as were his good-guy senses, and Mike Landry definitely wore the white cowboy hat, not the black, but the whole situation was hinky.

After twenty minutes, Marse moved his car to their driveway. The hope of hopes was that the nanny would be there to take care of the kids. He wanted to talk to both the doc and his missus before his gut feelings dulled. Maybe he should just say he'd looked into it and leave the whole mess alone. Nothing good was going to come from the investigation. Tolbert's body was long gone, and who really gave a shit? The guy was an A-1 asshole.

Doctor Landry came out of the door and approached his car. He had a smile on his face. "Good evening, Detective Marse. Rainie told me you came by while I was out of pocket. Please come in."

Marse was taken aback at Mike's apparent candor and relaxed nature. Usually, when people tried to hide something, they showed nervousness in their demeanor and body language. Mike was one cool customer, and either it meant there was nothing to hide, or there was a bleak darkness to the man's soul.

What no one had considered, including Mike himself, was the epiphany he would have in the shower. He'd rehearsed his thoughts over and over in his brain as the shower sprayed down on him. His conclusion—it was the right thing to do, and Marse was a man of honor. Who knows, maybe his idea might be the death of him, but he thought not.

〰️

They walked in the front door. "Rai, see if Allie can feed and watch the kids. Join me in the pool house, please."

He walked Marse through the house, into the backyard, and to the pool house.

"Nice set-up you got here, Doctor Landry."

"It's Mike, and since this isn't business, I'm going to refer to you as Rick, if that's okay? You want a beverage; we have non-alcoholic and alcoholic?"

"Non, please. Soft drink, water, whatever." Marse was pacing in confusion.

"Take a seat, Rick. Just want to catch you up to speed." Michael popped open a Coke and poured it into a glass, casually walking around the bar toward the seating area.

Marse scratched his head and looked down. This was a first. What exactly did he mean, up to speed? Rick watched his every move like a cat on the prowl.

Rainie looked equally as confused. Michael handed Marse the glass and sat in an adjacent chair. Rainie sat on the sofa across from the men, totally perplexed.

"Rick, last time you and I spoke was when Rainie had been kidnapped, right? You had given me Jake's info? Let me catch you up. Can I assume this conversation will stay between the three of us?"

"Can't say," Marse answered in all honesty.

"Alright, well, I'm going to assume you are a stand-up guy because I believe you are, and I can un-muddy the waters for you, and you can decide what you want to do with the info, but it'll be off my plate. I'm basing this on trust.

"I have a brother who has a Port Authority friend with benefits, if you will. When Tolbert took Rainie, I called my family. It just so happened my brother's friend was around—from what I gather; she's a dirty fed. Not my business." He lifted his hands in a shrug, giving an I-don't-give-a-shit expression on his face. "She found out where Rainie had been taken—probably before y'all knew. John told me, advising I wait for law enforcement. We're talking about my wife and unborn child at that time. Before I go any further—" Michael paused and did a Rainie with the hand in the air. Looking Marse square in the eyes, he said, "I was raised to revere women probably more than most families. We don't sit at the dinner table until my mom sits, then any other ladies; you get the picture." He punctuated the statement with a squint of his eyes. "Okay, so I've heard this piece of shit smacking and dragging my pregnant wife. She had hidden in my closet and called me. I heard it all, hence my severe panic and agitation." Mike took a sip of his sparkling water, glancing away from Marse toward Rainie.

He returned his focus to Marse. "Back to the story. I wasn't waiting for anyone to rescue my wife. I didn't care who got there first, y'all or me. When I got to the fishing camp, I went in and prevented Tolbert from shooting my wife. Frankly, he was fucking crazy, totally out of his mind. In doing so, I crushed his windpipe and then, for good measure, put one right between his eyes. Rick, Tolbert picked the wrong person's wife to mess with. I was more than willing to take the consequences of my actions. I still am."

Marse interrupted. "What'd you do with the body?" He had a look of curiosity but not a scowl or an assuming look.

"I'll get to that."

Meanwhile, Rainie sat, mouth almost agape with a total look of confusion and utter disbelief in Michael's confession.

"Rai, breathe. God and I had a talk in the shower, and I'm going for it." He looked back at Marse, who looked a bit astonished as well. "I get Rainie in the car. Needless to say, she was in shock both from the incident and by my actions, I'm sure. My phone rings, and a voice tells me to take my wife and go home. This person is sending someone to clean up the situation. Rick, I would have gladly confessed, but at that time, I wanted to get my wife home."

"Who was this person?" Marse's interest was gaining momentum.

"Didn't know and, ya know what, I wasn't questioning, I just wanted to get my wife home. The dirty fed spoke to someone on the phone and found out the body had been weighted in the swamp. You might find bones, but I tend to doubt it with the gators. Tolbert is dead, that I can promise. Fast forward now. What I'm going to tell you only three people know. You'll make four. Do you want to hear it, or are you good where we're at?"

Marse hadn't taken his eyes off Michael, and held his body perfectly still, waiting as the information dropped in his lap. "Shit, Mike. What do you want me to do with the information you've already given me? It'd be impossible to prove you killed Tolbert, other than you confessed. I felt certain you had, but he was a piece of shit, so he was a missing person from a cold file until there was a body. Do I want to know more? Hell, I'm a cop, of course, I want to know more, but can I live happily not knowing more? I don't know." Rainie and Marse were both fidgety with nerves. Mike was cool as a cucumber.

"Let me ask you, do you think anyone in your department is involved with a cartel? Like a plant of some sort?" Mike cocked his head to the side; his brow furrowed slightly with a truly quizzical expression. He had a sense of calm, not like a man who thought he was signing his own sentence.

"Maybe. There's one guy who gives me a dirty cop feel, but I don't know for sure. He's small potatoes, anyway, dirty cop, yeah I'd say so, but why would the cartel have interest in him?" Marse was still perplexed by the whole situation, and it showed in his body language. He sat tall, totally uncomfortable, like an animal getting ready to spring into the air after being spooked.

"Maybe someone has him fishing for information?" Michael asked, shrugging his shoulders, once again, in a blasé who-knows fashion. "Who'd think some uninfluential junior league NOLA detective would be connected to a cartel?" Michael leaned forward, elbows on his knees, toward Marse. He could tell Rick was chomping at the bit to know more. And again, why did he feel the need to air this information? What did he expect to come from it all? Information shared may bring peace? Was he looking out for Mateo? Certainly, Mateo knew who was after him and had chosen not to fight.

"Shit, Mike. Whatever you got on your chest, give it to me. It stays here. I'm taking it you want someone other than you, Rainie, and whoever to know, just in case. Hedging your bets?" Rick dropped his shoulders, unfolded his arms, and had clearly decided to hear him out.

"Are you familiar with the name Mateo Moreno?" Michael asked.

"Funny you should ask. Yes, in fact, he was supposedly killed when a bomb exploded on his compound." Marse slugged back his Coke and let out a muffled belch, excusing himself.

"Really? I hadn't heard." Michael leaned back in his chair. "What I'm about to say is maybe going to floor you, I don't know. Mateo Moreno is no longer." The statement couldn't be more accurate. "He was one class act. I know he has countless murders attached to his name, and he was the head of some big cartel—"

Rick chuckled as he clasped his hands behind his head. "Yeah, one of the main cartels in Colombia, Mike. Class act? You killed him, too?" He looked Mike directly in the eyes.

As though pondering the questions, Michael put his fingers to his lips. "Hmm." He got up, opened a beer, took a few chugs of it, and slowly walked back to his chair. He had a look of contemplation, maybe even satisfaction, with a calculated smile on his face and a brightness in his eyes. In a stammered laugh, he said, "I guess I did when you put it that way." He looked off as though in the distance. "Come see this." He led Marse from the pool house to Rainie's office, and opened the door, ushering in both Rainie and Rick.

Upon seeing the six-foot stuffed bear, Marse loudly commented, "What the—"

"Precisely our thought," Rainie chimed in. "With this came three dozen pink roses, absolutely gorgeous. The card read something like, Welcome to the world, Michaela. Signed with an M."

Michael led them back into the pool house. "Rai and I get a phone call the night Michaela was born, and the bear was delivered. When I answered the phone, I instantly recognized the voice as the man who had called me about the cleaner after the Tolbert thing. It was Mateo Moreno, and he wanted to meet with me. After considerable thought, I agreed. A couple of days later, he picked me up at my office, and we took a drive. He gave me a picture of a man and asked if I could create the face in the photo. I said yes. Reconstruction is my thing."

Rick cut in, "Did you have a choice, really? I mean—"

"He said I did, and I believe him. I'm not going to go into the whole conversation, but basically, he wanted out of the business for the protection of his family, and the only way he could do that was to fake his death. That way, his family would no longer be a vulnerability."

Rick got up and grabbed a beer. "Mind?" He slugged back a few belts and sat back down.

Michael smiled at him; this was a lot for the lawman to take in. "I'm a fairly good judge of character, I like to think, and there was an authenticity to him I liked. Yeah, he's not one of the good guys per se, but he's not a thug either. His competition had tried to take him out, and it was only a matter of time before they were successful. Rather than go into hiding and subjecting his family to possible torture to flush him out, he chose to give up everything.

"I can't even fathom giving up my family. If it had been me, I might have moved my whole family with me, but he'd have to keep guard around them all the time. He knew it would be no life for them. Rick, I don't know if you're a Godfather fan, but the way he spoke conjured up thoughts of when Kate tried to leave the compound and Tom, Corleone's consigliere, wouldn't let her leave, and she gets frustrated and angry, like a prisoner in her own home." He got up and grabbed a bottle of water, cut a lime, and pushed it down in the bottle. "Rainie, want a water with lime?"

She walked over to him, standing close so their bodies were touching. She took a sip of his water and gave him a quick peck. "I need to attend to Michaela before—"

"Gotcha. Come back when you finish and bring the princess." He kissed her forehead, and her eyes closed as she drank in his affection. Both men watched as she left the pool house. After only four and a half weeks, the pregnancy after-pudge was contracting. She didn't look like she had a four-week-old; maybe a three-month-old. His heart fluttered as he watched his wife through the window walk back into the house. If not careful, the warmth in his groin would heat up, leaving him in an embarrassing predicament.

Rick looked back at Michael. "Your wife is an amazing lady. She has such a unique look—very dramatic."

"Yep." He smiled. "I fell in love with her the first time I saw her, but fucking Tom snatched her up. Sorry, uncalled for—poor guy. His loss, my gain, though. Married with kids?"

Marse relaxed back. "I'm one lucky S.O.B. I have a fantastic wife and great kids. Divorce rates within the police force are astronomical; it's one of the biggest challenges being on the job. I'm one of the lucky ones to have an understanding wife. She's the best thing that ever happened in my life. Being a cop for me was like being in the family business. We have a strong blue line presence going back generations. But back to your story. I take it you did the surgery?"

Mike sat down again, swigging his water. "The surgeries have begun, yes. It's gonna be two, maybe three, possibly four to get the total transformation. I don't know if you've seen pictures of Mateo, but there will be very little left of him. He's a first-class act; I hope as we meet again, I'll get the skinny on why he chose the life he did. If you sat and talked with him, you'd never think he was some tough guy. He's a nice person with a gentle way about him." As he took another sip of water, he watched as Rick gave him an odd, unbelieving look.

"Mike, if he's such a gem, why tell me all this?" He was more than questioning. He truly wanted Mike to think about the possible ramifications.

While he should have had a queasiness in his stomach or rattled nerves, he didn't. "I don't know. He went to great lengths to camouflage his plans, but one never knows. I wanted one of the good guys, and a smart one at that, to have an idea of what was in the works on the odd chance something went a foul. I don't think it will, but I get a distinct impression there's someone on the inside at the NOPD in Mateo's enemy's camp. Someone he trusted, maybe. On the weekends, when I have to continue the transformation, I'd feel much better knowing I had a guardian angel for Rainie and the kids. Shit, she's already been through so much. Granted, my wife has a way of getting herself into some crap. She's too ballsy for her own good." He paused for a moment. "Any scoop on Grayson Smith? He's one slimy, cold bastard."

Both men laid back, draining a few beers like two friends shooting the shit. The conversation went on for another half hour before Rainie came back with Michaela. Marse indeed had a softness for babies. He put his arms out to hold her. The visit went well into the night, and around ten, Rick left with more information to process through his mind than he could've ever imagined. Marse liked Rainie and Mike. There was nothing he wanted to do with the information Mike had shared. He understood what Mike was saying—and the threat of trouble didn't emanate from Mateo, but instead from someone not buying into the assassination. Now there were only four people who knew for sure Mateo lived.

KISS ME MORE

The six-week visit with the OB went well, and Rainie was given a two thumbs up for returning to routine activities, even though Michael noticed she hadn't complied with all the restrictions, like driving. He hadn't missed an appointment, and this was going to be no different. She told him it was utter nonsense for him to attend; nonetheless, he was there. After all was said and done, she headed back home with Michaela in tow.

Before heading to the office, Michael stopped at their home in the quarter. As he pulled into the parking lot, he started to get a tingling of excitement in the pit of his stomach. The sensation was quickly moving from his stomach to his boys below. He moved to the house with long strides, trying to thwart the rising heatwave rolling through his body. It would be their first date night since a week before Michaela's birth, she'd been given the two thumbs up for sex, and he had arranged for the perfect intimate date. Their four hours were going to be sheer pleasure for her. He could feel his pulse quicken at the thought of her legs draped over his shoulders. He wanted all of her, slow, steady and methodical. He was going to crest her over and over.

Michael had the non-alcoholic bubbly chilling, rose petals sprinkled on the bed, and soft tassels hung from each of the bedposts. Everything was perfect. He placed candles around the room. He knew she had planned for a night of fine dining. It would be their first date without the kids since the week before Michaela was born. Little did she know, they were going to be feasting on each other. Knowing his wife, Rainie wouldn't be the slightest bit disappointed. She'd be thrilled. He knew she loved nothing more than to have his tongue exploring her every nook and cranny. She was remarkable in the sack for someone who'd never thought she had any sexual prowess, and was always willing to try new adventures. For this particular night, the first time for over seven weeks, he'd stick to her favorites, making her swoon with one big O after another.

His phone rang. "Where are you? I tried the office, and they said you weren't back." Rainie's voice sounded concerned, and a touch miffed. "You okay?"

"I'm fine. You told Allie we'd be leaving about seven?" he questioned, but more for assurance and to get her off her nosing track.

"Yes, but you haven't told me where we're going? How dressy do I need to be?"

"Think Antoine's, and you'll be good." He wanted to say, 'Just throw on a pair of scrubs,' but part of it was the surprise.

He had one more stop to make, and it was at the jewelers for the push present he'd picked out for after the birth. Since Michaela was a May baby, he'd picked out a simple but perfect emerald ring. After picking up the ring, he headed for the office. The day's schedule was medium to light with a few post-ops, some quick injections, and an interview.

Beth, his office manager, handled the initial interviews, whether for a new nurse or cleaning service, and it would be no different for a partner. The candidate had to pass her stink test first. He'd given her all the requirements, and she'd informed him that legally, she could not ask about being married or the church part either but would be on her toes and do the best she could. She had narrowed it down to three men. He had no hesitation in venturing down the paths Beth found uncomfortable and legally unsound. If anyone had a problem talking about their marriage or their faith, simply they weren't the partner for him.

"Where is the information on the guy coming in at three?" Michael inquired.

Beth was nearing fifty, but any joe off the street would have pegged her for upper thirties—early forties, tops. She had a full figure that probably could've dropped ten pounds and not been too thin, but she had a classic look with dark, wavy shoulder-length hair and blue-green eyes. He'd hired her the day he opened his practice; she had worked in a law office down the street and had been given her walking papers. Right was right, and wrong was wrong, and she had no problem communicating that to her employer, hence her termination. Michael admired her scruples. He remembered seeing her walking down the avenue, box in hand, with very determined steps, maybe a gloss in her eye but not a tear down her face. She was sensibly strong.

"Zeke Ramos. He's got a year under his belt at Children's in oral and maxillofacial. Nice guy, laid back. He wore a visible gold crucifix and had a wedding band on, just FYI—went to LSU undergraduate and med school, then finished his residency at Children's. He's got a warm smile. I have no idea where he placed in his class which probably means it's nothing to write home about; otherwise, I would've heard." She was sorting things on his desk for the upcoming interview.

"What's your gut on the guy?"

She laughed. "A definite possibility."

It was, by far, one of his and his wife's favorite impractical statements people made, and as a joke, it had become a phrase he found himself habitually using. "I have a few calls, but let me know when he gets here. I don't want to keep him waiting. Punctuality, you know." He knew she knew.

He called home. "You getting excited about our date tonight?"

Rainie could feel his smile through the phone. "Very." He could hear Michaela's grunts as she nursed.

"Tell Michaela she needs to grunt a little more ladylike; she sounds like an ogre."

"Michael, have you heard yourself when you're sucking on my breasts? What she sounds like is you." She blurted out a laugh from deep within. Then he heard a slight cry.

"Rainie, you scared her with your guffaw." He chuckled.

"What the fuck is a guffaw? You mean my laugh? Well, the little princess will have to get over herself. Guffaw? What happened to my deep, sensuous laugh from the pit of my soul that you can recall on command? Guffaw, my ass. Speaking of—"

Beth buzzed, so he quickly told Rainie. "Gotta go. I love you. See you soon. Dr. Zeke Ramos is here. Later."

He walked to the front. The sight nearly bowled him over. Black chin-length hair, dark brown almond eyes, chiseled cheekbones, straight nose, squared jawline, and a warm and gracious smile. He'd just ripped an identical face apart a little over three weeks prior. Could he ask if he was related to Mateo Moreno? Fuck, what if he was?

Michael put his hand out. "Welcome, Dr. Ramos. I'm Mike Landry. Come back this way." The two meandered back to his office. Indeed, Zeke did have on a crucifix, and wore a wedding band on his left hand. Michael's office wasn't overly impressive but classic enough, and it worked. "Please sit." He walked around his desk and sat to face the new guy.

"Dr. Ramos, you like Children's?"

"I do." He nodded his head almost with a bounce. "It's Zeke; my dad is Dr. Ramos." He chuckled.

"Why are you looking for a change then?" Michael studied his body language, and if he was covering anything up, it didn't show.

"It's time, I think. I always knew it was a jumping-off place. I only planned on my residency there. As I'm sure you know, I'm new to the game. I've always wanted to work in a small practice. I might find more autonomy and develop closer bonds with my patients, and from what I understand, you do predominantly reconstruction and are somewhat light on cosmetics? That's my purpose, I think."

"Gotcha, I know the feeling. Where's your dad's practice?" Michael continued to scrutinize every word the man was saying.

"He's a psychiatrist in Baton Rouge. We bleed purple and gold, I'm afraid." Zeke was about as open in his mannerisms as anyone could be, so if there were dark hidden demons, they were well out of sight.

Michael smiled. "I grew up around Baton Rouge, went to Catholic High before LSU, but I'm a few years ahead of you."

Zeke grinned in a knowing way. "You played football, QB, right? Dang, small world. You probably went to school with my older brother, Zach." The atmosphere was quickly relaxing.

Michael nodded with a smile on his face. All the stiffness of an interview seemed to fade. "Small world, indeed. Yes, I did." It felt like an old home week. This guy had to be the one to join his practice. They had so much in common. Maybe. Both had settled back in their chairs, and it felt like two guys jawing back and forth. Michael dreaded bringing on an associate or partner; however, this was all going well, and the tense knot in his stomach was gone. "I'll have the contract ready for you to look at, pass by your wife or lawyer, and then we can get back in touch if you're still interested. Since you've worked at Children's, you know some of the cases can be heart-wrenching. Knock on wood; I've been blessed to have good results thus far."

Zeke started getting antsy, or seemingly distracted. He closed his eyes and put his hands together, "Here's the thing, Mike. You need to know because it might be an issue with you. I don't have a wife." Mike glanced at his left hand.

"Sorry to hear."

"No, I don't have a wife because I have a husband. I'm gay. I know I don't have to disclose any of this, but if we're possibly going to work together, I gotta be honest." Michael wasn't sure what to say.

Staying cool, calm, and with a most professional demeanor, he said, "Not my business who you're married to. I do have a wife, Rainie, two sons, and a brand-new baby girl. Are you okay with that?" Michael smiled, shrugged his shoulders, and turned up his right palm. "You need to be comfortable, too. And my wife, holy shit, is a pepper with a steel-edged tongue." Both men laughed. Michael turned the picture around of Rainie and the two boys.

"Mike, she's stunning. Those eyes are killer, and the boys are both handsome guys." Michael pulled out his phone and scrolled to a picture of Michaela. "Y'all are gonna have your hands full. She has her mom's eyes." Zeke pulled out his phone and scrolled to the picture of him and a strikingly handsome black man. They both had broad, laughing smiles. "This is Damien. We've been together since LSU undergrad; he's a petroleum engineer and travels a lot. He's been home lately, but before that, he was all over the world and gone months at a time. It's been rough."

Michael gave him his card, told him the contract would be ready within a couple of days, and he could look over it and let him know. After Zeke left, Michael called Beth in. "Looks like we have another doctor. We need to get the contract together; I trust you know all it needs to say. Maybe do an option for partnership after a year or whatever you think. I'll pass it by Henry, Rai's dad, and send it to the accountant. I want to make sure we do everything right by him and us. His brother and I played football together at Catholic. It's a small world."

☙

Rainie buzzed him on the way home, "What's your ETA?"

"I'll be pulling up in ten—so much to tell. I love you."

"Love you, bye."

Nine minutes later, he pulled into the driveway. Rainie was waiting at the gate and watched as he pulled in. Getting out of the car, he was grinning ear to ear. "I think I have the perfect partner."

"Well, I think you're pretty perfect, too." She ran her tongue across her lips, dropped her jaw slightly just enough to part her lips, and winked.

He was like a kid bouncing out of the car doing the won-the-game dance. No matter how he tried to say it, the words got twisted around. "Not partner, like wife, but doctor partner, but you're fucking fantastic, too." He was sputtering—so un-Michael-like.

"Thanks a lot, I guess. Calm down, and I want to hear all about it." She put her arms around him, kissing him with a hard, deep kiss. "Seven weeks, Mr. Play-By-The-Rules. I've wanted you in the worst kind of way, ooh-baby!" she teased. "But, please, by all means, tell me about your new possible partner; you look like you're gonna explode. Then, we can get down to real business."

Walking into the house, he was like a chatterbox. "Zeke, that's his name, is from Baton Rouge. His brother and I played football together. Nice guy. Fuckin freaked me out at first. He looks just like a young version of—" and he whispered, "Mateo."

"You think there's a connection?" Suspicions were echoing in her voice.

"No, he's just a handsome Latino guy. Now that I know who his brother is, I see the family resemblance. He looks like his brother, just not as big. I'm sure we have the report from his background check. I'll take a look at it; no, now I sound paranoid. He's been at Children's. He's younger, maybe your age. He was looking for a small practice and really into reconstruction." Michael kissed the kids on the way up the stairs. "What a day. I'm gonna have your dad go over the contract. I want to be fair." She followed close behind.

"Michael, you're always fair. Well, maybe not right now because I'm dying to have you. Dinner is at seven, and we don't have much time to play." She started unbuttoning his shirt.

"Not right now." He was completely distracted.

"What? Are you kidding me?" She looked hurt. Her eyes were sad and almost cloudy in confusion. She plopped on the bed impatiently.

The pants came off, but he kept talking. "He knows all about you and the boys and Michaela."

She rolled her eyes. "Pictures and all, I'm guessing. Did this Zeke show you pictures of his wife?"

Michael stopped. He knew he was going to floor her and wanted to experience the whole reaction. "No. Pictures of his husband." For once, Rainie had nothing to say, at least at first.

"Hm. Your new doc is gay? I didn't see that one coming. How are you about having a gay partner?" Then she went on the path of many questions. She talked non-stop while he changed his clothes, grabbed her dress, draped it over her, and zipped her up. She quickly grabbed her shoes as he threw on his jacket.

"Come on; I don't want to be late." They gave quick instructions and were out the door. His enthusiasm was like a boy going to his first prom with the girl of his dreams. Time was of the essence. They flew toward the quarter; she was still buzzing about the new doc. When could she meet him? When would he know? They'd have to invite them over, and she couldn't wait to tell Mer.

He pulled into Place d'Armes Hotel parking, as usual. "Why are we here?"

"Gotta get something. Come on." He just about dragged her along.

"Good gracious, Michael. Slow down." They got to the door and went in. He went straight for the shower and got it going, then began lighting all the candles. She looked around the bedroom. He kept his eyes going back and forth to her as he lit the candles.

He peeled his clothes off. "Turn around." He unzipped her, pushing her dress off her shoulders letting it pool at her feet. He had her bra and panties off in an inkling. The kisses flooded down her neck down her stomach to the promised land. "God, I have wanted this. It's all I've been thinking about all day. Just placing the candles and the petals, I got rock hard. It's all for you." She touched him lightly. "No, tonight is all about you. Baby, I'm gonna rock your world." He lay her down, surrounded by a sea of rose petals. He draped each leg over his shoulders. "I love your perfectly pink, um. So gorgeous. I can see you glistening already." He fluttered his tongue back and forth around her little bud. In long strokes, he slid his fingers inside of her. He sucked hard and nipped lightly. He could tell she was in ecstasy. Her body moved like a wave rolling into his hand, and he could feel her body burst with sweet release.

"I want you inside me, Michael." He climbed up her body, rubbing the tip of his cock against her tightening pearl. "Let me feel all of you; go ahead, rock my world." She watched as he slowly penetrated her. His body was beautiful, perfectly ripped with just the right amount of muscle. She watched as he moved in and out. "I want you to spank me, then do it in my butt." His eyes widened like saucers.

"Maybe another time, baby. This is our first time out the gate in a while." He continued to roll into her, the waves getting more intense and faster.

"I know you want to spank me; you even said so, and I've been reading since it's all I've been able to do. You ever do someone in the butt? I've never had it; all you've ever done is fiddled. Fuck me, Michael."

Flipping her on her belly, he smacked her ass. He knew it would only be a slight sting, but he could feel himself getting hotter; he spanked her again and again, then pulled her up on her knees. He dropped lower on the bed, dripping saliva down her backside. He leaned in for a quick taste of bud and could tell from the dewy drippings she was getting off. "Rai, this is going to sting, almost burn. Tell me to stop if it's too much. Fingers and a cock are a huge difference." He started with one finger, then two, thrust in and out. He moved to three, she began to groan and beg for all of him. He coated his cock in saliva pressing the head up against her anus. Pushing, he could feel the resistance of the pursed ring, then it yielded. Yeah, her ass was clamping tight and felt great, but he still preferred her better part; it had a different texture and topography, not like the slick squeeze of her ass with little or no distinction, just incredible tightness. He fulfilled her request and knew it had to burn even though he tried to be tender. Once the pulsing began, his body took over. Pulling out, he rolled on his side and cuddled next to her.

She turned and looked at him. Her eyes were teary. "Oh God, Rai, are you okay? I shouldn't—"

"Michael, I wanted you to. In every book I've read, the guy character says, 'nothing feels as good as anal sex.' I wanted to please you. We've never done that, and I know I can't get pregnant with a butt fuck. Right? Now, how great was my ass?"

"Truthfully, you've got the best ass if I had to fuck an ass, but I'll take your sweet stuff every day of the week and twice on Sunday. Rainie, you have by far the most outstanding lady parts." Petting her ass, he sat up and looked at the redness from the spanking. He hadn't noticed the red marks during their interlude. "You're still a bit red from the spanking. What the hell have you been reading? Please don't tell me it's shit you've gotten from my mother."

She was on a roll. Laying on her side, pillow under her head, she began the barrage of questions. "What do you prefer? Twat, cunt, pussy, cunny, folds, slit, mound, vajay, honeypot, or the all-clinical vagina?" He blushed and started laughing as he got up, still half-erect. "Look at that swinging tool. Or should I say: Cock, dick, rod, sword, bat, or—" She crinkled her nose, "Penis? It's amazing all the names those books have for the anatomy." She sat straight up, Indian style. "What are your faves?" She tilted her head to one side like the dogs when she made squeaking noises.

"Oh my God, you are too fucking much. How long have you planned this?" He pulled a small box out of his jacket, turned, and presented it to her. "This, my love, is your push present. All the books said I needed to get you a push present. I think it's hysterical with you and your books, but I followed my book for a first-time dad. Rainie, you are a trip!" He watched as she opened the box.

Tears rolled down her cheeks, "I love it. An emerald, for May, Michaela's birthday." She slid it on her finger. "Michael, thank you. I love it."

Lying next to her, he looked at her hands, both donned in sparkling rings. "It does look nice. Beautiful on your hand." He turned his head to her for a sweet kiss. "Now I want to know, what were you doing while you were reading the books, hm? Because I know you don't do self-gratification." He chuckled.

"As you very well know, Michael, my mind is a powerful thing. I don't have to touch a thing to have pleasure. Nothing brings on an orgasm faster than thinking of you inside of me or running your tongue—well, you get the idea. And you were right. It did burn. What is your experience in the anal department?"

"Really? You want to know?" he asked. "Now?"

She propped her head on her hand in anticipation. "Why not? You know all of mine," she said amidst her throaty laugh.

"I've performed the act on a few girls, women, and—really?" She nodded. "I told you about the woman at the club who did things to me. One of the things she got into was using a, as you call it, a plastic pretend; that's how I knew it burned. It's not pleasant for sure. I know guys are supposed to like it because it hits the prostate, which is like a guy's magic spot, or G spot, but not this guy! It happened once, and that was that, no more."

She snuggled in his arms. "I'm sorry, Michael, someone did that to you for their jollies. What a bitch!" Rainie's angry face with a set jaw and squared eyes registered her disgust.

"Ancient history. Since I had it done to me, I never did it again to anyone else until tonight. And as far as terms, it's whatever comes out at the time. I don't have a preference. Also, it depends on the context. I certainly wouldn't tell a patient 'I'd fixed their blank.'"

"You fix yatchees?" she asked, with a curious Alice look, complete with a dropped jaw.

"I have worked with a urogynecologist on a couple of occasions. But no sad or bad talk anymore. You like your ring?" His body felt warm, and snuggling together made life perfect.

"I love my ring. By any chance, do you have condoms here?"

"No. I can pull out. I know the risk of conception is greater right now. We can try that if you want, or I can run out and get some condoms."

He started to get out of the bed. "Stay put, sir. We need to take a shower, because I'm not putting your magic wand in my love box after it's been up my poop chute!" He fell back on the bed in hysterics. "Besides," she added, "we're going to have an astronomical water bill. You turned on the shower when we first got here."

"You are one funny lady!"

HELL OF A VIEW

"What is it now, Russ?" Marse audibly exhaled. He'd had enough of the snooping detective. Russ was a pain in the ass. Every time he saw Tobin heading toward his desk, a fire lit in his gut as the acid from years' worth of ulcers spewed like erupting volcanoes. The guy rubbed him the wrong way. He'd seen his fair share of dirty cops, and they all had a slithering way about them, with half-hearted laughs and empty questions, and this turd was no different.

"Just out of morbid curiosity, I've been looking into some of the particulars on the Moreno hit and the medical examiner's report was far from conclusive. Nothing says pointedly that the body from the explosion was Mateo Moreno. I remember you saying you didn't think someone could get to him." Russ cocked his hip up on Marse's desk and half-sat, as though he owned the place.

Marse looked at the hip, then back at the man's face and back at the hip until Russ stood straight again and was off his desk. This guy was pissing him off. His chest tightened, and he could feel his fists wanting to ball, so he purposefully flared them out. With a forced calm, he began, "I misspoke, Russ. Anybody can be gotten, anybody! Besides, I don't give a flying flip over some guy in Colombia. In the grand scheme of things, it's just one more bad guy off the planet, and where the hell did you come up with the M.E. report?" He returned to his paperwork as though dismissing him, but the guy didn't move. Marse looked up with a set jaw and laser stare. "Yes? What now?"

"Since they haven't found Tolbert's body yet, maybe the cartel disposed of it. Maybe it was even Moreno, and someone tried to get retribution. Or, what about—" He leaned on the desk into Marse's space. "They made it look that way, and it was really—who was the girl he kidnapped, yeah, Rainie Landry, the plastic surgeon's wife— maybe the husband killed Tolbert. Whaddaya think, a possibility, right?" The guy was like a chihuahua yapping away. The only thing missing was the panting and bouncing up and down. His nervous body language and incessant questions could wear down a priest, and Marse was far from being a priest and completely worn down.

"For fuck's sake! Don't you have anything important or current on your desk? If not, I have a ton I'd be happy to float your way. Do you even know anything about the cold case? Cold being the operative word here. The Landry's are nice people; he's a freakin' surgeon, c'mon. Golden hands. The down and dirty of it, just so you get the picture— Grayson Smith was the cartel contact, and now he's somebody's bitch in prison, if not dead. I suspected, at the time, Tolbert was in on the cash shenanigans, as was Tom Todd, Rainie Landry's ex. Maybe Tolbert thought Rainie had some of the cash and wanted it, who knows, but her husband, the doc makes buckets of money, so that thought doesn't even hold water." Rick sarcastically tapped his head. "I got an idea; maybe you should go work for the police in Colombia if you've got such an insatiable curiosity about the goings-on of the cartel? Now, I have real work to do, Russ. If there's nothing else, I gotta get back to it." Marse got up and walked to refill his coffee. With any luck, Russ Tobin would be gone when he returned from the coffee pot.

Marse was sure his gut was right regarding Russ Tobin. Someway, somehow, he was involved in the behind-the-scenes curiosities. What the poor jack-off didn't realize was he was a dispensable link, and if his operation was to be covert, whoever hired him had done a piss-poor job. The mere idea of bringing him into any of the dealings spoke volumes about the cast of characters that stirred him into the mix. It'd be a comedy of errors. They would all be sloppy, sub-par, and transparent. Whoever was in power wouldn't be for long with imbeciles like Tobin working for them. The new boss wasn't too clever, evidently.

With all of this in mind, he'd placed a hidden mic on Russ's desk several days prior, and it was working perfectly. Marse heard him pick up his phone and punch in the numbers. "Hey, it's R.T. Spoke to Marse, yeah, I was cool. He has no idea. The Tolbert case is a done deal, and from all I gather, there's no way the Landry's were in on it. The old lady's ex was the muppet, and he's dead. Oh, since it's DEA stuff nobody here knows anything about what goes on outside of New Orleans, especially fed biz. Marse made it clear; I gotta drop this like a ton, ya hear me. If I get somethin', I'll call, but you don't hear from me, consider it done." He listened for nearly five minutes. "I don't care who told you Big M is still kickin' and is in New Orleans, he ain't, at least from all my intel. Hey, ma man Marse knows more than anyone else in this department about the law firm cluster. It's been dead for over six months, like dead silence, nada, nothing. Call me if you hear something else, and I'll run it. If not, shut it down."

Bingo, his gut was spot-on. His goal now was to find out who Russ's contact was. That was the person behind the big stir. Day moved into the evening, and Marse called his wife. "Hey woman, got something I gotta run down, and then I'll be home. Promise." He hung up the phone with a big smile. She was his girl and had been since high school. She put up with all the department bureaucracy, the stupid late nights required by some cases, and the all-hours-of-the-night phone calls. Retirement was getting close, like counting-down-the-time close.

Using his personal cell, he dialed the number of someone he could trust. In fact, he had relied on him back in the days on patrol years before. He was the one he'd gone to regarding Diane and Tom Todd's murders. He had the skinny on anyone and everyone in the crime world in NOLA. "Teddy, hey. Wanna grab a drink at College Inn? I wouldn't ask you if I didn't need a friend."

"Your wife okay?" Teddy asked.

"Like I said, I need a friend." Their code had worked for years, and Marse didn't call on him unless it was something worthy. His friend always made time, as did Rick anytime Teddy had called him. Using the term wife was code for the department, as in married to the job.

Teddy was sitting off to the side when he walked into the restaurant.

"Hey Rick, how's the wife? I swear y'all got more bullshit than we do with the Feds. What gives?"

"I got a dirty cop fielding for someone in a cartel."

Teddy's face dropped. "You know Moreno's dead."

"So, I hear. Who did the hit?"

"It's a fucking mystery, man. Some think it was Manny Lopez; there was bad, bad blood there. His old man Alejandro set Mateo up good in the organization, so the rumor goes. Manny's a two-bit whiny little pussy, nothing like the old man. He would've had to get someone to turn. Mateo coulda did something to someone. He could be cold-blooded, but from what I gather, it always had to do with business. Your guess is as good as mine. So, who's your mole?"

"Russ Tobin." Marse covered his mouth as he spoke in case someone was watching.

"That piece of crap. It has to be Manny. Only someone as stupid and pussified would latch onto Tobin for intel. I'm sorry, but it's laughable." He took a slug of his drink.

Marse handed over Russ's number and the recording device he'd used. "I couldn't hear the other person, but maybe you can enhance it and tell."

"I'll get back with you, and tell the wife I send my regards." He slugged down the rest of his drink. Rick settled up and headed home.

☙

Zeke was just as excited about signing the contract as Michael. They'd try the arrangement out, and if both felt it was going well, then a partnership would be up for discussion. Until then, it was salary, excellent benefits package, and like all the employees, profit sharing.

Rainie planned a celebratory dinner for the four of them. Michael suspected she wanted it on her home turf, which for some reason, always made her feel more in control and comfortable; as far as Michael was concerned, Rainie was always the maestro of any social orchestration. "Rai, what's for dinner?" He walked into the bathroom as she was in the shower.

"Your round chef is catering and serving. I thought you might like that. Gives us time to visit. I have two bottles of regular champagne and non-alcoholic; I'm sure the gay guys will understand. I don't want to have to pump and dump." She rinsed the conditioner from her hair.

"Gay guys? Really Rainie? How about Zeke and Damien?" He pressed his face against the glass, watching her naked body. She opened the door and pulled him in, clothes and all. "You're mad, woman," he said through laughter. "All you had to do was ask, and I would have stripped on the spot." He flung water from his face and gave her a big wet kiss.

"I thought this would be more fun." She lounged on the shower seat. "Come on, Michael, dance for your playtime." She started making the sounds of a striptease. "Dance, strip for me, Michael." He started swaying, then grinding as he peeled his clothes off. "That's it, baby, take it all off." She sat with one knee bent up on the bench and the other splayed out, showing off all her bits. She giggled even though she tried to put on her sexy stare.

"I'm cooperating, no complaints, now you cooperate, Rai. Show your appreciation. Touch yourself, and do it like you mean it. I want to watch."

"I don't do that," she argued.

"You do tonight, baby." He began stroking himself. "Come on, Rainie. I want to watch. I'll make it worth your while." Through his open mouth, he curled his tongue at her. "Oh yeah, but you first gotta get yourself there. Watch me Rainie, I know it'll make you cum; it has always fascinated you. Want me? Want me bad? How bad? Then, pleasure yourself. You know how you like it." She touched herself for him, obsessed with watching him. She massaged her hot spot, and while it was something different, the enthralling part was watching Michael.

He watched as her body responded and dropped to his knees, and buried his head in her excited folds, going for the big climax. She grabbed his hair at the pivotal moment. Draping her leg over his shoulder, she shuddered. "Oh God, yes, Michael. You feel so good. That's it, oh God, yes!"

He rested back on the shower wall and pulled her down on him to ride the rolls of his body as he flexed himself into her. "That's it, my love. I'm gonna give you a brilliant ride." He held onto her hips and ground her down; his hips pistoning him into her. It was raw and natural. With the jolting moment of truth, his eyes opened wide in panic. "Shit, I forgot about a condom."

She jumped up, pulled the removable shower head, and shoved the sprays to shoot inside her with the full stream flowing deep. "Hopefully this'll wash away your swimmers. I'm gonna have to remember this when reading my books." She laughed playfully. "If one of your little suckers beat the flow of water, then it deserves to land the prize."

Rainie realized what time it was. "Quick, Michael, get your clothes on. They'll be here any moment, and I want to be ready for our guests, not thrown together." Twenty minutes later, and just in time, she swiped on a last application of lip gloss when she heard the slam of a car door.

Michael gazed at her in the mirror. "Rainie, you look beautiful. I hope you get good vibes from Zeke. It's important to me that you like him. Bring those glossy puckers over here." He held her tight, pulling her body into his. "And you feel beautiful. Lady, we got a good thing going on!"

As Zeke and Damien approached the door, Michael opened it. "Welcome, y'all." The men shook hands as Zeke introduced Damien. Rainie greeted them and was taken aback by how equally handsome they were. It was hard to fathom that these two magnificent-looking men were a couple, and not just two guys going stag. Zeke was shorter than Michael by a couple of inches and gave off vibes like a Latin model, dark and dreamy. Damien had more of an islander look, dark-complected with gorgeous whiskey-colored eyes. Both had engaging smiles and genuine expressions in their eyes.

Damien was the first to speak to Rainie. "Love your place. It reeks of posh. Zeke told me you're an interior decorator, but I would've known it anyway. You did it up beautifully."

"Thank you," Rainie said. They walked further into the house. "Y'all want champagne to celebrate?" she was quick to offer.

"Would love some, please." Zeke's voice was satiny. Michael watched Rainie's body relax as the men spoke. He watched her as she continued looking at Zeke. Mateo had had the same effect on him the first time they'd met in person. The smooth Latin accent resonated with strength but had a tender quality all at the same time.

As always, the chef provided a spectacular dinner, completed by cherries jubilee flambé.

Michael could tell Rainie approved of Zeke. As she spoke to him, her eyes glittered. She was most enamored. "Zeke, how did you and Damien meet? I want the whole story." She spoke in typical Rainie style, with overly animated hands. Tie her hands, and the girl probably couldn't speak.

"Afraid it's nowhere near as romantic as the two of you, but it was out there and a lot of fun. I was bartending just off-campus. When Damien ordered his and his girlfriend's beverages, our eyes locked. I knew he was with a girl, but I also knew he was giving me a look over. They started coming in regularly, then one night, they invited me to their place for a drink. We were wild and crazy back then. Eventually, she got tired of vying for Damien's attention, didn't want to share him, and split, wishing us a happy life. No harm, no foul. She was a crazy, crazy girl." His smile was broad and his eyes enchanting.

It looked like Damien was waiting for some reaction from Rainie and Michael regarding the ménage a trois. No one would have ever given a second thought to the sex life of this hetero-bougie couple. But neither flinched. Mike liked the vanilla coating of his and Rainie's exterior; that people wouldn't necessarily know what they were into just from looking at them. Damien sent off a different set of vibes than Zeke, and while it wasn't theirs to judge, something wasn't quite right.

Michael could tell Rainie approved of the new partner. "Zeke, where is your family originally from, like where were you born? When did your parents move to Baton Rouge? I think it's the biz that your brother and Michael went to school together." Things got a little quiet in the room. Rainie and Michael exchanged glances. Had she pried too much?

Zeke looked relaxed and not bothered by the question in the slightest. "I was born in Colombia. My parents moved to the States when I was young. My father worked at the hospital, where my mom was on the housekeeping staff, maybe love at first sight as Mike felt for you. My mom was young when they married, seventeen, I think. They had two boys, a girl, and then me." Michael knew she wanted to ask about any relation to Mateo, but he was having none of his wife's battering of questions. He knew she'd pick up on his look, and she did.

"Coffee, anyone?" Rainie got up and headed into the kitchen.

"Mike," Damien pointed in the direction of the kitchen, "your wife is fabulous. Zeke told me how beautiful she was, but wow. I bet she can be quite hypnotic—lucky man." They were all relaxed at the table as the chef's helper cleared away the plates.

Michael laughed proudly. "Ya know, I told her right before y'all got here that we had a great thing going on. She's my everything. Don't get me wrong, I love our boys, and Michaela ties my stomach in knots already, but it's all because of Rainie. She, gentlemen, is my everything. She brought me the package." He turned toward Zeke, almost in reflection of his thoughts. "Zeke, I'm glad your folks moved to the States. Colombia seems extremely dangerous right now." Michael had a scrutinizing look as he shook his head slowly from side to side. There were too many similarities between Mateo and Zeke, and yet, his sense of suspicion had not been tagged. Despite his usual thoughts, there was, in reality, such a thing as coincidence.

"Sadly so," Zeke answered. The conversation continued for another hour, and then they called it a night.

Michael turned the lock to the front door. "Great night. What'd you think, Rai?"

She clasped her hands, pulling them into her chest. "They're adorable. And oh my God, they're both so handsome, but, um, never mind."

Walking to the bed, Rainie turned toward Michael, expounding, "I won't ask, but dang, I wish I could. From the way you described Mateo and the pictures on the news, I wonder if there is any relation. I guess time will tell."

The boys were long asleep; regardless, Rainie and Michael tip-toed into their room to deliver goodnight kisses. She brought Michaela into their bed to feed. "Michael, recently, I've noticed you've been getting a little, um..." She thought for a second.

"Um, what?" He rolled on his side and watched as she fished for words.

"Kinkier, I guess. Do you miss your old life?"

"That came from out of left field." It was like a dagger plunged straight into his heart, and his chest tightened; it was hard to take a breath. "Are you kidding me? No, the only life I want is with you. All you ever have to do is say no if you don't want to do something, and if I'm making you uncomfortable, we need to talk about it. I'm not complaining at all, but it seems like you've been the one to pull out the stops. The other night I just wanted to make love, and you started the anal stuff, and then tonight, you wanted me to strip in the shower." His eyes narrowed, holding back his hurt feelings. The pain in his chest was more than he could bear. "Rainie, I'm fine with whatever you want, but you gotta let me know. I thought we had a great thing going on; I told you that before going downstairs."

Looking down at Michaela, adjusting her sleep sack, Rainie responded casually, "It's not that big of a deal, Michael. And I'm not complaining at all, I'm loving it and having fun, and you're a blast. You put up with all my craziness. I was just making sure I'm all you need. Ya know, checking if you missed the wild stuff." She didn't understand that her words held a sharp edge at times.

"We've taken it as wild as I want to. You're way beyond plain old vanilla, and there's not one boring bone in your body. I love our fun play, but that's what it is, fun. At the end of the day, Rainie, we make love, period. If we never did anything but cuddle for the rest of our days, I'd be fine with that. It's all about being close to you. I love you."

He stroked Michaela's silky, soft dark hair. She had more than fuzz but not quite actual hair; it was almost like a delicate fringe. Rainie touched his hand gently. "Michael, I didn't mean to upset you. I love you. I want to be all that you want." She pulled a sleeping Michaela from her breast, trying to stir her. "I like Zeke and Damien, and I think both are sweet as can be, but I get the distinct feeling Damien had his eyes on you, Michael, which made me want to call him out. I don't trust him."

Michael propped up on his elbow, gazed at Rainie but with a different contemplative look. His face, genuinely thoughtful and searching for the right words, became stark serious. "Funny you say that. I kinda felt he was scoping your body like another guy would—not like, well, Zeke. I wanted to say at one point, hey, I thought you're with Zeke, and my wife isn't up for grabs, asshole. It makes me angry and sad for Zeke. He even said in the interview that Damien traveled the world with his job, and it made it hard sometimes. My mind immediately went to how much I missed you and the kids those few days I was gone. My thoughts didn't even go to a chance of infidelity—like he maybe had lovers in other places. That kills me. Zeke is such a nice guy. Other than thinking Damien was scoping me, did you feel his eyes wandering your body? You get any weird vibes off him?" He softly caressed her hand, observing the mother-daughter bond—complete trust and dependency drenched with pure love. The love he had for her was indescribable. Rainie was his everything, and he desperately wanted things to be perfect.

She readjusted the baby so she could look him better in the eyes. He knew his eyes probably looked sad, revealing an aching heart and bummed spirit for his new partner, knowing the closeness and faithful relationship he and Rainie shared. "Not really, Michael, but I did feel like Zeke was so open and into Damien. You could see it in his eyes when he looked at him. Damien is damn lucky to have him. He is, and don't take it the wrong way, but Zeke is beautiful. Fucking unbelievably gorgeous. He obviously doesn't have the sexy swagger you have, Michael, but I think he's insecure, and if Damien is fooling around, I get it—been there, done that." She finished with Michaela handed her to Michael for a little skin-to-skin time with him. It wasn't long before he put her in the cradle and snuggled next to Rainie. "I have sexy swagger?"

She snuggled closer, "Oh, my gosh, yes, Michael, your sexy swagger turns me on. Sometimes watching you walk in my direction, my knees buckle, and my yearnings get pretty dang hot. It's like a tickle you can't wiggle away from." She shivered, "You're not even walking right now, but just the visualization, yowzah!" She leaned forward and kissed him. When their lips met, he was sure fireworks were going off over their heads, complete with the whistles and fanfare. She was the real deal, from the tip of her head all the way to her toes, and she was his and only his—the forever kind of deal.

ALMOST MAYBES

"Rick, hey, it's Teddy. Got something for you. Mother's in thirty?" Just the thought of a debris po-boy made Marse's mouth water and reminded him how empty his stomach felt—no one did debris like Mother's. Thoughts streamed through his mind, and the more perplexing his theories of what Teddy may have discovered, the more his gut twisted, and the more restless he became. Whether he'd be there early or not didn't matter; he couldn't sit still, so he hoofed it to his car, racing to Mother's. It had only been a couple of days since he'd given the recording to Teddy. Whatever was on the device must've captured his attention for such a quick turnaround.

When he got to Mother's, Teddy was seated with both their po-boys—waiting, drumming his fingers on the table and nervously jiggling his knee at top speed.

"You got my attention, Teddy." Marse handed him a ten for the sandwich. "Thanks."

"It's on me." Teddy looked thrilled, like a young boy copping his first feel. The excitement electrified as he flipped through his pocket notebook. Without a doubt, he had info and was bursting at the seams to cough it up. A couple was sitting next to them within earshot, but since both were probably nearing ninety, there was no worry of them hearing or understanding the coded conversation.

"Remember St. Marten from before a couple years back? His lady was the smokin' chick?" Teddy asked.

"Yup," Marse said with a mouthful of food and gravy dribbling down his chin as he grabbed for another napkin. Gravy stains were the price one paid for a Mother's debris po-boy, and they were so damn worth it.

Teddy explained to Marse that after enhancing the recording he heard that Delores Moreno, Mateo's sister, had something to do with the explosion on the Moreno compound. Either she had moved up, or gone to another cartel, or even set Mateo up. All this info came from her boyfriend, St. Marten, who was like Marse's Chatty Cathy in his office. The boyfriend was the one digging into finding Mateo, but that inquiries about Mike Landry had re-surfaced. By this time, Marse had not taken his eyes off Teddy, but had managed to scarf down six inches of po-boy and created a heap of dirty, crumpled paper napkins. He'd also guzzled a half-bottle of Barq's root beer.

Teddy tucked into his sandwich while they both thought over the new facts. "It galls the hell out of me when someone's gone dirty. Good to know who we're facing, at least. Sad to hear about the hot chick. It always disappoints when family turns on family, if that's the case. My doc, Teddy, is clean as a whistle for sure, and not a party to the hot mess. I'd stake my life on it."

Po-boys downed, they sat finishing their drinks, munching on ice, and re-living some of the good old days. "Rick, any more stuff to listen to, I'm up for it. Right from the get-go a couple of years ago, this has been nothing short of a fucking train wreck. Remember the crap from the shoot-out at the O.K. Corral? This is all tied to those same people, mark me."

Rick had his device back and would re-plant it when he got back to the office. "Sad to say, I bet there's more. By the way, next sandwich is on me."

◛

"After all your brother did for you, Delores, I can't believe you're not gonna go after Lopez. You know he's the one who called the hit. We gotta hit back even harder. All's you got to do is say the word, and I know Mateo's men would take them out." Diego sprawled out on the warehouse sofa. He had a cigarette in one hand and a beer in the other, like he was the head kingpin. Diego fancied himself more important than reality.

Filing her dagger-like claws, Delores didn't even look up when speaking to him. "For the time being, I have to play nice with Manny, even though I think he's too fucking stupid to have gotten to Mat. Something tells me Mateo is soaking up the sun on a beach in France or Spain. Who knows, but maybe since my brother moved his whore to Cartagena, he got sloppy? And get this straight, Diego, Mateo didn't do anything but hold me down. He's always been too soft for a man in his position." She pushed his legs off the sofa. "He's never approved of you. He didn't think you were good enough for me. So now, what do you think? That change your mind about my brother?"

Done with the nails, she sat next to him with her legs under her like a cat ready to spring on an unsuspecting mouse. This position made her sit taller than him, and she looked down at him like she was the one with power, not him.

"He was only actin' like a big brother," Diego said. "Like no one is good enough for my little sister. I watch them come 'round and know what's on their minds. I give them the mean mug; they know I know. Same thing, chica. We both know why you want me." He stubbed his cigarette, grabbed his crotch, and laughed.

The TV, tuned to a Spanish sports channel, broadcasted a heated soccer match, but a news flash raced across the bottom of the screen during the play. It continued to report on the explosion and the investigation. Anyone with half a brain would've known the authorities wouldn't waste man-hours on a cartel hit; it was pointless. Delores watched but knew there was no investigation. The policia didn't chase between cartels; they let them handle their own business. It got way too messy; besides, most of them were on the payroll of someone. She played with her phone as they waited for the guys to return with the boosted SUVs.

"I think I'm going back to Cartagena—a short trip. Try to get close to Manny. When I go, you'll need to run things here. You got the stones for it?" She looked up from her phone at Diego, raising one perfectly arched black eyebrow.

"What, and you'd take off and leave me, jus' like that?" He snapped his fingers.

She looked down at him, lightly passing her claw-like fingernails up his neck. She pouted, "You think I should take you? I need you here, mi amor. You don't trust me, is that it?"

He looked away from her. "I trust you, Delores. What I don't trust is all those macho Colombian men. They'll treat you like a whore. That's all they'll want from you, but I love you, and would make sure no one would disrespect you." He stood up over her. "I know what people say. They say you keep me around like a toy. I ain't no toy." On his way to the refrigerator for another beer, he pulled out his knife and stood behind her with it pressed hard to her throat. "See, I am good to you, Delores, and yet you treat me with no respect. Maybe together we go talk to this Manny Lopez, and you find some other office boy."

She didn't flinch. They heard the horn, and as she got up to open the garage door, she pushed Diego's hand and the knife out of her way. "You do that again; I'll use your own blade to cut off your balls." She sent shivers up his spine. She was cold, crazy, calculating, and dangerous. The blood coursing through her veins was like ice. Her frigid expression showed no signs of love; in fact, there was no expression at all. Her eyes were dark and soulless.

A brand-new black Jeep kitted with the whole package pulled into the warehouse. A short, dark-haired man jumped out of the ride. "Them college kids, no one never taught them to watch their stuff. Car was unlocked, windows down with keys under the visor like they didn't care. What a chump."

She slinked her way to the vehicle, looking it over. "Good work, Tomas. We'll get a good price for this one." She peered inside the car, reached under the passenger seat, and came out holding a wallet with a handful of credit cards. "Yeah, definitely a spoiled brat. He's gonna have a hard time telling his daddy that not only is he missing his car, but all of the credit cards, too. We could sell these cards—no, destroy them." She spoke as she turned and headed back toward the sofa. "Diego is gonna run things while I'm gone. Don't want no trouble. He's my ears and eyes, what he says goes, got it?"

Delores grabbed Diego's collar as she passed him. "Take me home."

Like a dog on a leash, he followed her out the door to her car. "Putting you in charge shows how much I trust you. Don't fuck anything up and watch the men at all times. I guarantee Tomas won't give you any trouble; you can trust him. The others, not so much; they'll need close watching. I leave for Cartagena in a week, but I want to see how the operation works when everyone thinks I'm gone. How much will the mice play while the cat is away?" She grinned. They jumped in the car and took off.

☜☞

Six weeks had passed since the first surgery, and Michael was anticipating a call for phase two of the transformation. His nerves had started getting a little raw, and his even-keeled disposition was taking on a far more impatient tone. Every muscle was tense, his comments at home edgier. His movements were more manic and not like the ever-so-cool Michael, and the familiar feeling of loathing himself lurked out from the deep hole of his past. Michaela had started to get a little whiny, and he knew she was picking up on his intensity.

He turned on the shower, stripped down, and stood as the water beat on his neck and shoulders with a forceful intensity. The heat had streaked the glass of the shower. He could just barely make out Rainie's shape. "Mike, you've got to get a grip." Her voice sounded more distant and not as boisterous. "Do you hear me? You're making the baby cry. Daddies aren't supposed to do that."

He wiped the shower door with his hand. "Rai, you okay? I hope you aren't getting sick."

He peered out the smudged circle he created, and saw a face planted up against the shower door. His stomach leaped into his throat as his heart raced. He threw himself against the back wall of the shower. The vision he saw was like that of Rainie, but it wasn't it was Rand. Rainie's dead twin. His body nervously trembled inside, his mind trying to process the insanity of it all.

"Mike, do you hear me?" Rand's tone was aggravated.

"Yes, yes, I hear you. I've been preoccupied." He continued describing his feelings, how he was nervous knowing the next call would be coming any day and how he didn't want to leave the family again but knew he had to. As he spoke, he choked up with emotion. He slumped on the seat in the shower and cried. The door flew open. He tightly closed his eyes and held his breath.

With a look of panic, Rainie stepped into the shower. "Michael, are you okay?" She knelt down and put her arms around him, holding him as his chest heaved. His sobs were from his soul. "Michael, what's wrong?" She took his face in her hands, looking him directly in the eyes. Her face showed fear and confusion.

His heart began to slow down, and his usual peace and calm took over. The intensity that plagued him was gone. All he could say was, "Rand."

A slight smile formed on her lips, and a warm, understanding look emanated from her eyes. "I know Rand's been upset because Michaela has been crying. I'm so sorry." She turned off the water and pulled two towels off the rack. She wrapped him in one and herself in the other after peeling her soaking dress from her body. She dabbed the towel on his face, stretched up, and kissed him. "Better?" They walked into the bedroom.

"Looking through the misty glass, I thought it was you, but it didn't sound like you. I could clearly tell it was you until her face pressed against the shower door. I've been an asshole, I know. Waiting for the call is the worst thing, but I guess it pales compared to travel and surgery. I'm on pins and needles, like the long-tailed cat in a room full of rocking chairs that you so handily refer to when you're uptight. That's me. I'm sorry my tension has affected Michaela, you, and the boys. I love you."

They stood naked in each other's arms; her comforting and him relinquishing to her gentle embrace. "Well, you can sigh in relief because I have a hand-delivered envelope for you. No more waiting; it's here. While you hate the anticipation," she tapped the tip of his nose, "I hate you being gone, even if it's only three days. It feels like an eternity." She walked to his closet and pulled out his overnight bag.

The tension of waiting turned to the thrill of living on the edge—a feeling juxtaposed by his loathing at leaving her. A tingle triggered in Michael's body, and the anticipation was like a wild aphrodisiac, igniting all his senses. The adrenalin roared through him as he packed a few things. Glancing over his shoulder, he saw Rainie watching him. "What's that look?" She stood, arms crossed, with her head at a slight tilt.

"Michael, your moods are like a roller coaster. I'm supposed to be the one keeping you insanely curious, but the roles have reversed, which is pretty damn scary. I'm now the steady, reliable, calm as a cucumber one, while you're teetering on a tight rope. If you want this damn envelope, you better get your ass over here. It's gonna cost you." She put her hand toward him, beckoning him with the finger she had pointed at him. "You ask, 'you think I have a sexy swagger?' Oh, but yes, sweet Michael."

Rainie plopped on the bed. He reached around her to grasp the envelope. She stuffed it under her, forcing him to put his arm around the back of her body. She pulled his body down, scoping out the well-defined muscles in his chest and shoulders. He maneuvered to the far side of her and onto the bed, pulling her on top of him. Holding one arm around her, he easily took the envelope from her hand. "Are we reading it together right here and now? Or do you want me to tell you the details?" he asked with a teasing smile as one side of his mouth turned up, fashioning a coy look.

She giggled. "Open the letter and get on with it." He opened it and, with a grin, began to read it silently to himself. "Are you shitting me? Ya know, I could've opened it before giving it to you and read it first." Her nose wrinkled in playful disapproval.

Clearing his throat, he began aloud. "Mike, everything you will require is enclosed. Leaving Friday at 4 AM, returning Sunday at 6 PM. Same routine, though an hour earlier, different driver, pilots, but Noir will meet you. Safe travels."

He rolled her over and straddled her hips, gazing down at her.

"Michael, it must drive you crazy that he's so verbose." Her laugh was contagious. Her lips were tempting, almost teasing. They were a kiss waiting to happen. Delicately, he kissed her once, twice, and a third time. Gingerly, he began stroking lightly from her chin, down her neck, and ventured to her breasts. "Careful how close you get to the nips; I suspect you'll get more than you bargained for." He kissed between her breasts and moved down to her stomach. He pushed his mouth against her belly and blew hard, creating a loud, tickling raspberry. She coughed out a laugh and a poor attempt at a squeal. Her throaty voice plainly didn't squeal a typical high-pitched sound; nonetheless, it was a sound of sheer delight and friskiness. "And here I thought you were getting all sexy on me, but no, you tickled and tricked me. I'm going to have to watch you, buster, like a hawk."

They gazed into each other's eyes. "Are you asking me to get all sexy on you? Just what is it you want me to do, hm?" He blew on her belly again. She laughed, wiggling herself over on her belly. Leaning forward, he whispered in her ear, "I'll gladly taste your delicate little bud, or is it pussy, twat, or vajay?" He kissed her neck. "But there'll be no back end, um. I far prefer—"

"No? You don't like my ass? I'll have you know; I think I have one hell of an ass."

He lifted her hips, kissing each side, then stroked his tongue down into her. He nipped the insides of her thighs, then traced all the pleasure points with his tongue. With one quick flip, he had her turned over on her back. He placed her ankles on his shoulders. Sliding into her felt like a soft, warm hug; tight, with the right amount of squeeze. He thrust deep into her, sliding back and forth. The slow, melodic pace was intoxicating, and began throbbing from the core of his being until he felt the imminent pulse and pulled out, spraying his seed onto her belly and breasts. "No baby-making this time." He jumped up, dampening a warm washcloth to wipe her down.

She crooned, "We need to get a box of condoms. I don't believe the old wives' tale about nursing preventing pregnancy; I know too many Irish twins."

Her sexy, throaty laugh enthralled his heart like the vertical plunge of a roller coaster after chugging up to the pinnacle. He felt his breath catch before letting a more subdued chuckle follow. It was her laugh that had first intoxicated him, setting her apart from the rest of the freshman girls during rush week. After their brief conversation, she'd been imprinted forever on his heart.

"I don't go for the old wives' tale either. John and I are dang close in age, maybe not Irish twins—" he grinned, "but close enough. I think we should wait another year before the next one."

She wrapped her arms around his neck, pulling him in close. "Next one? Don't count on a next one, sir. I want my body back for good." She gave him a quick peck before releasing him and padding to the bathroom. She drew her bathwater. "Are you going to bathe with me, Michael? I know you already showered, but I want you to be with me. Those three days will feel like an eternity."

☜☞

Friday morning came fast, and he was off again to the far corner of the world. He quickly fell back into the role of Monsieur Marchand. After a day of travel, it was a relief to see the black car appear as the helicopter neared. Once again, the pilot was skilled and set down with precision. Unlike the initial pilot, this one spoke not a word, did his job, and nothing more.

Noir greeted him with a handshake, maybe a stroke closer to showing some personality, but only by a hair. The building came into view and was as he remembered. It looked like a scene from a James Bond movie. Once again, there wasn't any deviation from the original itinerary.

Since Michael already knew the layout, he walked to his room, dropped his bag, and went in search of Mateo. It was good to see his patient again. The healing was going remarkably well. The two men sat down with a glass of wine and some cheese. This time, Mateo inquired about the baby and seemed more personable. Michael felt a warmth, perhaps a longing from his patient. Thoughts crossed his mind as he watched Mateo. The man gave up everything. Did he have regrets?

"Tout va bien?" (Everything okay?) Michael took a small bite of cheese.

"Oui," Mateo replied, but his eyes said much more.

"Besoin de parler?" (Need to talk?) Michael asked. "Je pense que tu fais." (I think you do.)

Mateo instructed Michael to follow him. They walked to his private quarters, and when he locked the door, he flipped a switch, like in the military SKIF top-secret security rooms. The button eliminated any chance of a breach. "Mike," he said in English. "I miss my wife, my lover, and my children, but I know I will have a new life. I need only be patient, yet I still mourn them. Once the transformation is complete, I can leave this place behind and begin a new life, a more relaxed life. I no longer need the extravagances I once desired. As you would say, I have been there and done that and have paid the price for my indulgences. Who knows, maybe I will find another wife, even father a child or two. I missed much in the profession I chose."

Mateo's quarters were comfortable, but nothing out of the ordinary. It reminded Michael of an apartment he'd had while in medical school—plain walls, a desk, a sofa, a dinette set, a bed, a side table, and a dresser—nothing reminiscent of the luxury Michael would have assumed of Mateo's former life.

Michael sat on the sofa with his glass of wine in hand. Mateo pulled up a chair, sat, and ran the tip of his finger around the rim of his glass, looking into it. There definitely was a sadness.

"You, sir, are a contradiction." Michael crossed his legs. "Mateo Moreno, the most powerful man in all of Colombia, but what I see is a kind, caring man behind your eyes. Forgive me if I speak too boldly. Out of curiosity, what's your story? Were you born into your status? Family business?" Michael tilted his head to one side in ponderance.

Mateo seemed to find the question amusing as he gave a melancholy chuckle. "No, not at all." He took a sip from his glass. "I was born to a hard-working family. I would see the long black cars drive down the streets and think one day I would like to ride in one of those." A smile of remembrance crossed his face. "The men in the cars had beautiful women on their arms and rolls of money. I did not know what they did, but I knew they were to be respected." It was like a spellbinding movie that moved Michael to the edge of his chair. The rumble of anticipation ignited a need to know.

"I've always thought it was a family kind of business, no?" Michael questioned, more as a statement of fact. From what he'd researched, all indicators expressed a familial alliance. Mateo stood, walked to the small fridge, and grabbed a bottle of water. He held it up, offering Michael a bottle. "No, thank you." Michael wanted to know; he needed to know who this man was.

"You are correct; in most cases, who would one turn to, but

family? The trust is in the blood, my friend, or should be, yes? As a teenager, my parents managed the necessities, but I needed a job and went to work at one of the richest resorts in Cartagena as a cabana boy, riding my bicycle five miles to get to work. I would serve beautiful libations complete with spears of fruit and floating flowers to add to the temptation. I added a heavier touch to the beauty of the beverage, wooing the guests to ask for me as they basked around the pool. Some would tip me handsomely, some not. I waited on a boy at the poolside, about my age. He ordered like a big shot with little to no respect for anyone, especially me. I thought it was odd, but then I saw his father call to him. His father was one of the men I had seen riding in the big black cars. I stepped up my service to the boy. At first, the boy talked down to me. I just smiled and did my job. After a time, he became friendlier, but this was after seeing me many times. He was never with friends, always alone. One day his father had called for him. He made a passing comment, completely disrespectful, regarding his father. He said it right to my face. I am certain my face showed the fear and shock." Animatedly, Mateo reenacted the look of surprise and, yes, much concern.

"Mr. Lopez—I inscribed his name on my brain—walked over to the boy. It was as though he glided, completely poised. He was the essence of control and sophistication." Mateo watched Michael's expressions closely as though trying to read him. "The man told his son, in a quiet way, but I could tell he was outraged: 'Since you have no respect for your father, I suggest you leave now and think about what it means to respect. The car will take you home, this minute.' The man apologized to me for his son's insolence and hoped he had not been offensive to me. I told him the boy had always been kind to me, then he handed me a sizeable tip and said he appreciated my work. He had been watching me over time, and perhaps when I was older, I might want to work for him. He admired young men willing to work hard. And so, in time, I did things for him. I washed his cars, ran errands, and even drove him a few times. Before I knew it, he treated me more like a son than his own son, Manny. Thus, my life in business developed under his guiding hand. The son was nothing more than a spoiled child, even as a man. He did not have his father's respect. In time, his business became my business and his men, my men. When Mr. Lopez passed, it crushed me. He had been a father figure to me since my father had always worked and had no time for my sister or me. Manny tried to take the business, but he was imbecilic, and no one wanted to work for him. No one chooses to work for a child. But after Seignior's passing, there were many looking to move up and take over. Men with far more experience and much older than I. When one amasses much power and wealth, there is always another in line, trying to take it away. Like my own father and Seignior Lopez, my life was all about business or work. My father worked sun-up to long past sundown, sometimes working two jobs. Neither man enjoyed his family, and there I was, like them, not being able to enjoy the fruits of my labor and always looking over my shoulder. I hardly knew my wife, my lover, or my family. Not that I wanted to be the cabana boy again, but I wanted to live my life. I wished my life were simpler." Michael understood.

Since Mateo had been so open and candid about his life, Michael felt comfortable sharing his feelings on Rainie; it came as naturally as breathing. Michael spoke about the boys, Michaela, his upbringing, and his practice. He mentioned his new partner, leaving out a few of the personal details. The more Michael spoke of Rainie, the more heartsick he became—no way would he want Mateo's life. As the hour was getting late, Michael needed to retire for the evening. The next surgery, while not as intense as the first surgery, would still be quite taxing. He left Mateo's room and went to his own in hopes of a peaceful night's slumber.

Fretful nightmares took him back to Rainie's abduction, and then a whirlwind of fears— the thought of what would have happened if he hadn't been able to save her plagued him. The oh-so-familiar tremble of his body soared with anger as his mind played a loop of the sounds and feelings he'd felt when she was kidnapped. Randy Tolbert was one sick fuck. With a jolt to attention, his body glistened with sweat; his respirations were elevated and choreographed in duet with his racing heartbeat. While still captured between wakefulness and sleep, it was a relief when the alarm went off.

After a half-hour on his knees, giving thanks and asking for God's help, it was go-time. The thrill of testing his abilities and creativity sparked butterflies in his stomach and kicked his adrenalin into overdrive. He loved the creative aspect of his profession and the ability to change people's lives. The twist on this one with its sense of espionage may have seemed fabulous and daring at one time in his life. Still, with Rainie and the kids back home, it was more like a major inconvenience and pain in the ass, but there was no denying the underlying excitement. The one comforting thought was he would be back home the next day and into her loving arms.

Mateo smiled at him as he entered pre-op holding. He was prepped and ready. "Bonjour, mon ami." (Hello, my friend.)

"Comment vas-tu, Guillaume? Nerveux?" (How are you, William? Nervous?)

Mateo smiled as he shook his head, "Non pas avec tes mains habiles." (No, not with your skilled hands.) His smile instilled confidence in his surgeon.

"Bon!" Michael held his patient's face carefully, studying as he drew purple marks. "A bientot. Dormez bien." (See you soon. Sleep well.)

Welcomed by an entirely different surgical team, Michael felt the need to acquaint them with his expectations. From all accounts, this new team was equally as skilled as the first. It was more than obvious they had been instructed not to engage in small talk and pleasantries. Docteur Marchand was perhaps the most arrogant, self-absorbed person on the planet. Hm, he thought, similar to some of his colleagues in the profession. Many of Michael's acquaintances from the medical sector, particularly the surgeons, regarded themselves way too highly, and came across with a God complex. He knew how he needed to act; he'd witnessed it too many times. As he scrubbed, he observed the team prepping the surgical suite to perfection. One attendant turned on the music as instructed, and he could see the telltale signs of smiles beneath the masks. Marchand or not, Michael needed his music like some surgeons needed their chewing gum. It set his pace. On cue, one of the nurses rolled the patient in, strapped him down, and prepped him. The anesthesiologist began the sedation, and Michael entered.

Mateo had already assumed the life of William La Salle after the first surgery. His hair was bleached blond, his skin lightened to almost look Caucasian, and his face had an entirely different landscape. There was little likeness to the man once known as the most powerful person in Colombia. Mateo's second surgery proved to be transformative, with a concentration on the soft areas of the face. Fatty implants filled the cheeks and jowls. The new staff was completely unaware of the first surgery. The only common thread throughout the whole ordeal was Noir. At their first face-to-face meeting, the photograph presented to Michael riding in the black limousine was coming to life before his very eyes. Michael accomplished more than he had expected, translating into one more surgery to go, not two. Although it had only been twenty-four hours, it seemed a lifetime since he'd snuggled next to Rainie in bed.

With his patient sleeping comfortably with round-the-clock monitoring, Michael slipped into his swimsuit and then into the tepid pool. It was warm enough to relax him but not so much that he was rendered limp as a boiled noodle. His exhaustion level crept high, as though he'd been days without sleep; perhaps that was why the young brunette went unnoticed as she entered.

E. Conners had assisted in the surgery. Not that she was necessarily flirting, but the fact that she was in the nude made him feel most uncomfortable and validated his decision to promptly exit. "Je n'avais pas l'intention de vous deranger. Je vais partir" (I did not intend to disturb you. I will leave.)

"Non, je partais juste." (No, I was just leaving.) He wasn't and could've used a few more minutes in the pool but wanted to avert any possible rumors and stave off any unwanted advances.

She glided gracefully through the water, watching him as he toweled off. "Dommage que je pourrais vous aider a vous detendre." (Shame, I could help you relax.) She sparked a seductive smile.

He ignored the overture and went straight to his room. He couldn't help but question the situation and wonder if someone was trying to set him up. He hadn't given anyone from the surgical team even the slightest sign of interest. No, he thought, this was definitely a set-up; it reeked of it, but by who and why? It was a puzzle. Who would've been behind it? Mateo? Noir? Or maybe it was the girl herself, seeking the thrill of banging the surgeon?

Once back in his room, the shower beckoned him. The pulsating force of the spray felt good on his neck. The chlorine odor as it swirled the drain picked at his brain. Not only was the incident strange, but it set off a creepy crawl up his spine to the tips of his ears, alerting his senses that things were amiss. Most unsettling. He padded into the bedroom and was startled to find the brunette naked in his bed. That was it; he was pissed. This was undoubtedly not an overture he had invited and one he had declined in the pool. He reached into the bed, grabbed the naked girl's arm, and marched her out the door in search of Noir. It took but a minute.

Noir looked from him to the naked girl and back again. Michael was tired and impatient. "Garder cette trollop sous controle." (Keep this trollop under control.) He shoved her into Noir, who, from all appearances, was equally as mystified. As he returned to his room, he heard the pop of a gunshot. He hadn't meant to get the girl killed, but that was their business, and maybe she was working for someone else. Random thoughts ran through his mind like a treadmill permanently stuck in the on position—going and going with no end in sight. Since he was wide awake, with sleep being the furthest thought in mind, he strolled down to Recovery. Mateo was groggy but beginning to return to the land of the living.

Michael smiled at his patient. "La chirurgie s'est bien deroulee." (The surgery went well.) He patted Mateo's hand. "Un de plus." (One more.) Mateo gave a thumbs up. The men spoke for a minute. Michael explained the odd situation with the nurse in the pool and then in his bed. He voiced his concern about it being a set-up, but that Noir had handled things in Noir's way. Mateo nodded in acknowledgment, saying the girl had acted inappropriately and he was sorry, but he didn't think it was a breach in his security, merely poor judgment of a foolish girl. Either way, Noir had taken the situation in hand, even if he'd been a bit over the top. Michael assured Mateo he'd check on him before he left in the morning.

The return to New Orleans went without a wrinkle and any more inappropriate encounters. It was good to be home. The boys were watching out the window and raised the alarm that Michael was home. He was welcomed by cheering boys, a plethora of hugs, and a sweet, flirty kiss from Rainie. Allie took the boys back to the den and let Rainie and Mike have a few minutes alone before dinner.

Dropping his case, he took her in his arms. "I missed you. Come with me while I unpack; I had some strange happenings."

Like a puppy, she trotted behind him up the stairs. "You have my curiosity up."

He mumbled something to the effect that she had something of his up. Upon entering their bedroom, he wasted not a moment to start undressing her; walking her to the bed, he tossed her onto her back and plunged into her hard, with purpose. "I need you in a bad way." Wham, bam, and done, so unlike Michael.

Taken aback by his wanton urge, she wasn't quite sure what to say, so she fell back on a sarcastic teasing swipe. "Michael, tell me how you really feel."

"Sorry, babe, for going all Neanderthal on you." He pulled up his pants. "I wanted you, no, needed you desperately. Strange coupla days. Travel was perfect, Monsieur and Docteur Marchand were impeccable, surgery couldn't have gone any better, and it all came together, leaving me with only one more short surgery." He watched as she put her clothes back on. Knuckling his eyes, he rubbed the tired feeling away. "I've told you about the facility before, I know. This time I brought my swimsuit thinking it would loosen my muscles, get rid of some of the tension, ya know. There I was, swimming a few laps, and one of the surgical team, a young brunette, comes in to swim, fuckin' buck naked. Needless to say, I left and went to my room."

Rainie unpacked his case while she listened. A big grin crossed her face. "Aw, Michael, it was like a schoolgirl crush, only grown-up style. I hope you weren't rude." She walked toward his closet to put his case away.

"I guess I wasn't, because when I came out of the shower, she was naked in my bed!"

She turned around slowly. "What? Bitch! Michael, no means no, right? What'd you do?" She sat next to him on the bed and rubbed his thigh. "Little miss surgery girl got you so hot and bothered that the first thing you wanted to do was jump my bones. Is that it, or did you miss me that much?"

Michael laid back on the bed. "I feel bad, Rai. I grabbed her arm and brought her to Mateo's man and complained. Walking off, I heard the pop of a gun. I didn't mean to get her killed. I was tired, and she was an annoyance. When I told Mateo, or should I say William, about it, I might as well have been talking about the weather. It was like no big deal. I think I know the man, and he's a caring, loving man, and then, life, it's like nothing. I was concerned maybe she was a plant or something like that, ya know? No, just some stupid kid wanting to get her jollies with the doc, and now she's dead. I shoulda—"

"What? Just fucked her and sent her on her merry way?"

He jumped up and coiled back, aghast. "No! I shoulda sent her on her way, yes, with a scolding or something. Why'd I bring her to—" She saw he'd blanched and looked devasted. "It's all I could think about on the way home."

"C'mere, you." She wrapped her arms around his waist and hugged him. "Michael, my love, had you any idea that Mateo's man would have killed her; you'd have never said a word. That's who you are. It's not your fault. Who knows, maybe Noir told the girl you could have pulled out a gun on her for her audacity, and then he shot the gun in the air to make a point. Did she scream? Or did you hear the body fall?"

"No, but—"

Rainie grabbed his hand. "No more bad thoughts. You have three kiddos waiting for you, and dinner's gonna get cold."

ᏮᏭ

Delores straddled Diego's hips. "Tell me how business went today without me being there. The cat was away so, did the mice play?"

"It went like usual, whatchoo think? Chica, you bein' at the shop don't make no difference. The only thing that ever fucked up business was crazy Santa and his junkie ass. I know it ain't right to speak ill of the dead, but he was one off da rail's motherfucker. All's good, my sexy minx," he purred at her, staring at her lips while flexing himself between her legs. "Take me to your bed," he whispered into her chest. "Sure you don't want me in Cartagena with you? You gonna miss me, bonita." With her legs wrapped around his waist, he carried her to the bed.

☙�

Emile, Manny's closest friend, sat in a chair with his leg hiked over the armrest as they watched the television. "Hey Manny, they find Mateo's body?" Emile pried.

"No, I told you, and they won't. The investigators might find a foot or a finger, but he's in a million pieces. What you so worried about? I got it under control. Delores Moreno is coming to see me. She wants to talk." The two men grinned at each other.

Emile walked to the bar and poured a couple of shots. "Is that what you call it, talk? I say she's gonna try to get to you through your cock, Manny. She is one fine piece of ass. She'll make one helluva inamorata. Heh, heh." He cupped the air in front of him like he was squeezing her buttocks. He took a long draw on a joint, followed by tossing a shot back, all the while coughing and choking for air.

"You smoke too much of that shit. Put it down; you're fuckin wasted." Manny changed the channel to a game, swallowing down the other shot. "Another, Emile." He handed the glass to the man. "I want to hear what Ms. Moreno has to say. Maybe she'll want to join forces, but I don't think Mateo's men will follow her. As far as I know, they've made no allegiance to anyone, and there's no word about who's taking over. Course, there's not too many from the inner circle still alive, and the rest probably scattered, shittin' themselves. I wonder maybe the sister called the hit."

Manny's compound was a quarter the size of Mateo's and his army of soldiers less than half. His father had been a reasonable businessman, given the subject of his affairs. Rarely had he raised his voice; rather, his silence struck fear. Manny was mouthy, loud, and emotionally charged without much wisdom, so Señor Lopez and his associates favored Mateo. Only the most disreputable wanna-be wash-out considered working for Manny. No one of substance associated with Manny, no matter the money he offered. The question in his mind was still about Mateo's murder and who'd called the hit. Manny didn't try to stop the false rumors that he had ordered the hit, though he hadn't. He didn't deny, and with his coy answers, he tried to give teeth to speculations. Some suspected the call had come from Mexico; another rumor was Argentina, but the most likely hypothesis was Delores, Mateo's sister. She was known to be cold, but a hit on one's own family was more than cold. Emile rolled another joint and fired it up.

"Go smoke your shit outside. You sit there, eyes glazed over like a brainless joke. What good are you to me like this? Besides, my children will be here soon." Emile shrugged one shoulder as he passed through open arches onto a stone veranda overlooking the garden and pool. He sat on one of the sofas and pulled out his phone. "Heads up, Delores Moreno meeting with Manny in two days." He waited. "I'll let you know."

❦

"Sarge, I might have some legit info on the Moreno hit." Russ Tobin strutted across the squad room like a peacock. "Heard through the wires, Delores Moreno is headed for Cartagena in a coupla days. It seems there's a meet with Manny Lopez." He stood with his arms crossed in front of Marse's desk with a cocky grin on his face like there was some point to prove. "Seems I mighta been right on thinkin' that hot bitch was behind the hit. If I was you, I'd start trustin' the Tobin gut. Hasn't failed me yet." He hiked his hip on the corner of Rick's desk, and once again, Marse stared him down. "What is it about you? You got a problem findin' out who blew up Moreno, or you just skatin' down short-timers boulevard? If I didn't know better, I'd think you didn't want to know who did the deed."

Rick pressed his fingers into his temples. "You make my head hurt, Tobin, and get your ass off my desk. I don't want to have to tell you again, got it? Why don't you put in an application to DEA? You seem to be obsessed."

The more Russ Tobin smeared his mug and boisterous opinions in front of Marse, the more suspicious Rick became, and the more pungent the stink on the whole damn thing became. Just the sight of Tobin sent the feeling of crawly insects up Rick's neck, and he could feel the hairs tingle as they stood at attention along his neck and arms. No doubt about it, Russ Tobin was one bad cop. He reeked of being on someone's payroll other than the NOPD, or at the very least a wannabe. Tobin wouldn't have been the first of New Orleans' blue line to stray. Unfortunately, in his career, he had seen quite a few throw their lives away for extra scratch in their pockets.

To say Rick Marse had had his opportunities to walk on the dark side of the blue line was an understatement. Seemed like the more upright and forthright the officer, the more significant temptation for the crime syndicate. He'd had offers from high-priced cars, to boats, to his kids' school tuitions. With a smile on his face and a flutter in his heart, he scratched his head in amusement—tuition had been the hardest to pass up. Fast cars and boats didn't even offer the slightest tickle to his fancy, but his kids' schooling was a colossal temptation; however, nothing was worth his integrity or the shine he had on his badge.

Tobin had returned to his desk, but like a freakin' boomerang, he was back in front of Marse. "What is it Rick, you think you're better than the rest of us stiffs? You talk to me like I'm a piece of shit. I walk the same damn line you do."

Rick hadn't even looked up from his work. He merely said, bemused, "I doubt it." He continued with his work.

Tobin slammed his fists on the desk right in front of Marse. "You know what, you're the one that has some sort of deal going on. You can't even look me in the eye. Aren't you supposed to bleed blue with your grand pedigree? You and your hoity friends, the good doctor, and his lovely Mrs. Landry, I'm gonna make it my priority to investigate that shady relationship. Maybe the missus and Delores are friendly, go to the same nail parlor, or maybe even the good doc gets his designer drugs from the Moreno operation. A lotta docs got a nose problem and sure as shit have the money to do it. You even checked the circles they travel in?"

Rick tightly squinted his eyes with a set jaw and pursed lips as he drew in a deep breath. Should he even entertain a conversation with the man? It wasn't going to change anything. A stream of insults passed through his mind like a pictorial montage. He looked up for one second, winked, and calmly said, "You do that, Russ." By Russ' huffy puffy exit, it was apparent the sting of sarcasm had been felt.

Deja Vu

The dull, empty ache she felt in her heart was nearly immobilizing. As she watched the endless loop of the explosion and the constant stream of reporters hypothesizing as to who'd murdered the infamous Mateo Moreno, the tears rolled down her cheeks in a continual stream. Marguerite, now legally named Rita, had not met Mateo's beautiful Colombian wife. Considering everything, Marguerite was thankful that Mateo's wife had been traveling with their family and was safe instead of being blown up with her husband. Mateo indulged his family in the most refined things, she knew, and while his death was a hazard of his business and tragic for his family, perhaps the wife, too, would find liberation. Mateo had told her many times that he knew his wife had been in love with another man for years, and he held no ill will. Their marriage was a means to an end—a beautiful family and an heir to his lineage. Maybe in this tragedy, she might find some peace in his death.

Mateo had provided a beautiful home for Marguerite in Cartagena; however, it wasn't her home. New Orleans had always been home, and she missed it desperately. She knew the likelihood of Grayson's survival in prison was improbable, Mateo had even said those very words, but she had not received a letter or any indication of her husband's demise. To that point, Marguerite had not heard he was alive either. She had been cut off from everything she had ever known, but in hindsight, Mateo had been attentive, provided for everything, and she knew she had been the love of his life. The news of his death struck her hard, but in the same breath, the freedom to leave and return home was an answer to a prayer.

A few days after the explosion, Marguerite received a package containing an airline ticket, her old passport, and identification papers plus fifty thousand in U.S. currency. All the old accounts in New Orleans were still open and had plenty of money in them. Mateo had also maintained her home in New Orleans. Marguerite had a debt of gratitude held deep in her heart. He had taken care of her, as promised, even though at the time she'd held much resentment. She felt like she'd been taken prisoner—whether for her own good or not. It was most displeasing at the time. The wellness clinic, as Mateo liked to call it, managed to melt away twenty-plus pounds and gave her skin a more youthful glow. He had insisted on her growing her hair from the short bob, and she felt more attractive, more desirable. He had kept her with all the luxuries one might want after completing eight weeks in the wellness facility, which was top-notch, and while she hated to admit it, she needed some serious help.

Packing up her things to return to New Orleans resurrected dormant ideas and predilections she'd once favored. She wondered what had happened to the redhead married to the doctor. Had she just gone about her merry way, or had she been one of the nails in the coffin of the law firm? She would've liked a chance to have her in the sack. Old conversations swirled through her mind. Nobody had taken her seriously back then. Had they, then maybe it wouldn't have ended the way it did. Randy Tolbert was still missing, presumed dead. Thibeaux had gone through a nasty divorce and been disbarred, ruining his life. Then her Grayson was sentenced to years in prison, and more than likely been just another tragedy of prison violence. She had had no word of certainty, but Mateo had said it was probably the case; or had he said he would make sure it would be the case?

As she opened her carry-on, she found a handwritten letter from Mateo. She plopped amidst the stacks of things needing to be packed and began reading.

My darling, my dearest, the one true desire of my heart, I look forward to our Greek holiday away from the bothers of life in Cartagena.

My heart has melted watching your journey to wellness, leaving the horrible nightmares behind. I beseech you, my love, never look back, only forward to many years of our blissful happiness together. I love you with all of my being. M.

She felt her heart sink. How quickly she had reverted to old ways of thinking, and the darkness had already taken a foothold. Maybe a few more visits with her shrink would help her through Mateo's death. She wasn't strong enough to move home just yet. Why hadn't he told her about the vacation to Greece? She had no idea. The gates of her heart opened as she gave way to a waterfall of tears. She called the wellness center and set up an appointment.

ॐ

Michael was already in his office when Zeke came in. "How's it going, Zeke? Still feeling fulfilled here?" He looked up from his desk with a smile.

Zeke had a pensive look on his face, not his usual bright smile and sparkling eyes, always so full of life and vigor. "Got a minute?" He slunk down in Michael's chair and crossed his legs, spinning his wedding band around and around his finger. "If this is too personal, say the word, and I'll stop. I need to unload."

Michael came from around the desk, shut the door, and then sat in the other chair, turning toward Zeke. "What's up? I don't know if I can help, but if I can't, at least I'm a good sounding board." The corners of Michael's lips turned up in a warm smile, and he spread his hands as though saying, 'Go on.'

A single tear rolled down Zeke's cheek; he pinched his nose and tried to look away, gathering his emotions. "It's Damien. I think he wants to—" He cleared his throat. "I think he has found someone else and is planning on leaving me." He looked at the floor with his head held low. Looking up, he slightly shook his head, cleared his throat again, "No, I know he has someone else. I can't even begin to compete with this person for his attention. I, frankly, don't have what it takes."

Michael leaned back in his chair with his fingers steepled. His expression was deadpan. "This is just my opinion, and I feel awkward in saying this, but if you're looking for my advice and you are, I take it?" Michael stayed silent for a second, giving Zeke a moment to confirm. "Firstly, if someone is cheating on you, they aren't worth your time or your heart. I know, easy for me to say. You say you can't compete—"

Zeke, rather red-eyed, briefly stated, "The affair is with a woman. I've seen her; I know who she is. Her name is Connie Tolbert, and in a lonely housewife kind of way, she might be considered attractive."

Michael let out a long sigh. "Fuucckk! I know who she is and if he wants to be with her, best let him go. She's one messy, messy person. It's a long story and one for another day, but my advice, my friend, is cut your losses and fast. Run, don't walk. Your heart will heal and you, sir, are a great catch. Any man, um, with your, um, preference or, um—"

"I get it, Mike. It's heartbreaking, that's all. Sorry, really." He glanced at his watch just as a knock sounded on the door.

"Come in, Beth. Lucky you, you got both of us at one time." She blushed, looking at Zeke but handed each of the doctors their printout of patients for the day. While she was friendly, Beth was all business at work, and the day was never to start late, unless one was having a baby or a major familial crisis; otherwise, she expected punctuality. Looking at Zeke, Michael said, "We can go over that case today at lunch?"

"Good deal." Zeke glanced at his patient list, then thanked Beth and left the room. He had pulled himself together just in time.

☙☞

Heads turned as Delores strutted through the airport in her tight black mini, cropped jacket over a hot pink spandex tank and five-inch stilettos. She was one gorgeously sexy woman, no ands or buts about it, and she knew it. She also had ice running through her veins—one stone-cold killer, proven several times over. The chauffeur held up a sign with bold letters spelling out Mrs. Rodriguez. It could have just as easily been Smith or Jones, but that would've been more conspicuous in Cartagena.

Delores nodded to the chauffeur. His eyes glistened as he watched her walk up. He wasn't expecting his passenger to be quite so tasty.

The passengers were usually fat men in black silk suits two sizes too small and dark glasses, or obnoxious, brightly printed island-type shirts sucking a fat cigar under their straw-brimmed hat. But always dark-tinted sunglasses.

"Bienvenido. Aviseme si puedo ser de ayuda durante sue stadia." (Welcome. Let me know if I can be of assistance during your stay.) With his sexiest Don Juan smile, he tricked a wink at her. This foxy Latin goddess made his cock hard just watching her walk in front of him. Her tight round ass performed under her skirt as her hips slinked from side to side. He could imagine sliding his mighty steel up and down her spine. She looked over her shoulder and thanked him, knowing damn well he'd watched her with eager anticipation and a heart of wanton lust. She knew she had that effect on most men and used it at will. It worked like a charm. He was handsome enough, and she wanted to keep her options open for male company, so she resisted making a rude comment. "Negocios o placer?" (Business or pleasure?) He handed her his card. "Yo si necesitas algo." (Call me if you need anything.) He opened the car door and watched as she slid in. She glanced at his handwritten card. It was barely legible, but from all accounts, the name read Seb, probably short for Sebastian, followed by his number.

After a tumultuous ride of constant horn blowing, darting in and out of traffic, taking turns far too fast, and hard braking, they pulled up to a gated residence. Unlike the rest of the adventurous car ride, he pulled up to the house at a much-reduced speed, almost a glorified roll. Outside were three armed men in view—one at the door and one on either corner of the house.

One of Manny's gun-slinging soldiers led Delores to the study. The round, dark haired man came from behind his desk. "Dedee, I'm so sorry for your loss. I feel like I've lost a brother. You know how close Mat and I were. We grew up together." He placed his hand over his heart and took on an expression of profound sadness. What a pathetic snake was all she could think. They did the exaggerated air hug. "I was most surprised to hear from you. What can I do?" He ordered his soldier to have someone bring them a glass of wine.

Arching an eyebrow with her head at a slight angle, she inquired,

"Any idea who murdered Mat, Manny? At first, I must tell you the truth; I thought it was you." She watched his expression closely. He pantomimed an appearance of someone appalled; his mouth dropped in exaggeration, drawing his hands to his lips, and completed the act with a gasp.

Sputtering, "N-no! How could you think that? For a brief moment, I thought, and I am sorry even to hear the words pass my lips, but I did, just very briefly, may I add, wonder if you had—"

She interrupted, "How dare you say such a thing? I knew there had been bad blood between you and my brother, and if he had stepped out of line, which he has—er, had been known to do, I was prepared to say, such is the life we've chosen. I wanted to hear it for myself from your lips, Manny."

His eyes glassed with unfinished tears. "I promise you, on my children's lives, I had nothing to do with Mateo's death. You must believe me, Dedee." He still had the expression of a fat, spoiled boy, too weak to do anything but pretend to order people around. In his forties, he had yet to become a man, and if she had anything to do with it, he never would develop into a man. He had enough power to be annoying and get in the way, but not enough to wipe her out; she was far more cunning, so she thought, than her brother, Mateo, certainly more cold-hearted.

She leaned forward, held up her glass, and offered a toast. "To Mateo, may his soul finally rest in peace." They both held up their glasses. They spent the next half hour talking about his family, but the conversation was beginning to drag. "It was good to clear the misconception, Manny, and give my best to your wife and children. Now if your man could take me to my hotel. Thank you for the wine and good wishes. I'll only be in Cartagena a week if that. Hopefully, I will be able to see my sister-in-law, niece, and nephews." The pretend farewell hug commenced. He then bowed, took her hand, and kissed the top as though she were royalty. She slowly batted her eyes and turned to leave as Manny's gunslinger led her to Seb, the driver.

Once back in the car, she spoke briefly with the driver and said she might take him up on his offer to show her the sights; it had been some time since she had been to Cartagena and played tourist. She'd call him.

Just the happenstance she might call put a bulge in his pants that was increasingly growing more obvious, and she imagined uncomfortable.

She scrolled down her phone and wondered if the contacts still applied; after all, they had been numbers of Mateo's top-ranking confidantes. One she knew intimately well and had polished his knob on more than one occasion. She hoped Javier hadn't been collateral damage; he was such a good lover. She knew Diego was jealous when it came to Javi, and with reason. By mistake, while making love one time, she had spoken his name, and it had been months until she'd heard the end of it.

৩৩

The resort was as lovely as ever. Delores called the number she had for Javier. He picked up on the third ring. "Hola Dedee. In town, I'm guessing? Where are you staying, Casa San Agustin or Hilton? Like last time, are we going to dine in the suite? I do hope so."

"Hilton. I love the view; it is the best. Am I right, no? Come up to the suite, say eight? Repeat performance, I hope." He gave a slight chuckle to her playful suggestion.

"Cartagena is not the same without Mat," she continued. "It feels different, but we'll talk when I see you. Handsome as ever, I am sure." She giggled like a schoolgirl. Javier had always been a heartthrob for her, and while Mateo had ignored her indiscretions with his close friend, it was hardly a secret. Javi had been her first love, and he was the perfect bodyguard and confidante for Mateo, tall, strong, and intense—a Latin version of James Bond. Just the thought of him made her temperature rise. She knew how much he'd loved her brother, and Mateo's death, she was sure, would have toppled his world. The hope was that she could sway him to stand by her as she tried to take the reins of Mateo's organization.

৩৩

It had felt like a long day, and Michael was sad for Zeke. The poor man was heartbroken, which was not his area of expertise, not even with the ladies—well, maybe one in particular. It was good to be home.

"Rai?" he called out. Her car was in the drive, and the boys were outside playing ball. Allie was sitting outside on the phone and pointed to the house, indicating his missus was inside. He loped up the stairs to find her in the nursery with Michaela, changing a diaper with her phone pressed tightly between her ear and shoulder. She put up a finger to tell Michael to wait a second.

"Look, Mer gotta go, Michael's here. Talk later, my friend." She beckoned him over with a curl of her finger. "Give us kisses, Daddy. You might get a sloppy from her; she's been nursing." She took a closer look at him, with eyes looking deep into his. "Someone stole your yo-yo? You look sad, Michael. Everything okay with your patients today?"

He nodded and told her about Zeke and Damien and Damien and Connie. "Connie? Shut the front door! I told you I got a weird feeling about Damien. Poor Zeke. Michael, who do we know that's gay and single? Maybe Allie knows someone." Michaela was clean and ready to go to Michael. "I have a couple of things to finish in the office. Either give her to Allie, or may I suggest some Daddy-daughter time?"

Try as he might, he couldn't get a word in edgewise. He followed Rainie down the stairs, Michaela in his arms. "Glad you asked; my day went well, and I've been looking forward to being with you, so it's all good times here." He slathered his comment in sarcasm.

"Michael, don't be such a baby. I'll be back in a few, just a couple "i's" to dot and—" She was out the door.

He and Michaela joined Allie, who had just hung up the phone and was beginning to follow Rainie into the office. "Allie, hi, how'd the day go?" he asked cheerfully.

"Great, Doctor Mike. Gotta see the boss-lady for a second." Allie slipped into the office. He started feeling like second-day news, not how they typically made him feel when he came home. A little put-out, he brought the princess back into the house, put her in the swing, and turned on the television.

World news was on. A reporter, during her segment, highlighted the disappearance of Emmanuel Lopez. She also referred to the past assassination of Mateo Moreno. Without any plausible information and with misguided assumptions, the reporter tried to connect the dots between the two Colombian men. Aside from cartel affiliations, the two were of entirely different calibers. He found the speculations to be intriguing, having been so intimate with one of the men. Could Mateo have been instrumental in the disappearance? Michael doubted it, being that Mateo had gone to such extremes to fake his own death. Surely he wouldn't have risked it all for a strike at Manny. It didn't make any sense. The longer the report went on, the more interesting the what ifs became if one were not in the know. He could see where the story might gain traction for an audience unawares. Both Allie and Rainie came in at the same time, chattering away. He turned to them. "Shh!"

Ready for a curt comeback, Rainie stopped abruptly when she saw the picture of Mateo side by side with another Spanish-looking man. She sat on the arm of Michael's chair. Sliding his hand down the curve of her hip, he stroked the side of her buttock, resting along the side of his armrest. He felt her body quiver. She locked her hand in his to stop the tickling, looking down at him with an arched eyebrow. He grinned. "Who's that other guy, Michael?"

"Emmanuel Lopez, head of a rival cartel to Mateo Moreno. According to the news, the guy is missing. That's the gist of it. I guess the reporter is trying to link Mateo's assassination. Who knows, maybe they think there's a new kid in town trying to take over." He turned the TV off. "How was your day, Rai?"

She slid into his lap and put her head on his shoulder. "I've been missing you today, extra more than usual." She kissed his cheek.

He stroked her hair. "Extra more? Never heard that one before. That must mean lots and lots, to quote the boys. Why'd you miss me so much? Anything got you down, in particular?"

She got up with him right behind her, began pulling things out for dinner, then stopped and put it all back in the fridge. "Michael, take me to dinner." She looked at Allie. "Hot dogs and chili for the boys. We're going out."

Taking Michael by the hand, she led him upstairs.

"What's up, Rai?"

"I told you. I missed you today more than usual. We need grown-up time away from it all. Just you and me." She folded into him and hugged him tightly.

"Okay, you got me, and wherever you want, we'll go." She let go of him, turned on the shower, started going through clothes in her closet, undressing at the same time. Michael followed her into the closet. "I'm dressed to go anywhere, you decide." She grabbed a casual knit dress, and as she bent over to pick up her shoes, he cupped her from underneath and dropped to his knees. "I know how to change your mood. Before we go out, I'm having an appetizer." He ran his tongue over his teeth, stopping on his eyetooth, and arched his eyebrow. "Any complaints? Speak now or—"

She turned around, grabbed a handful of his hair, and buried his face into her. "Oh, God, yes, Michael. Don't stop. Don't s-t-op." Her release was intense; he quickly dropped his pants, brought her down to him, and plunged inside her. He was throbbing hot and held back nothing. His penetration became more purposeful, harder, and faster. "I want it rough, Michael. Do me hard." She could feel the sweat forming on his body as he worked his magic.

"Well, I was ready to go anywhere, past tense. Now it looks like we both need a shower, and if this brings on another kiddo—It's. Not. My. Fault." He pulled her into the bathroom. Once in the shower, they discussed their days and re-visited the subject of heartbroken Zeke.

The knock on the door was light but loud enough to hear. "Javier?" she asked as she opened the door, already knowing he would be standing on the other side. She had watched him as he'd pulled into the hotel drive and followed his movements, as though tracking him through the hotel to the elevator in her mind, so she was more than ready to greet him upon hearing his light tap. "Still as handsome as ever. It is good to see you." Throwing both her arms around him, she held on tight. "Are you doing okay, Javi? What a miracle you were not with Mat. I feared the worst and was afraid when I called that you would not—never mind, you answered, and you are here." She cleared a lump out of her throat. Emotions were a rare commodity with her, had been since she was a young girl. Despite her beautiful face and drop-dead body, she had developed into a cold and calculated woman—use or be used out of necessity. When her heart took over, for those rare split seconds, it was overwhelming. "Want a beer, wine, soda, water, or pretty drink? I'll have them bring one up if you want." He grabbed a bottle of water out of the fridge.

"Bonita, how are you? Other than tickle your fancies, is there anything else I can do for you?" He made his way to the living area. She watched him, admiring his smoothly fluid gait. He could've swaggered or strutted, but he was more like a big cat, a lion, or maybe a beautiful jet-black panther—graceful and sleek, with a killer smile that he flashed on occasion. "It was odd, the day of the—er, accident, no, no accident—assassination, Mateo sent me out for a case of wine. Me. Not one of the house boys, no, me. It was like he wanted to be alone in the house. Many of the men were on the compound, but no one in the house. He was somber, to himself, even more than usual."

She sat next to him on the sofa, leaning her body into his as she watched him speak. "Probably unhappy because of something his American whore said to him. He was too good for her. What a cow! She drew him off his game, made him weak." She stroked his strong hands.

Javier turned abruptly with a fierce scowl on his face. His black eyebrows, usually slightly tapered and benign, were furrowed and angry. "Not even you, will I afford the mistake of speaking ill of your brother. Mateo was anything but weak, and as far as Marguerite, he loved her. He was good to his children and Alicia always, but Marguerite was his love. The circumstances would have never allowed Mateo to marry her. Like it or not, she loved him deeply as well, and if they had been allowed to be together when they were young, life would have been different for them both. No, Mateo was the strongest man I've ever known." He stood up and went to the window. His body was tense. He turned back around, his ebony eyes glossed over, "Never again shall you say anything against him."

She threw her hands in the air. "So sorry, forget I said anything!" She approached him slowly. He put his hand out to stop her. "Can we just talk? I misspoke." Trying to manipulate the situation, she pouted with a demure expression.

Javier was still pissed, holding an icy stare. She opened her satiny lounge robe, exposing her naked body. She ran her finger from her bottom lip, down her throat to her right breast, and began encircling her nipple with a dagger of a fingernail. "Diego not giving you enough at home? You want me to fuck you, is that it, Delores? I'm not in the mood anymore." Now she was pissed. Drawing the sides of her robe together, she tied the sash tightly around her waist.

"Too bad. It would have been nice for both of us, but I wanted to ask for your help in another matter as well. But forget about it. Just leave. If I were only looking for a roll in the sheets, I have a line of studs waiting for an invitation. I just always thought we had something special. I see I was wrong." She turned her back on him.

With a few long strides, he grabbed her by the waist and threw her on the bed, pinning her with his legs. "I thought it was different between us, too. What do you want from me, Delores?"

She looked up at him and with an expression void of any emotion. "I want to kill Manny. I have no problem pulling the trigger, but I need help in acquiring him. I'd say kidnap; however, I don't plan on ransoming him." The iciness of her voice was alarming. The thought of taking out Manny had crossed his mind, but he wasn't completely sold on the round cretin having the smarts or the balls it took to assassinate Mateo. Staring her in the eyes, he confirmed his interest and willingness to help her with a nod. She watched as his mood lightened. He reached for his zipper.

"Let's seal the deal."

ONE TOO MANY

Meredith had regained her trim figure quickly after the twins. Rainie watched as her classy lean friend prepared food for dinner and buzzed around the kitchen, putting away bowls, plates, and a chopping block. "Look at you, all domestic. Bet the hubs is digging your transformation, but I do miss you in the office. After this next project, I'm thinking of calling it quits; I know, I've said it before, but this time, whatcha think?"

"I think—" Mer paused with a dishtowel in hand rested on her hip. "You'd go absolutely bonkers and end up in some kind of trouble. Rainie, your idle hands are definitely the devil's workshop. Indeed. Plus, I'm almost ready to be back at work full time. The girls are ten months, almost eleven. Gotta find a good nanny for them, and no offense to Allie, I want a pro. Your boys were already what, two and four? I've put an application in with a service and have a few interviews set up. I'm not looking for live-in, just like eight to four, at least for the present. Now, aside from that, tell me about this thing with Connie Tolbert and Zeke's beau, or soon-to-be ex-beau. It's odd, Rai, too odd if you ask me, and I don't think it a coincidence. The whole thing smells. Where'd they meet? You have to see the oddity of it all, yes?"

Although it was a big city, New Orleans was like a small town where everyone knew someone who knew a friend or a cousin that somehow linked back to them. All the coincidences started rolling around Rainie's mind. Zeke was a nice guy, but maybe it was a tad strange his brother had gone to school with Michael and even played ball with him. While realizing the connection had felt a bit heartwarming at first, the new Connie info raised some flags. Does Michael feel it, too, or is he as naïve as I am? she thought. Growing up in New Orleans, weird connections were just the way of life, and nobody ever gave it a second thought.

"Mer, interview at the nanny place. Whatever you do, don't bring them to the house. You've awakened the inner skeptic in me, now, and you know I won't rest well until we know everything about the nanny for those precious angels. Maybe I can get Marse to look into whoever the lucky chosen nanny might be." She smirked. "Gives me an idea; perhaps he can look into Zeke and Damien. The poor detective didn't realize he would have a terminal case of pain in the ass when he started with me." She had been doodling on a piece of paper, literally connecting names through a myriad of arrows. Hmm. Michael needs to pick Mateo's brain regarding Connie, Damien, and even Zeke, but Zeke's so sweet; surely he isn't bad news. The thought weighed heavy on her heart.

❧

Rainie made tracks after leaving Mer's with an array of what-ifs. Her heart picked up pace, and that old horrible vice-like tightening in the chest started rearing its ugly head. The panic attacks had almost vanished, but this turned them on with a vengeance. "Shit, I thought I was done with drama, or at least this kind of nasty guy drama." She paused for a moment. "What, Rand? Have an opinion, do you?" Rand's hollow voice took on strength. "No, Rai, I think Mer made a good point. It's worth looking into, but you don't need to get all goofy with your hyperventilation and incessant worrying—making up all kinds of possible b.s. Check it out, be cool. Wait to go into hysterics." Rainie turned the radio louder, trying to drown out Rand's bossy rant, not that it worked. She could hardly wait for Michael to get home.

❧

All was well at the house by the time she turned into the driveway. Calling Marse was first on the list of things to do after calling Michael. Rather than call the office, she texted him.

Mer had an idea. Going to call Rick Marse just to check a few things. Love, love, love you! MUAH!

Her phone started buzzing before she sealed her message with a blown kiss. "Rai, what are you calling Marse about?"

As she sorted the mail, she answered nonchalantly, "Mer pointed out how the whole Connie-Damien thing was suspect and for that matter all the coincidences, like Zeke being from Baton Rouge, you playing ball with his brother, that kinda thing. It wouldn't hurt to get Marse to look into it. But maybe it would be better for your private secret patient to give some input next time you meet. Your opinion, oh wise one?"

Silence from the other end of the phone was deafening.

"Michael?" She tapped on the phone with her nail. "Hello? Are you there? Earth to Michael."

An irritated voice emerged, his words clipped at the end, and some of the Southern charm fell off as well. "Yes, I'm here. Does Mer really think things are, as you say, hinky? Maybe your girl needs to get back to work and lay off the TV dramas. Before you say it, I'm not blowing you off, and yes, I think the whole Connie thing is odd, but Zeke? I don't get any weird vibes from him. I think Connie went after Damien, and maybe she's the one having some point to prove. If you want to call Marse, go ahead, but I'm sure the man has enough on his plate. Remember Zeke was one of three candidates for the job, and I could have picked one of the others, so I think you're barking up the wrong tree with him. Gotta go, getting the evil eye from Beth. Later."

Before she lost the courage, she called Marse. "Detective Marse, this is—oh, I'm programmed in your phone. Is this a good thing or a bad thing?" Her laugh was like a low rumble, sexy yet husky. The conversation was light for the first few minutes, the customary niceties. "I bet you're wondering why I'm calling." Momentary silence. "Well, you remember Connie Tolbert?" Of course, he did. "It appears she is dating Michael's new partner's husband." More silence. "Course he didn't know he was gay at first, not that it matters, I'm not saying that, but I guess the husband swings both ways because he's having an affair with Connie. I just think it's strange. Don't get me wrong, the guy is handsome and funny, but—" She stopped rambling and gave Marse time to process what she'd said.

"Um, Mrs. Landry, now what is it I'm supposed to do about this? Do I think it's a coincidence? I don't believe in them, coincidences, that is. As you well know, Mrs. Tolbert is a piece of work. My advice is to stay clear of the situation." Silence again.

Rainie's brain was pinging in all different directions. "Could I get a background check on him and Michael's partner? Michael doesn't think it's anything but Zeke, that's the partner, is from Baton Rouge and went to the same school as—"

"There are services that do background checks, and you know as well as anyone, just because your husband's partner is from the same area means little to nothing. If, by chance, you get any other information, please let me know before getting involved yourself. We know how that ends up. Tell the good doc I send my regards, and you have a good day. Take care, Rainie, I mean it."

Who was he kidding? She could hear the curiosity in his voice. He thought something was awry, she was sure. How could she just sit idly by when the monsters were maybe back in the picture. Rand's voice was clear as it rattled around her brain. "Rainie, leave it alone. You're getting hyped up." She rolled her eyes and thought, whatever, Rand! The train had left the station, and there was no way she was just letting it go. She went to the computer and looked up investigative agencies. Triple-A Agency and Secret Affair were the ones with the most significant ads and were licensed and bonded. She called both, and they asked the same questions. These were businesses to check on cheating husbands. She quickly switched gears.

So, at the end of it all, nobody wanted to play ball with her. She called Mer as she walked into her office.

❧☙

"Seb, hola." She put on her most girlish, flirty voice. "This is Delores, the ride from the airport the other day? I am happy you remembered me, as I am certain Manny has you quite busy. Are you open any evenings for the rest of this week? I leave Friday afternoon." The young man was so beside himself he called out his calendar for the rest of the week— where and when he was taking Manny on different appointments. From that moment until Friday afternoon, she knew where Manny would be and with whom, proving his vital role in Manny's organization. He was a man in the know. "Ah, so you would be available to take me to see the sights Wednesday evening? How marvelous. No, I won't peep a word to anyone about our meeting, but I don't want to get you in trouble with Manny if he told you to stay away from me. Well, yes, you are a grown man and can do as you please with your off time." She played it perfectly. Seb was to drop Manny Wednesday afternoon at the home of some side piece. She couldn't imagine who would want to go to bed with Manny, but each to their own. Small world: indeed, the woman lived a few doors down from Marguerite, so when Javi went to grab Manny, it would not be odd to be parked so close as his car had been there many times. With a slight pang of jealousy, she wondered if Javier was servicing Mateo's whore now that her brother was gone. Manny was going to be easy to get to, especially with a tell-all chauffeur like Seb.

The plan was in place, and Manny was soon to be food for the fish. There would be no big murder scene; he'd just vanish. No blood or gore, no, just disappear. Javier would put him on Mat's boat and then pick her up from the hotel Thursday morning. Once it was done, she and Javier could spend the last night together. He was excellent at wielding his sword, and what a mighty weapon it was.

Wearing a blood-red shimmery dress cut to her navel and sequined stilettos to match, Delores looked like something out of Victoria's Secret catalog. Her firm round breasts, flat abs, and perfectly tight ass were a walking ad for male enhancement. Seb's eyes twinkled as he looked her up and down. "Oh my, bonita, you raise my temperature just looking at you. First, we'll go for a drink, then dinner at this great place in the old part of town, then dancing if you want and whatever your heart desires."

Delores had to admit he was charming and most easy on the eyes. There was no doubt he would put every effort he had into pleasing her. He was young and an obvious walking hormone. The evening went as planned with great drinks, dinner, and the boy was wonderful on the dance floor. She danced more than she had in years and was more than happy to reward his efforts by bringing him back to her room, where his youthful inexperience was more than made up for by his eagerness to please and plentiful endowment. She greedily accepted his deep-mouthed kiss and left with promises to hook up again next time she was in town. The night ended well.

❧

After a few trumpet sounds from her phone, she answered. Javier was ready for her and promised to pick her up in an hour. She said she'd be waiting outside. Clad in a bathing suit covered by a sheer sundress, wide-brimmed sunhat, and large dark shades, she patiently waited for her ride. The head of every man walking into the lobby turned as they passed her, and finally, he pulled up. The valet opened the car door for her, and off they went.

"Dedee, I never grow tired of your beauty. I feel like the man of the hour having you with me. If you could have seen the looks from every man that came your way, it would even make you blush. I cannot wait to suck those lips later. But, as far as business, it was a piece of cake. Clapped a chloroform cloth to his face while his lady friend was in the shower, and he was out like a light. No fight, no noise, too fuckin' easy. I threw him in the trunk, and by the time we got to the boat, he had choked to death on his vomit. Manny did not fit the business; he was always a spoiled boy. I put a hat on him and sunglasses and threw my arm around him like he'd had too much drink. No one seemed to notice or much less care. All we need to do is toss him overboard once we are far enough out. Then, my sexy girl, you'll be all mine, and I plan to ravage you until you beg for mercy." He took her hand in his, kissing the top with a slight touch of his tongue.

Leaning across the car, she kissed his neck. "Aw, I would have liked to punish him, but that gives us more time to relax on the boat. He did the deed himself. Ravage me until I cry for mercy?" She squeezed his crotch. "Maybe you'll be begging for mercy, ever think of that?" Their sexy banter continued as he pulled up in front of the dock.

After getting on board, she started to fix drinks. "All you want is water, no wine, no beer?" He shook his head as he loosened the lines, and off they went, just the two of them and dead Manny down below. She went down below for a peek; Manny was wrapped in a tarp and tied to a cinder block, then she returned to the deck. Javier drove the boat out into the ocean for about an hour. The breeze felt good on her face. He watched her as she sashayed around in her tiny bikini. Undoing the ties to the top, she nestled behind him, rubbing herself against him. He cut the engine. "Let's get rid of the dead weight first." He went down to the cabin and threw the body over his shoulder, and then into the water, where it dropped like the dead weight it was. "Now that business is over, take off your bottoms and lay on the cushions. Delores, I want to see all of you first and get myself ready." He took hold of himself, rubbing himself with force. "Now suck me, suck me hard. Wrap your luscious lips around my cock. That's it." He pulled himself from her mouth, grabbed her hair, tipping her head back, and kissed her with a hard passionate kiss, almost enough to bruise her lips. He mounted her, then parted her with an angry sexual attack. She thought she heard some movement but quickly dismissed it to the cushions, the hungry quest from Javier, and the rocking of the boat, but no.

Seb leaned over and looked her in the eyes, almost with a look of sadness. Javier aggressively nodded to him. Seb exposed his throbbing manhood while Javier, still plunging her cleft, clutched the joints of her jaw, forcing her mouth open. With a wicked smile, Javier gestured for Seb to slide his cock into her mouth. There seemed to be reluctance on Seb's part at first. "See Delores," Javier said through gritted teeth, "You were right, the studs are lined up for a whore like you. What is it? You can't get enough with Diego's cock that you needed mine and then needed Sebastian's? Have her for yourself, my brother." She started to fight back. "Seb, she likes it hard. You, Delores, use your body as a weapon; you've used too many men to get your way. Nothing ever satisfies you." He pulled out, shooting his load onto her chest.

Javier growled in a menacing tone. "Delores, you've been asking for this for a long time. Always teasing men with your body, but you have the heart of a cold bitch. You've made yourself nothing now.

I know you wanted to take Mateo's place but being a cock-hungry bitch you don't have what it takes. Join your weak friend Manny. He picked her up and threw her from the boat. She saw Seb's eyes plead in defiance.

She struggled in the water. "Please, no, Javier, no," she choked as she fought to stay above water, but it was overcoming her. The motor turned over and began to pull her body with it. He had wrapped the line around her leg at some point in the brutality. Her mind began to drift as her consciousness departed.

Hands grasped her arms; another set reached down from above, pulling her upwards. She sputtered for air. "She's still alive, thank God. Javier, I can't believe you treated her that way. She's Mateo's baby sister." He laid her naked body across the cushions and covered her.

"You foolish boy. She has twisted you with her charms." Javier looked at Delores. "If not for Sebastian, you'd be sleeping with the fish. I once loved you and would have died for you, but you spoiled yourself playing the whore to so many. I could never love you again." The boat gunned and headed for the harbor.

❧

"Michael!" He pulled the pillow over his head. An emergency from the night before had kept him at the hospital until three in the morning, then Michaela had woken up when he came home, and with a gracious heart, he'd picked her up before Rainie woke up. Two hours of sleep was hardly what he called a night's sleep. "Michael!" He rolled over, squinting to awaken and gain focus. With exaggerated blinks and knuckle rubs to his eyes, his body broke the gravity from his mattress.

"I'm up, Rainie," he mumbled. She made her way into their room. She could tell he was exhausted from the slight stagger he had as he made his way to the bathroom.

"You look like a zombie. What time did you get in?"

He was ready for a morning piss. "Ahh, so needed." He sighed.

"Lovely, Michael." She put her hand on her hip and turned toward the bedroom.

"I didn't invite you to watch. That's on you. I got in about four, and then the princess woke up as I was coming up, so I gave you and Allie a break and did the daddy thing, and you're welcome. Now, what in the hell is all the hollering about?" He grabbed a pair of knit joggers and slid into bed, turning on the side lamp.

Rainie shoved an envelope in his face. He arched his eyebrows, and suddenly he was wide awake. Silently he read the letter. She plopped on the bed next to his legs. "And?"

"Next Friday, and that'll be it. Over and done." One side of his mouth curled into a thoroughly delighted grin. "Done. Life back to normal. No more stealth getaways, pretending to be Marchand, back to plain old me. Amen!" He reached out to her, dragging her onto the bed with him. He leaned over and kissed her deeply, exploring her mouth, then pulled her on top of him. She hovered over his crotch and began lightly rocking back and forth. It didn't take much encouragement for his soldier to rise to the battle, and within seconds he had his pants off. "You are one sexy lady."

"And as tired as you are, you're sure you wouldn't rather sleep?" She pinched his nipples.

"Won't be pretty, but it's gonna feel so good." He grabbed her hips, moving her to his body swells. "This is for me, sorry." He flipped her over onto her back and began with diligence, hard and pounding. It didn't take long; he quickly kissed her, turned off the light, pulled the covers up, and said good night. "Call the office and let them know I'll be in at nine."

"You're welcome, Michael. Shush and get a good hour of sleep." She closed the door and went to the kitchen for the kids and the call to the office.

The hour and a half flew by, and before she knew it, Michael was entering the kitchen spryly. "Good morning, all." He kissed Michaela on the forehead, mussed both boys' hair, and planted a quick peck on Rainie's lips. "A bagel for the road, and I'm off. Talk later, my love."

She ran after him. "Michael, find out where Damien met Connie? I'm curious."

"Rainie, you're always curious," he said, and out the door he went.

The days marched on, and soon Michael was back on his way to the airport. Odd thoughts scrambled through his brain. Part of him was going to miss Mateo. Even though their encounters were brief and with specificity, they were intimate. Other than John and his dad, Michael didn't have friends. He'd made social connections with people at school, but never someone he guy-talked with. The relationship with Mateo was a closer bond than he'd shared with anyone except family. Life threw odd twists, and the closeness he'd developed with Mateo was just one of those oddities.

Like last time, he saw all new faces during his travel. The pilot was a good old boy with a strong southern twang, maybe Georgia or Tennessee, but he had obviously missed the memo about not bothering his passenger. He was about five-ten and looked as though he could've been on the offensive line in high school. His physique looked strong as a bull, but a paunch betrayed his lack of discipline. His midsection rounded over a belt buckle that would make any cowboy proud.

"Hey, buddy, welcome aboard. We should have quiet skies. My name is Clarence, but all my friends call me Bubba. You are?" Michael just stared at the jolly pilot but finally answered briefly.

"Je m'appelle Marchand." He twitched his lip into a cock-sided smile with a touch of arrogance and continued to his seat.

"No parlez the francais. It looks like it'll be a quiet ride for the two of us. You no English and me no French. Who woulda thunk it? Well, I guess that's the way the cookie crumbles." The pilot laughed to himself and waved as he returned to the cockpit. On the other hand, the attendant had received the memo and spoke only enough to ascertain he had everything he needed as far as beverages and food. She spoke both French and English, managing to take care of everything for the flight.

The entire flight was consumed with his memories, his thoughts drifting to the first time he'd heard Mateo's voice, then the gifts at the hospital. Life with Rainie was like a dream, everything he'd ever wanted, and yet with her, the doors opened up for madness like none other. Just that curious thought sent a pang of remorse for even allowing such an idea to cross his mind. He'd gladly take any oddness life threw at him as long as he had Rainie in his life. Life was good, and he loved her with every ounce of his being.

The jet landed, and the copter awaited—same routine, just different pilots and people. By the time his travels ended for the day, his mind and heart were ready to see the patient and get some downtime. The day had been an emotional roller coaster; perhaps what he needed was a holiday with Rainie and the kids to get away from life's stressors. Maybe they'd visit Wendy in Washington, at the very least go to his parents'. Since the baby, he had seen Jack and Missy a great deal. Their visits were almost a weekly standard, but always at the house, never in Baton Rouge. As the helicopter touched down, he saw Noir standing outside the vehicle, waiting for him. Come to think of it; he had a few questions for the giant regarding the gunshot.

"Bonjour, Noir."

"Bonjour, Docteur."

The trip to the complex, rather than the usual painfully silent trek, induced Michael to switch gears, and he asked about the wellness of Monsieur LaSalle.

"Mattie's good. He pines for his children and Marguerite. Once he has a new woman and moves out and starts his new life, he'll be better." Mattie? English? Michael had been under the assumption Noir was French or Canadian and knew William LaSalle, not Mateo Moreno. Had he misunderstood all this time? He figured Noir knew there was some clandestine activity in the midst and maybe some broad strokes, but Michael was shocked that Noir called him Mattie.

"Since we're so frank and open with the English, which blows me away, by the way, did you kill that nurse?" Their eyes met in the rearview mirror.

"No, but she thought I shot her and passed out. When she awoke finding to be alive, she was most regretful of her improper action. Don't worry; she is no longer on staff. You have all-new team." Ah, so English is not the giant's first tongue, he thought. He hadn't any trace of an accent but certainly did not sound or come close to looking Colombian. If Michael had to guess now, Russian would be his first attempt. He looked like an actor who played a KGB officer or bad guy—big, strong, and stiff as a board. Noir was like a walking wall, with biceps probably nearing something obnoxious, like twenty-four inches.

They pulled up. Noir took his case and led him to Mateo. The change in the man was a marvel—there wasn't even a hint of the old face. They met in Mateo's soundproof room, where their conversation was protected. Once the door closed, Mateo grabbed Michael by the shoulders and hugged him. "It is good to see you, my friend. Life here is beyond boring and lonely. Noir brings the occasional girl to me, but, eh, it is not the same as true companionship, no. Feels good while it lasts and breaks up the monotony though." Mateo's eyes sparkled with intensity as he looked at Michael. "Something is troubling you, my friend; I can see it in your face and your body. How can I help?"

It was shocking to think he could be so easily read. Where would he even begin? Michael was reasonably sure Mateo honestly didn't want to hear, but he did seem to ask with authenticity and a sense of caring. "You don't want to open that box. There's a lot of shit to unpack, and you don't need that before surgery, or at all, as a matter of fact."

Mateo grabbed a bottle of water and tossed one to Michael. Opening it, he slugged down half the bottle. "But there is where you are wrong. I do want to know, and I do need that. For many years, as you would say, the buck stopped with me. Always a problem to solve, an answer to be had, you know, and now life is too peaceful. I know once I leave here and rejoin the world as William LaSalle, I will not always be at peace, but you have given me a new life; let me at least listen. I may not have the answers."

"You got anything stronger than water like a beer, a whiskey?"

"But of course. Sit down, put your feet up, and whatever you want. Beer? Bourbon? Sit, sit." He took Michael by the arm and led him to the sofa. "I cannot have my surgeon upset, no!"

Michael laughed as he sat down. "Just who is Noir? KGB? And what does he know about me?" Mateo chuckled as he poured bourbon in a glass and handed it to him.

"Noir is the brother I wished I had. He has known me since I was a boy. We were both cabana boys. He is the bastard son of Alejandro Lopez. His mother was a Swedish maid at the resort. Alejandro always cared for him and his mother, not lavishly, to draw attention, but he lacked for nothing. As far as you, he knows you are a surgeon and that your name is not Marchand but does not know your name. Noir is the only connection I have to a life once lived, and he would go to his grave gladly to protect me. He has taken two bullets for me and saved my life countless times. The most important thing is that no one in my organization or family knows of him. He's a ghost. Now, what else perplexes you, sir?"

Michael held his bourbon high to toast Noir. "Here's to Noir. Oh, I found out he didn't kill the girl from last time." Mateo shook his head as though he knew but held a smirk on his face. Michael took a mouthful of bourbon, tightened his lips, and let out a sigh. "That's smooth. What kind of bourbon? And what's that smirky look about you?"

"This is Eagle Rare, a fifteen-year-old bottle, not that glamorous, but it does have a nutty, mild spiced, yet smooth velvet quality. It is far from expensive, but I am fond of it." Mateo tilted his head to the side with a chuckle, "Elizabeth is the nurse's name, and evidently, when she came to, let us just say she thanked Noir ever-so-thoughtfully for not shooting her. Now, what else grieves you so?"

After a couple more sips of his bourbon, Michael got up and poured another two fingers of the lush liquid in his glass. He stretched out on the sofa. "You my shrink now, Mateo?"

"How about two ears to listen eagerly, Mike. Michaela, Rainie, and the boys okay?"

Michael laughed, holding the glass to his forehead. "Yes. I told you about my associate, Zeke, last time we talked. What I didn't tell you is...Zeke is gay and married to a man named Damien—"

"The black man, right?" Mateo steepled his fingers, putting them to his lips.

"W-wait, you know about Zeke and Damien?" Michael raised an eyebrow, then took another gulp of the bourbon.

"Slow it down, Mike, enjoy the bourbon, do not abuse it. Enjoy, relax." Mateo's voice was as smooth as the bourbon. He even chuckled a bit.

"Okay. I don't know what you know and what you don't, but are you aware that Damien is having an affair with Connie Tolbert, the widow of the man—"

"That kidnapped your wife. I thought as much, but I think it is more the woman's doing than the man; he is a weak person. Your

Zeke, I know his people in Colombia. They are good, hard-working people. Too bad the boy has not found a suitable partner. He deserves much better than Damien."

Mateo had all of Michael's attention at this point. "So, you don't believe Damien is trying to get Zeke to dig into the Randy Tolbert thing? What is that all about? Is it Connie?"

"Can I have a bourbon, or is it too close to surgery?" Mateo had crossed the room toward the bar. "Let me get us some food, I know I have to limit what I eat, but you can have whatever."

"Have a small one, and as far as food for me, steak and potatoes sounds good, but I'm going to want lots of bread to soak this up." He held up the glass with a grin.

Mateo picked up the phone to the kitchen, ordered the food, then poured a shot of bourbon for himself. "Salute, Mike!" Michael put up his glass and nodded. "Connie is jealous of you and Rainie, as are many, I am afraid. There are people in this world who want to do nothing but rob other people of their joy, such as my former lover, Marguerite Smith, and that, my friend, is a story for another day. Back to Connie. She wants it all: money, lavish gifts, a beautiful house, but mostly a faithful husband, as we well know Randy was not. She is just stirring the pot to fluster you and your wife. As I said before, on that frightening afternoon when your wife was abducted, go on with your life. Ignore the ugliness. Nothing can hurt you or your wife. Damien is the closest she can get to you and Rainie. If she tears Zeke apart enough, poor boy, then maybe he will leave your practice, taking you away from Rainie and perhaps making you overworked, unhappy, and perhaps leading to you or Rainie seeking comfort in someone else's arms, but that will never happen. You two are connected spiritually; even I can see it from a distance. Zeke is loyal, and he will find someone, and one day he can take over your entire practice if you want, and you and your wife will live without worry, as they say—happily ever after." By this time, Michael felt a bit full of drink, light-headed, and loose with his words.

Swirling the liquid around the glass, he closed one eye and held it up to the light, then passed it beneath his nose. "I'm going to miss you, Mat." He glanced over at Mateo, who had a slight melancholy smile on his face. "Oh, any chance you're related to Zeke? He looks very much like you. I know you said you are familiar with his family, but—"

"No relation. You know we all look alike." And he laughed. "I, too, will miss you, my friend. Once I settle, you, Rainie, and the children can visit me. Or maybe I can visit you in Baton Rouge. We will be in touch if you so choose. It is strictly up to you, my friend." He tossed Michael a bottle of water. "Drink up. I want my surgeon in tip-top shape and not hungover. As you would say, hydrate." Just then, there was a knock at the door, and the food arrived. Deep conversation, bourbon, and English were done for the night. Michael felt a sense of closure and could answer all of Rainie's questions. The thought of her tugged at his heart.

With a full stomach, only a slight buzz remaining from the whiskey, and a soul at peace, Michael threaded the way through the corridors to his room. After a quick wash-up, he slipped into bed for a night filled with dreams of Rainie and the kids.

In his dream, they were playing in the park, Allie rocking a carriage to the delighted coos of Michaela. Everyone was happy, smiling, and laughing together. It was idyllic. He collapsed by her side on the blanket, gently touching his forehead to hers, gazing into her eyes. In a soft voice, he whispered, "I love you more today than yesterday and will love you into eternity. Nothing will ever come between us, my love. You are the air I breathe."

She sweetly kissed him and whispered back, "And I feel the same for you. Michael, you are mine forever."

The urge to touch her was intense. A tiny peek of her breast was revealed, and it took all he had not to nuzzle into her. From that point on, all he could concentrate on was having all of her. He laughed in his dream. "There's no place like home." He awoke to burying his head into the pillow with a throbbing desire for her and repeated the sentiment.

❧

Two days later, he arrived home earlier than the six o'clock dinner hour, which was both a treat and a surprise for Rainie. Hugging him close, she said with true relief in her voice, "It's over now, thank God. Right Michael? Over?"

"Yes, my love. As over as I want it to be." While he was clearly happy to be home, she knew there was melancholy in his voice. Had the situation been different, and perhaps if their lives crossed for other reasons, he knew he'd found a friend in Mateo and felt wholeheartedly the feeling was mutual. They shared a bond, not only because of circumstances, but also because they held similar values and passions and merely walked alternate paths.

She stepped back and tipped her head to the side, her eyes sizing him up. "As you want it to be? That means over for good, yes?" She knew the look, and the answer was not yes but a loud, unspoken no. "Just what aren't you saying, Michael?"

They heard the boys in hot pursuit of attention. He was still standing in the foyer, the front door wide open and his bag on the first step from the welcome home. He bent to grab Henry but continued to look in her eyes., "It'll hold for now." *Oh really, it'll hold for now. What will hold?* she thought disgruntledly.

A bigger distraction was impossible as Leslie and Henry pulled into the driveway.

"Mimi, Poppy!" Henry ran to Rainie's parents with open arms. She couldn't help but think, Yep, it'll have to hold now.

After a brief visit, the grandparents invited the boys for hamburgers, and as usual, it ended in a family affair, including Allie and Eric in the car following. Ever-present in Rainie's thoughts was the something Michael was holding back. Yes, it was going to wait until everyone was tucked away in bed—until then and only then.

She and Michael doled out good night kisses and well wishes for a restful sleep, then Rainie headed for their bedroom.

Michael closed the door behind them. "That was nice being with your parents. Time gets in the way, and before you know it, the weekend is gone. We have to make more of a point in spending time with your folks. Since Michaela, my parents have monopolized the grandchildren's time." She was dressing in her pajamas and completely silent. "Rai, you've hardly said a word all night. Something wrong?" He moved toward her.

"What'll have to wait, Michael? When I said I was happy the whole thing with you-know-who was over, you said—"

"I know what I said, and I have full intentions of talking to you about it." Clothes off, he climbed into bed. "Now come to me, my sexy vixen. I've missed you, and I have much to tell, as well as, on a different note, show." The corner of his mouth curled up, and he patted the pillow next to him. She slipped in next to him, face to face.

She stroked the side of his face running her palm against his rugged stubble. "First the chat and depending on how I like the nature of it, we will proceed from there, buster," she said, lightly tapping the side of his face while holding her own cocky smile.

There was much to tell, starting with the chatty pilot, his melancholic thoughts on the flight, then the conversation with Noir, and a few too many drinks amidst some heart-tugging moments. "I don't have friends, Rai. I have John, but I don't have a Meredith in my life and never have. I think Mat is my Mer, even though the circumstances have been awkward at best. I feel like I've lost a friend." She could feel the sadness creeping into his psyche like a shroud darkening everything it touched. "If you knew him, you'd like him. Would you have a problem if we went and visited him?"

She sprung on top of him, locking each of his hands in hers. There was understanding in her eyes. "Of course, we can visit him, Michael. The key here is we. I resented you feeling obligated, almost held at ransom, to do, well, you know what you did, and not really having a choice even though he said you had a choice. Now it's like the night after giving yourself to someone, thinking they were into you and not getting a return call or them answering your call. A wham-bam-thank-you-ma'am." She kissed him and, in a laughing whisper, bent close to his ear. "I promise to call you in the morning. Each and every morning, for the rest of our lives. Now, what were you going to show me?"

OH, ME

Time became irrelevant with hectic schedules and non-stop go-go-go—just a blur in the blender of life. The death of Mateo had dropped into the chasm of no man's land and Manny's disappearance was hardly a blip on the radar. Life as they knew it ticked over day by day, nothing different than any other normal family. The calendar pages flipped from one year to the next and the next.

It was days from Michaela's third Christmas. Her soft dark ringlets framed a cherub face brilliant with ice blue eyes and a porcelain complexion. The personality was mostly Rainie paired with a most pensively observant perception she came by honestly from Michael. Sometimes it felt like she looked right into her mom's soul, and like any child her age, "No" was her favorite word, although she'd mastered a vocabulary of well over fifty words, used only if and when she so chose. Thomas had gained the knowledge of the Christmas secret but held it close for his younger siblings. Henry was on the edge of either knowing or milking the innocence for what it was worth. Regardless, the merriment soon to be experienced in Baton Rouge never became old and continued to be a family affair between Rainie's parents and Michael's. After the first Christmas Rainie's family had spent with the Landry's, each subsequent year continued to amaze them with the magic and newness of the festivities. It had not staled in their time of celebrating together, and the sacred day hastened and was upon them.

"What time are you closing the office today, Michael? After all, it's

Christmas Eve?" Rainie tugged at the collar of his shirt. "Michael, you need to wear a Christmas tie today." He walked into his closet and pulled out a red tie with a design of Christmas tree light bulbs.

"Good enough?" He gave her a cocky smile. "I'll wear it today only if you promise to wear it tonight." With a wink of the eye, he rolled his tongue along his teeth, stopping at the eyetooth. They didn't hear the door as it slowly crept open.

"Mommy, why you wear Daddy's cwoves?" Michaela stood with both hands on her hips, back arched in scrutiny. "Why?" The look she gave came out of an old black and white Shirley Temple movie—a perfect pout if ever there was one.

"Yes, why indeed, Michael?" Rainie arched her eyebrow, holding a sassy smirk, fighting desperately not to laugh.

"Well, because it's getting close to Christmas, and I know Santa is watching. I wanted to share with you, Mommy." Michael looked at Rainie. "That's why. McKay, don't you think I should share, and wouldn't Mommy look beautiful in my tie?"

The tot scrunched her face as though something smelled awful and looked at Michael shaking her head from side to side in a most exaggerated fashion. "No!" She turned on her heel and ran down the hall, where she heard the boys playing. "Me too play, me too." Silence followed for a second, then came the growl. Michaela didn't always screech like most frustrated little girls; she growled sometimes. "Thom-mass, Henwy, me too. Mommy!" The tease came quickly to an end with her shout for Rainie.

Rainie heard Rand whispering in her ear,. "Oh my God, Rainie, she sounds just like you. Hopefully, she'll have Mike's good sense, and God, let's hope his self-control. Oh, and if you two want to do your thing, a-hem, make sure the door's locked. Please don't twist your kids; y'all are like dogs in heat!"

Michael was perplexed. "Did you check out or something? You almost looked catatonic."

She put on a swagger as she drew close to him, grabbed the tie, and slipped it under his collar. In a hushed voice, she leaned to his ear. "Are you going to blindfold me or restrain me with the tie, Michael? Hm?" She kissed his neck. Inside her head, Rand fussed, "Thanks Rai,

I needed that visual. You didn't lock the door; if you had, I woulda known you'd be up to something kinky."

Michael took a step back and looked at her. "Where did that come from?" He chuckled. "We haven't played those games in quite some time." He brusquely pulled her into him; biceps flexed for a hard squeeze.

Rainie coughed a loud laugh. "That was strictly for Rand's appreciation. Apparently, if we lock the door, she doesn't come around but occasionally overhears us flirting and evidently finds us kinky." The room took on a coldness while a vapor formed into Rand. She was equally as animated as Rainie, hands full of animation and expression.

"Rainie, how dare you tell him I said that, but if you must know, maybe I wished I had had the kind of fun y'all have. I've never been tongue kissed, ya know. Made out a few times with my lips pressed together, nope, no tongue, eww, but maybe not eww. I wish I could feel what it was like to have sex, maybe. But, the point is, lock the door!" Just as quickly as she appeared, she disappeared, and there was no doubt she'd left the room. Rainie hugged Michael.

"Makes me sad. Rand died right when the hormones of lust and sexual desire started heating up and running rampant. Neither one of us were, ya know, that kind of girl." She held him close. While she was silent, he felt her thoughts sprinting through her imagination. She was electrified. Pulling back, she looked into his eyes as though searching, "Michael, don't think I'm crazy, but if it's even possible, could you—"

He threw his hands up and backed away in horror and disbelief. "Don't even go there, Rainie." She started to speak. "Shh, I mean it. I know what you're thinking and, hell no. Sister or not, dead, or not, it's not right what you've got swirling in your brain. I'm sorry, but if you want someone to kiss or, oh God, make love to Rand, I'll not have anything to do with it. I mean it. Do you hear me? Just the thought feels sacrilegious. That is fucking crazy, Rainie."

She sat on the bed. "Okay, okay. I get it. I don't even know if it's possible. Certainly, there's gotta be other dead teenagers that she could find. I don't know, Michael."

With exaggerated gestures, he tied his tie and turned to her. "On that note, my sweet but twisted wife, I'm heading to work. Start packing the kids. You know they'll want to stay the week between Christmas and New Year's at my parents' with Wendy's kids. I'll see you when I get home." He started for the bedroom door, then stopped and walked back to her, leaning over for a quick peck goodbye. "I love you, and I understand your motive." He sighed. "I hope you understand my point." *Yes, Michael, I get it, I guess.* She smiled and wished him a good day.

Following him out of the room, she hugged him again then went into the playroom where Allie sat watching the kids goof around. "We need to pack the kids for Missy and Jack's. The boys will probably stay for the week like usual. Except for Miss McKay, it'll be quiet around here. I'm assuming you'll be spending Christmas with Eric?" Allie nodded yes. "I'm gonna take a bath, and then I can help with the packing, too."

Rainie went back into her room and locked the door. "Rand, I know the door's locked, but it's just me. I want to talk." Silence. "C'mon, Rand, really. I have a plan. I feel you in here, I'm sorry if I embarrassed you, but I do have an idea and a question." She could feel Rand stirring in her mind. "Contemplating forgiveness, are you?" Rainie asked.

"What is this brilliant idea of yours?" Rainie flinched, startled, not expecting the voice to come from behind her. Rand was lying on the bed propped up on her side. "This I gotta hear."

Rainie mirrored Rand on the bed. They looked at each other, eyes latching in a fixation. How many times had they laid on one of their beds with the same posture? Rand looked so young, her skin perfect, without the slightest blemish, wearing the dress their momma had pulled from the closet to bring to the funeral home. It was a pale green self-belted slimline with pearl buttons to match the pearls around her neck. "Well?" she asked impatiently.

"Do you know other teenagers that died? I mean, do you have friends in Heaven?"

Rolling her eyes at Rainie, Rand was slow to answer and simply glared for a moment or two. "You don't get it, do you? I could've gone to Heaven. God is kind and even lets us have free will in death. It's not like I'm stuck here like some others, but I wanted to stay with you as long as I could manage. So, are there teenagers in Heaven, I'm sure, but I don't know, and no, I have no friends. Sometimes the angels come and check on me. Most people don't want to hang around because Heaven is so all that, but I want to be with you until the time we both go to Heaven. Besides, Rainie, who else is gonna keep you out of trouble? So what's your big idea, hmm?"

Weighing whether to say it out loud or not, she struggled with her internal debate. Then heard Rand's voice. "Dammit, Rainie, I hear everything you're thinking. You don't care if Mike kisses me. God, it'll be like kissing my brother. Gross! As far as the other thing, eww!"

"Rand, think about it. You can feel what I feel. Just try possessing my body; I don't know if you can even do it." She rolled onto her back. "Now, get on top of me and see if you sink inside me."

"I don't like this game, Rainie. I'm going to see what the kids are up to." She vanished. Rainie got up, pulled the suitcases out, and started stacking the clothes she planned on bringing to Michael's parents. She stacked Michael's, but figured he'd look it all over later when he came home from work. The whole Rand body invasion stuck in her mind. Taking leave, she went into the study and her computer. For the next four hours, she read articles about channeling, spirit stance, personhood, and intentionality. From what she gathered, the key to making sure it was only a temporary thing and not a permanent total displacement was meditating on the purpose and functionality. All these new facts intrigued her even more and increased her desire for Rand to have the experience, but it could only be one time. Her thoughts began to race. What if Rand likes it? Who wouldn't like it? Of course, she's gonna. What if she isn't willing to come out of my body? Maybe she was pushing the envelope too far and should leave well enough alone.

The shrill of the phone interrupted her thoughts. "Hey Mer. I'm packing and doing some research."

Mer was inquisitive regarding the research. "How many jobs we got lined up for after New Year's?" While Rainie's mind still spun on the body possession, Mer dug in, "What's got you in the crazy zone? You're fixated on something; I hear it in your voice or lack thereof. Is it your research? Two heads are better than one or two computers are better than one, I can help with the research."

The silence began to mount. "We were, what, sixteen when we made out with those boys from England? I know that was my first French kiss and yours too, if I'm not mistaken."

Silence followed by a huffy breath, "Rainie, what the hell are you going on about? Yes, if it hadn't been for the accents, I don't think we would've paid them the time of day. They were such assholes, come to think of it. Why?"

"Rand never really kissed a boy or had any kind of sex. We talked about Sydney and Heather, remember, the girls that had done it? We giggled and wondered. I remember wanting to try things with Patrick since he was your brother, and he'd never tell." Thoughts zoomed through her mind like a meteor shower—first one strike, then another, and another.

In a loud voice, Mer shouted into the phone. "What the hell is wrong with you?"

In a concise delivery, Rainie highlighted Rand's reactions to the morning playfulness with Michael, her abbreviated comment to Michael, his utter horrification, and her sharing the idea with Rand, then Mer blurted. "You said what? Are you kidding? Mike has to think you are totally nuts. You really want Rand to have a first kiss with your husband? Look, I'm sorry Rand hasn't had some of the pleasures of this world, but she has also been spared many of the trials of growing up. You forget growing up is a real mind fuck. Do you have any idea what kind of hurt your suggestion could put on Rand, on Mike, hell, on yourself? Good God, Rainie, you're not thinking right."

Rainie immediately went on the defensive. "It was just a thought, for crying out loud! Look, I gotta go, gotta pack up for his parents. Merry Christmas to you, Paul, and the girls. Love ya."

"W-wait, Rai—"

"Gotta go, love ya."

Maybe she was out of her head, and perhaps everyone was right, and maybe it would mess with Rand and Michael. For right then, she'd let go of the idea and re-group. There were bags to pack.

Rainie occupied her mind by engaging in the busyness of packing up a family, but the absence of Rand was a deafening silence. There was no calling for her or trying to smooth things or explaining herself; no, Rainie thought, let sleeping dogs, as they say.

Between mid-morning snack, packing, lunches, researching, and packing some more, it seemed no time had passed when Michael pulled into the driveway. The thought of Michael going to another woman's bed made her heart feel as though a vice of steel had been clamped upon the beating muscle extinguishing her very life. It tore her in two, and yet the thought of Michael introducing the loving touch of a man to Rand brought peace. He would never be cruel, disrespectful, or any of the horrid personality defects exhibited by a hormone-ridden adolescent attempting to cop his first feel or sexual exploit. While she was sure young girls could be equally cruel to young boys, it seemed far more prevalent for sweaty, lying young lads on folly adventures to be hurtful. Perhaps she saw it from only one side. Meredith had been right about one thing; Rand hadn't experienced the horrors of a first heartbreak or unscrupulous rumors of grave falsehoods only to have them repeated as though God's only truth. How many young girls had been labeled slut or whore as a result of being voluptuous? All she had to deal with were comments linked to Amazonian women. Like she had any choice in her height; and to think, Mer had always been a couple of inches taller than she. It was the most daring of young men who talked smack about Mer, who had a houseful of brothers who'd have beaten the living pulp out of anyone talking trash about any of their sisters, especially sweet, quiet, and undeniably beautiful Meredith.

Michael slipped in the kitchen door, stealthily wrapped his arms around her waist, and held her close. "I'm looking forward to a few days with you and the kids." Dropping his voice to a low whisper, he added, "When's the last time I had you in the barn or on the levee?"

"Michael, you make me blush. I remember well the first time on the levee. We missed getting caught by Levee Patrol by a mere ten minutes." She laughed. "And you, in all your wisdom simply telling me, if patrol did catch us, they'd have to sit and watch because you—"

He pulled her tighter with his rock-hard missile pressing into her back. "I stand by my words; with you, it just doesn't get any better. Feel what you've done to me now, Christ, how I want you. I can't even begin to count the ways!" He chuckled. "Before we get busted by any number of souls residing in the house, we better go upstairs and lock the door." He kissed her neck lightly, "C'mon, you." And he grabbed her hand, leading the way to the stairs.

🕉

An hour later, bags skillfully packed in the car; they took off for Baton Rouge. Rainie's mind drifted back to thoughts of Rand. Like the sun bursting forth over the horizon, an idea exploded inside her mind. But, of course, Missy would be the one I needed to seek counsel about the whole Rand-Michael thing. She almost felt gobsmacked, and a sense of peace showered over her body.

BEAUTIFUL MISTAKES

The gates couldn't open fast enough for her liking. Desperate to talk with Missy, Rainie jumped out of the car just as it pulled to a stop.

"Rai, do you mind if I turn the engine off before you leap out of the car? I thought the boys were car antsy, but you beat the cake. You gotta pee or something?" She glanced at him and rolled her eyes. He was right; she needed to calm down; otherwise, he'd figure out what her plans were.

Missy was her usual cheerful self, and happiness beamed from her smile. She welcomed everyone with a big hug then hooked her arm in Michael's. "Mom, I need to get the bags," he reminded her.

"Get the cases, dear, but we have to talk as soon as possible. It is most important." With a curious look, he nodded. Running through his imagination were a myriad of explanations. Of course, the first thoughts landed on the topic of health. Michael didn't allow himself to do a Rainie and start fretting or going over the top. His calm had rubbed off on her, and her animation and jumping to conclusions had mixed into his personality. He took a deep breath and determined to fight the urge and not yield.

Although they wanted to run to Poppa Jack and the barn, the boys reluctantly grabbed their bags and headed toward the stairs. Michaela was right on their heels. "Mommm," Thomas yelled, "McKay is trying to climb the stairs by herself; you, Dad, or MaMiss need to get her."

Thomas tried to hold the toddler tightly, but she squirmed and turned, making all attempts to break free from his grip, all the while screeching like a wounded owl and growling with a deep guttural wolf-like terror. "No, McKay, no, no! M-o-m-m, Missy, help." Sam rushed down the stairs and picked her up. Thomas had to do a double take. It looked like Sam had boobs, like a girl. He tried to ignore it, grabbed his bag, and high-tailed it to his room. "What the heck?"

Michael made it to Michaela first and, startled, noticed the change in Sam immediately. Swift as a flicker of a bulb, thoughts rampaged through his mind. He gave a sigh of relief that it wasn't bad news from his parents, but he certainly wasn't ready for Sam with breasts.

After dropping their bags, Thomas and Henry took off for the barn. Sam stayed behind with Michael and Missy. Rainie approached, and upon seeing Sam exclaimed with shock, "Oh, my. Well, I guess the cat's outta the bag." Missy cleared her throat. Rainie sheepishly uttered, "Sorry."

Missy looked at Sam, or was it Samantha? "I told you to stay upstairs until I had a chance to talk to them," she scolded.

"But, Missy, Thomas was having a time of it with McKay. I had to help." Missy put her arm around Sam's shoulder while Rainie grabbed Michaela.

Missy nodded, looked at Michael, and said, "We need to talk. Let's sit and chat, everyone. Coffee anybody?" While Michael and Rainie were way out of their element, they quickly sat, turning down the offer of coffee. All they could think was this story was bound to be interesting.

Sam began, almost as if rehearsed. "All my life, they told me I was a boy, treated me like a boy, I even liked boy things, but I knew I was missing the boy part." His head leaned toward his right shoulder as he whispered, embarrassed, "Ya know, a penis. I guess I'm just dumb." He looked around at Rainie and Michael, who all but sat with their mouths agape. "One day, I started bleeding, from, you-know-where. I'd heard of girls having that, so that's when I knew for sure, my grandma had lied about me being a boy born without the part. I didn't tell Missy or Poppa Jack, or anyone, until Missy found my—well, you know. We talked to the doctor about making me a real boy, but then when I kissed Marybeth from down the road and felt like I was going to throw up, I realized maybe I really was a girl."

Rainie interjected, "So, we need to refer to you as she or her?"

"Uh, yes." She gave Rainie a nu-duh look. "I've been able to strap these down," she said, grabbing her breasts, "but when they took me off of the boy pills, they grew a lot bigger, like overnight almost." Missy had already told everyone except the children about Sam being transgender, so there was no surprise in her physically being a girl. It was the part where she'd figured out her true identity that had Rainie and Michael a bit sideways. "You can still call me Sam, but I'm a girl. A real girl, and I'm not pretending to be a boy anymore. I guess deep down, I've always known, but I didn't want to disappoint my grandma, and then when I came here, I didn't want Missy and Poppa Jack to throw me out, being I wasn't a boy, cuz ya know, they only take boys." Sam inhaled deeply, eyes jumping from Rainie to Michael back to Rainie, who almost seemed to be holding their breath, waiting for the conclusion of the story. The air was thick with all the rambling thoughts. "Missy changed my school, so I'd only be with girls, and maybe learn how to act like a girl." She looked down at the floor, fidgeting her feet and nervously twitching her hands. "Y'all still like me?"

Rainie, tearful, jumped up and went to her, "Oh my, of course, sweet girl, yes, we love you." She hugged Sam. "I'm sorry your grandma didn't tell you when you were little." She kissed the top of the girl's head. "And as far as Thomas and Henry, they won't care. You can tell them just like you told us or any which way you want to; they love you. So, you knew but didn't want to know and wanted to please everyone else. I'm happy it all worked out." Missy glanced at Michael, who still seemed to be very much in thought, and then at Rainie with a look of indescribable love.

∞

Thomas and Henry raced to the barn, Henry lagging by a smidge. "You're getting pretty fast, dude," Thomas said through winded breaths, his hands on bent knees as his entire body struggled to settle into a regular respiratory pattern.

Henry piped back, "Give me more time, and I'll beat your butt." They walked to the spiral staircase. "PopJack, you up there?" When they heard him answer, they flew up the stairs.

He hugged the two of them. "How're my boys? Getting excited about Santa coming tonight?"

Thomas knowingly winked at him. "Yeppers! Poppa Jack, did you know Sam has boobs?" Thomas asked. Jack just smiled.

Henry looked at him like he was crazy. "No, duh, Thomas, she's almost a grown-up, like fifteen or sixteen. Grown-up girls have boobs." He paused when he heard Thomas's guttural moan. "What? You thought Sam was a boy? I've known since we met her. She didn't smell like a boy. Sure she plays like a boy, but so do a lot of girls." Henry watched the horses in the paddock. Jack was taken aback by Henry's astute intuition and had a hard time fathoming that the little guy had known all along, while nobody else had even suspected.

Once the whole Sam ordeal settled in the house, things became more like their usual visits. Michael went over to the barn to hang out with Jack for a check-base, and Rainie sat with Missy, gearing up for an intense conversation.

"I'm so glad I have you to talk to right now. I know my parents are due anytime, but maybe you can chew on some of my thoughts for a while, and then after the Christmas chaos is over, we can get down to the nitty-gritty. I know you can feel my head buzzin', and while the Sam bomb was pretty outstanding, I'm worried this will blow your socks off."

Missy rocked back in her chair, sipping on her coffee. "Before you start, Rainie, and I hope this doesn't upset you, but your sister has been hanging around here today. She's been watching me but hasn't said a word. I think she wants to talk, though."

Rainie called Sam and asked her to keep an eye on Michaela so she could talk to Missy. Rainie got some of McKay's treats from the kitchen and grabbed a bottle of water before returning to the Hearth. She surveyed the room before sitting, as though looking for something.

"You're upset?" Missy swallowed loudly. "I—"

"No, heaven's no, Missy. I'm glad to hear Rand's been hanging around here. I haven't seen, heard, or felt her for most of the day. I'm happy." Rainie's face flushed a light pink. She chugged her water, trying to figure where to begin. Her heart began to race as her nerves picked up.

Almost screaming in her head came Rand's pissed-off voice. "For crying out loud, Rainie, this is between you and me, period. Don't you bring Mike's mom into this. It's you and me!"

Missy's body startled as she heard Rand's voice clearly in Rainie's head. It was the first time she had heard an exchange between Rainie and Rand. Until then, Missy had only heard the thoughts of living people, and that was only some people and only some of the time.

Rand's rant began, "Oh my God, she heard everything I said to you, didn't she?"

Rainie's jaw tightened as her eyes creased in the corners from a hard squint. "See, Missy, what I'm talking about with Rand? I saw you flinch; I know you heard." Rainie closed her eyes tightly, taking in deep breaths. "Dammit, all I wanted to ask her, Rand, was what she thought of my idea, nothing more, but forget it!" Rainie abruptly stood, clenching her coffee mug with one hand, her other hand balled in a fist out of frustration. "Fuck it!" She stormed out of the room and went up the stairs to the bedroom.

"Oh, no, you don't, Rainie," Rand said. "You can't run from me. Maybe everyone else on the planet, but not me. So you want me to kiss your husband? Oh, because," and she changed her voice to a sickeningly sweet exaggeration of Rainie's earlier thoughts, "Michael would be gentle and kind and do it properly? Maybe I don't want to kiss your husband; he's your freakin' husband, not mine. What is it with you?"

Rainie rolled on her side as Rand's shape formed, and the two of them stared eye to eye, mirrored with the same squinted eyes and a fire of anger frothing in their expression. The silence was piercing. She put her hand out to touch Rand, but all she could feel was a buzz-like tingle. Her heart weighed heavy, sinking into her chest, and the once-angry face turned to one of sadness. Her mind was void of thought.

"What now, Rainie?" she said, taunting her like a teenager.

"Nothing, Rand. You were the one to complain about not having a real kiss. I wanted to make it happen for you. That was all. I love you, and it saddens me that you missed out on so much, but, ya know, Mer was right; you also didn't have to go through all the hurt and bullshit. I'm too tired to deal with any more of this nonsense," she said, and got up. "I'm going downstairs if you want to continue to berate and harass me."

Missy was busy in the kitchen when Rainie and Michael walked in from different directions. "C'mere, you two." She spread her arms like angel wings; Rainie gladly accepted the comfort. Michael put his arm around his mom's waist, reaching through far enough to tickle Rainie's ribs. "Our girl has had a rough hour, Michael." Looking into Rainie's face with a small sympathetic smile, Missy warmly asked, "Things better between you and Rand?" Rainie nodded. "Michael, y'all better get dressed, and I hope Wendy, Dave, and John will hurry with the boys; it's almost time for Christmas Eve service."

"Oh, God, Missy, I totally forgot, in all the madness, that everyone was here." Almost bemused, Rainie asked, "Where are they? And everything good with Sam?" She raised her brow.

Missy nodded, "Fine. Everybody's fine. John was a bit aghast, but he and Jack live in their own existence. They went for a ride on the levee, and I bet they're freezing their tushes off." She pulled out her phone to call Wendy.

"Quickly, Rai." Michael turned to go up the stairs grabbing Rainie by the elbow. "We need to jump in the shower, and you can tell me about you and Rand." She didn't have her usual spark and tried to force enthusiasm. "That doesn't work, Rai, whether it's frustration, sadness, or hurt, it's written all over your face. We'll talk in a minute."

Once the two were in the shower, Michael reeled her into his arms. "I love naked hugs. They make everything better. Now, Rand?" He pulled back, evaluating the depth of her honesty by the intensity of her eyes. She pulled him close.

"She ran away, is the best way I can describe it. She's been hanging with your mom. She's a fucking sulky teenager, is what she is. One minute she wants a real kiss; the next, she's acting like I'm some deviant. Yes, it was my idea to use you as the giver of the kiss, but then,

I dropped the subject. You and Mer let me know I was wrong. She's throwing a pissy." She held him tighter. "Kiss me, Michael. I want a deep, passionate kiss. Do it like you love me."

He snorted with a laugh. "I do love you, so how else would I kiss you? Oh, my beautiful lady." He turned his head slightly and leaned down, glancing from her lips to her eyes and back to her lips as he delivered a most passionate and loving kiss. He could feel her body melt into his. Kiss for kiss, she matched him. "Rainie, stop. We don't have time. I want our next interlude to be slow, sweet and filled with meaning, not a wham-bam. I hope you don't mind." He handed her a towel and with his towel dried her back. "You good with a tumble later tonight?"

Rainie smiled. "Of course."

Like every Christmas Rainie experienced with Michael and his family, the celebration held promise from the past, and it was glorious, never ceasing to delight. Once again, presents filled the house, and everyone felt the generosity of their blessings. The special grown-up gift was a five-day excursion on a Caribbean island schooner. Rainie reflected on her and Michael's honeymoon, and while the passion level might not hit the high notes like the honeymoon, the beauty and splendor of it all would be second to none. Since everyone in the family had had the experience it wouldn't be a shocker first time for anyone.

Unfortunately, the morning for Michael to go back to work came too fast, and she found herself waving as he drove toward the gate and River Road. Walking back to the house, she detoured and strolled by the pond. Looking down into the still, reflective water, Rainie remembered the time Rand had let Michael see her reflection in the pond and smiled with a melancholy heart. She and Rand had finally grown apart, and the feeling was horrible. Her eyes filled with tears mourning the fracture of the bond.

Rainie went inside, intending to lay down. She didn't feel much like socializing. Wendy and Missy were yakking in the Hearth, but all she wanted was to be alone. Missy called out for her to join in, but it wasn't in her heart, so the trek up the stairs continued. She sunk into the bed staring at the ceiling. Rand's presence was strong. "I'm sorry, Rainie. I've been a total bitch. You're so happy with Michael, the boys,

Michaela, and even the world. I guess I'm jealous. Before, the most important thing in your life was me, and well—"

"Oh, Rand, I love you, and my relationship with you is like none other. Don't misunderstand; you've been monstrously out of control, but no more than I was at your age. I think maybe that's the difference you're feeling; you realize my age. It happens to me with the kids; one day, they just seem much older than they did the day before, which I know is silly, but it feels that way because we get busy and don't notice." Rainie rolled on her side, facing Rand, and as they had earlier, Rand turned on her side and ran her hand down the side of Rainie's face. The same tingling of static passed over Rainie's cheek, and they laid there, looking into each other's eyes, both heavy but filled with love.

"Rai, I think you're right, but I want to be older, not stuck as a fourteen-year-old forever. I've heard once I go to Heaven, there'll be no age; we'll all be the same. I wanted to wait for you, but I don't want my being around to piss you off or cause trouble. It never has before, and I always felt like you needed me, but you don't need me anymore, do you? I'm just a big old pain in the butt." Rainie smiled, pouring out every ounce of love she had for Rand and softly shaking her head, mouthed no.

An hour went by. Rainie could hear Michaela giving Missy and Wendy a run for their money, so she headed downstairs. Rand was like glue, following her every step, every move, and holding onto every word but remaining silent. Rainie figured it had something to do with Missy being able to hear her.

Michaela raced to Rainie. "Mommy, Mommy." Rainie picked the little one up and made her way across the room to Missy and Wendy, apologizing for being gone so long, hoping Michaela hadn't been too much.

Wendy laughed, "She's a pepper, that one. Ooh, you and Mike are gonna have your hands full." Rainie apologized again. "No, no, Rainie. I'm not complaining; she's a hoot, and just as rough and tumble as the boys were."

Michaela put her head against Rainie's chest. It wasn't long before the toddler was fast asleep. Even though she had been a relaxed infant, her mind was active, and now that she could speak some and run, the whole complexion of watching Michaela had changed. She was a ball of curious energy.

❧

Every time he had to leave Rainie, Michael resented it more and more. He wanted to be with her and the kids. He thought back onto the fun times they'd had during the holiday, and then his mind drifted to the Rainie and Rand situation. While he could appreciate Rainie being so cavalier about him kissing Rand, and even though she said she'd let it go, something about the whole thing felt hinky. Michael felt quite sure Rainie would not be so inclined if it had been another female, or if Rand was alive. His mind drifted to thoughts of John, had the situation been reversed. How would he feel about John kissing Rainie to see what it was like, or what about sex? Michael violently shook his head, casting that thought as far as he could. "Hell no!" he exclaimed with force. But what if it were just a kiss? He reflected back to Rand. Could he even do that? It would be like kissing Wendy. "Hell no!" resounded again inside the car. The shrill of the phone snapped his thoughts back to reality. It was Beth, with a reminder of a new patient first thing and telling him not to drag ass. "I'm on my way, and for your information, I'm hitting about eighty and not going any faster. I shouldn't be late, but if I am, oh well. Tell them I'm coming from Baton Rouge. Give me a break. See you soon."

❧

There was a knock at the kitchen door. Missy startled but got up to answer it. Rainie could hear her, and Wendy had a look of question about her face. No one ever came to the kitchen door. If it had been Dominique or one of the usual kids from River Road, they knew just to walk in. It was two teenage boys asking for Samantha. Missy called Neverland. The next thing they heard was running from upstairs and a loud clambering down the stairs. Sam had on a pair of tight-fitting jeans and a tee-shirt knotted above her navel, accentuating her breasts.

Rainie noticed she even had on mascara, eyeliner, and earrings. No doubt Sam looked like a girl, and an attractive one at that. Rand's presence lessened. Rainie could tell she had moved closer to Sam, and as the three teens headed out the door, so did Rand. Almost in a motherly manner, Rainie worried about Rand. Her peculiar behavior had sent up warning flags, almost like cannon fire over the bow of a ship—not just mere little flapping flags, but like giant fucking cannonballs.

Missy sat and gave Rainie a crooked smile. "You're not her mother, sweetheart. Rand will be fine. Things okay with y'all?"

Rainie adjusted Michaela in her lap, and Wendy was all ears, not missing a beat. "Wait, y'all catch me up. I'm confused."

As though it was the most normal thing in the world, Rainie simply said, "Rand is feeling our age difference and is acting out. It all started when Michael and I were feeling a little frisky, flirting, and such. Rand got pissy, saying she'd never had a real kiss, and I started thinking maybe she could possess my body and kiss Michael once just to experience a kiss. Your brother quickly showed me the error of my thinking, and he was right. Rand was pissed that I'd even think something like that and threw a dang temper tantrum. We had it out, and it is all about the age difference and life experience. I think she's fascinated by Sam—"

"Aren't we all!" Wendy exclaimed. She showed no sign of being surprised about Rainie and Rand's communication and, from all appearances, acted like it was a typically normal thing to happen. Maybe this resulted from Missy's gift of hearing thoughts, or as some said, reading minds.

❧

As Michael prepared for his first appointment, Zeke rapped on his doorframe. "Busy?"

"Just going over notes from Clark Tuller about his patient coming to talk about a rhinoplasty. She was insistent that she sees me from what I gather in his comments. Sounds odd. If you're not too jammed, could you sit in on this one with me? Something sounds off."

"Sure thing. I have my first in half an hour. So no prob, Mike."
Beth poked her head in to let him know his patient was ready for him.

Michael and one of the nurses walked into the first treatment room to find a beautiful woman. She was petite with black hair past her shoulders, dark olive skin, and extremely dark eyes. Perhaps one of the most attractive and sexiest women he'd ever seen. Michael smiled. "Good morning, Ms. Wright. Dr. Tuller said you wanted to see me? What can I do for you?" He held her chart in one hand. "Please, have a seat." He handed the chart to the nurse and sat on a rolling stool facing her.

"Yes." He detected a well-camouflaged Spanish accent. "I had an unfortunate accident and now have this atrocity on my nose. I want it fixed." She pointed to what he thought looked like a perfect bridge to her nose. "Here, feel. You will feel what I am saying." He gingerly palpated the bridge of her nose, and while there was a slight difference on one side, it wasn't visible and barely present to the touch. She had a sharp edge to her voice. "Do you feel that hideous thing?"

There was a slight rap on the door; the nurse opened it, moving to the side so Zeke could enter. The woman's eyes widened, and her manner changed. "Ms. Wright, this is Dr. Ramos, my—"

Zeke interrupted. "Delores. What a surprise! I did not know you were coming in today. What brings you here? So good to see you." Zeke lowered his eyes and slightly moved his head from side to side. "My condolences on your brother's death." The woman became more agitated.

Michael held his expression, but the dots began to line up. This gorgeous woman was none other than Mateo's younger sister, Delores Moreno. He now saw it in the almond-shaped eyes. The name on the chart was Bridget Wright. Something was definitely amiss, and his warning alerts were blaring.

She stammered a bit. "Z-zeke R-ramos, I didn't know you were a doctor." She held her composure, but there was a significant density in the air that had not been present before Zeke entered the room.

Even though it had only been a few years since he had joined the practice, Michael and Zeke had learned to read each other well, and both men had suspicion mirrored in their eyes. With zest, Michael began, "What a small world! Ms. Wright and I were just getting ready to talk regarding possible solutions regarding her injury." Michael looked at Zeke. "Is there something—"

The deadly minx interjected. "Zeke, I had a terrible fall and injured my nose. Dr. Landry was just feeling the horrible distortion it's left. The injury happened some time ago and is still there, bothering me. Do you want to feel it, too? I don't want to sound like a vain woman, but it is all I see when I look at myself."

Zeke stepped closer to the woman and felt the nearly non-existent injury. "Delores, I do not think you need to do anything about the injury. The scar tissue from surgery could cause the distortion you feel to become greater, and I'm sure Dr. Landry will give you the same advice, but I will leave you to discuss this issue, and once again, my condolences." He turned to Michael. "Come by when you get a moment?" Michael nodded, and Zeke left the room.

After another twenty minutes, Delores Moreno, a.k.a. Bridget Wright, left without incident or the need for another appointment. When Michael offered his condolences, she asked if he'd known her brother, Mateo Moreno. Michael said he had heard the name from the television but had never had the occasion; nonetheless, losing a loved one was always difficult.

Over lunch, Zeke talked with Michael about Delores, explaining who she was and that they had briefly known each other as kids in Colombia, but someone as strikingly beautiful as Delores was hard to forget. He said gay or not; he could appreciate her beauty and raw animal magnetism. Michael acted unaware of the Moreno family, other than having heard the name on the TV. He listened as Zeke told of the many rumors he had heard and what he knew. Michael's last appointment couldn't come fast enough. His heart ached for Rainie, and, boy, did he have a story to tell her about the day.

Driving back to Baton Rouge, Michael called Mateo, or rather his alias, William. Over the last few years, they had spoken only a few times, to confirm all had healed well. Michael felt as though he needed to inform him of Delores's odd appointment.

The phone rang twice, then William picked up. "Good evening, my friend. I trust all is well with you and yours?" Michael breathed deeply. It was good to hear his voice. Even though he knew the face on the other side of the line was that of William LaSalle, the face he conjured in his mind was Mateo's, only the voice was distinctly different with French inflection. His tone was livelier, and the once satiny-smooth verbal swagger had vanished. Was he happier, or was this a pretense that could win him an Oscar?

"I'm well," Michael answered, followed by an elongated pause. "Today—"

Mateo interrupted, "Your wife, the children, they are all well?" An urgency had formed in his tenor.

"Yes, yes. Family is good, They are growing before our eyes, and the little one already is giving us a run for our money. No, this is business, maybe monkey business, but certainly curious." Michael tried to choose his words wisely, putting an edge on the conversation. "I had a patient today, which I would typically, under different circumstances, never disclose or discuss, but the woman I saw today, Bridget Wright— I'll start at the beginning. While reading her intake questionnaire, I started feeling something amiss, so I asked my partner to attend the appointment. Although I always have a nurse in attendance, I felt strongly enough about the oddness that I wanted another set of eyes. The woman complained of an irregularity along the bridge of her nose. I detected nothing; then she asked I feel it. As I palpated the virtually non-existent or barely existent injury, my partner knocked and entered the room. His first response was to call the woman Delores, and then say the customary niceties ending with a somber condolence regarding her brother's death. It wasn't hard to put two and two together and figure out the woman's true identity, but then my mind went to, why? Why the need for an alias, if you will?"

"Sorry to interrupt, but you are correct as to who that was. I am not sure why the visit, but I promise you I will have answers," William said. "There are a few possibilities that come to mind—not to worry, my friend. Onto brighter things. Have you ever been to Tadoussac, a small village in Quebec? It is a lovely quiet place to holiday, usually in the summer months. You and your family, or just you and your wife should go." Michael couldn't help but think how random. The message was clear that his friend was residing somewhere near the area, but Michael had made a point of not saying any names other than Bridget or Delores, why the transparency of Mateo's statement? "We will speak again soon; I know it. Until then, I wish blessings for you and your family." The conversation ended moments later. Michael's thoughts looped back to the transparency and lack of urgency for secrecy and discretion. It was so unlike Mateo, but then again, this was William, and he was no longer the man from the past.

Michael reached into the glovebox and pressed the button to open the gate and just that small motion sent his heart racing. The blood raced through his body like a river once dammed, rushing through a newly formed breach.

When he got to the house, Rainie was waiting by the fountain. The glow of the gas lamps spotted around the drive electrified her glowing russet locks. The tickle in his stomach spread like wildfire, and his every thought was of being in her arms.

"Michael, I have missed you so much today. Miss me?" She threw her arms around his neck.

"Rai, you're shaking. It's too cold for you to wait outside." He put his arm around her shoulder and walked her in. "It's been a most unusual day. Wait 'til you hear."

After dinner and time with the family, Michael and Rainie headed upstairs. "Michael, I do want to hear all about your day, but first things first." She locked the door and sauntered up to him with a no-nonsense smirk on her face. Draping her hands over his shoulders, she reached up for a kiss. He held her close, locking his mouth to hers, their tongues dancing in perfect synchrony as he cupped her breast. "Michael, get naked with me in the shower; I promise you'll have no regrets." She laughed in a deep, sultry tone.

"Naked with you? There is never regret, my love." Slowly she unbuttoned his shirt, not taking her eyes off his. Copying one of his moves, she grinned with her mouth opened enough to run her tongue across her teeth, resting on the canine, then withdrawing slowly into her mouth, enticing him to seek its slick temptation. His eyes twinkled as though dusted with specks of gold.

"Woman, why do you tease me so? You are a tantalizing minx."

Letting his shirt cascade to the floor, he stepped out of his pants while relieving her of her clothes. As he lifted her, Rainie wrapped her legs around his hips, raising the bar of passion. With one hand, he reached behind his back, turning the water on to beat on his back until the temperature warmed. Their kisses heated up, encouraging his devouring hands into exploration. Abruptly, almost savagely, he turned her away from him and bent her forward, so her palms flattened on the bench. He pulled her hips to him, grinding against her perfectly round ass. She welcomed Michael's wanton lust as he placed himself inside her and took her completely. Like the perfect duet, engrossed in the moment, their bodies thundered. "Oh, God, Michael, don't stop." Her thighs quivered in response to explosion of his body. He spun her around with force, embracing her beneath the spray of the shower. "Michael, I have wanted you, just like that, you beast." She let out a throaty laugh as she threw her head back, welcoming a bath of kisses. "Now, my sexy man, you wanted to tell me about your day."

"Let's just savor the moment. It's always outstanding, but sometimes it edges just a bit more." They held each other under the warm jets of the shower. "With a naked shower hug, the love passes back and forth between us, and everything feels right, ya know?"

They melted into bed, the warmth of the shower and pleasure still cloaking them from the outside world. Rainie whispered, "Now, Michael, tell me about your day. It seemed ever-so-important before—"

He rolled onto his side. "It is important, but I don't think it's anything we should worry about." He told her about the odd appointment with Delores Moreno and then his call to Mateo.

Just the sound of Mateo's name caused Rainie's stomach to tighten and her breath to catch. Nothing to worry about...is he fucking kidding me? "My body says otherwise, Michael. The name Mateo brings up too many feelings of apprehension—afraid for you, for me, our family. My stomach is in knots, and I can hardly swallow. Why didn't you call me instead of him?" She sat upright in the bed.

"It's over; calm down, Rainie. You're way over the top, my love, and getting yourself into a state. It's over." He nestled next to her, taking her into his arms. Her board-like stiffness started to subside.

෨෯

"Delores, where you been? What you don't answer my calls anymore? Too fucking important, is that it? News flash, you ain't your brother or Javier; I hear he's the new main man in Cartagena. So I guess you'll need to report to him now." She blew past him and went to the bedroom, followed by an icy wake.

Diego followed and stood leaning against the door frame. "You want something or just waiting for a show? And, by the way, I don't answer to no one. The business I got here is all mine; let fuckin Javier try to take it from me. I'll blow his fuckin balls off. Now, if you ain't man enough to work for me, then I suggest you get the fuck out. Now leave; I got some business to take care of."

She sat on the bed with her phone and waited until her contact picked up, "Russ, I saw the redhead's doc husband. He's so squeaky clean, he didn't even know who I was, and that was after his partner came in calling me by my real name. Zeke, his partner, has family from where I grew up. No, your plastic surgeon didn't even acknowledge when Zeke said he was sorry to hear about Mateo's death. The guy is clueless, so unless you got something else to go on, you got nothing. I'm telling you; I've talked to my people in Cartagena, and my brother is dead. I don't care if there's no DNA to prove it. It's been almost three years since the assassination. I'll tell you who I think did the deed. I think it was his best friend Javier, because he slipped into control right after Mateo's death. I tell you, my brother didn't take a piss without Javier shaking it for him, so when he told me Mat sent him on an errand, I knew for sure. He murdered my brother. No one else could've gotten close to him. That's it now, don't bother me about it, and you and your detective pals leave me and my business alone. I've more than taken care of you."

Another five minutes on the phone went by as she listened. "Your detective friend is your problem. No, you make him leave my stuff alone. You say he won't, then fuckin get rid of him, or I'll handle both of you." Call ended. Russ could feel the hairs on his neck rise with caution, or maybe just downright fear. Delores Moreno was one hard-cold bitch.

⊚

Morning came faster than Michael would have liked, and the trek to New Orleans was about to commence. Rainie walked him to the car. "Michael, next year, how about closing the office from Christmas Eve through New Year's?" Her bottom lip purposefully stuck out a bit farther than usual. "The kids and I miss you, not to mention John, Wendy, Dave, and their kiddos. The kids are all about their Uncle Mike. They say," and she put on a kid-like voice, "'A-Rai, when's Uncle Mike gonna be home?' I'm telling you, Michael, everybody misses you, especially me. Just think of all the great private time you're missing. Last night was better than wonderful. I bet it's gonna make you stiff just thinking about it," she teased playfully.

He held her close. "Your mean like this? Rainie, talk about not fair. You know how it goes—Christmas break is the time for kids to have their procedures done since they're out of school. But I'm planning a trip for us, just us. It'll be a surprise and right around Mardi Gras. Sound good to you? We'll bonk morning, noon, and night, oh horny one. The kids can either stay here or with your parents if Allie and Eric do their Mardi Gras ski trip like last year. Before you ask, no, we're not going to Colorado to ski; if we were, I'd take the kids, too." He kissed her goodbye and took off.

Rainie, Missy, and Wendy spent the day corralling Michaela. Finally, Rainie called Sam's cell. "Hey sweetie, any chance you could play with McKay for a bit? I wanted to take a bubble bath and not strap Missy or Wendy with Michaela. The boys are all with Poppa Jack, or I'd ask them."

Samantha said she would, but she had to finish something first. Missy could hear the two teenage boys in the background. Wendy saw her mom frown before ending the call.

"Mom, what's wrong? I saw you scowl, and I know that look." Rainie sat on the floor with Michaela, stacking blocks, but listened closely to the conversation. She quickly glanced at Missy, and no doubt there was a register of disapproval clear as day on her face.

"I don't think these new boys Sam's hanging with are up to any good. Sam's so backward, understandably, that I worry they could take advantage of her. Girls are so different than boys, Lordy, lordy. All we need is for her to get pregnant, or catch God knows what." Rainie's mind went to Rand and her obsession with Sam. She worried that Rand's fascination might not be a good thing. Thoughts ran through Rainie's mind. She'd have to talk with Rand and find out what was going on with Sam and the two boys.

An hour later, Sam returned to the house. Her hair was somewhat disheveled, but that could have been from riding bikes, climbing trees, or just playing, not necessarily playing around with the new friends, but just as Missy's alarms were going off, Rainie's spidey-senses were tweaked, as well. "I'm gonna take a bath while Sam has Michaela if y'all don't mind." Wendy and Missy waved her off.

Upstairs, she began to undress and could feel Rand's presence. She turned on the bathwater. "Where've you been? I know you've been around Sam."

"You mean Samantha," rang through her head.

"Sorry, Samantha, but that doesn't answer my question." Rand started to get in a pissy—Rainie could feel the coolness taking over the room, and then the mist began to form. "Rand, I'm not getting into it with you. One minute you're apologizing, the next, I dunno. I just wanted to make sure everything was above board."

In a hollow voice, Rainie heard, "Oh, I don't know, what would be above-board to you? It seems you don't have any boundaries when it comes to doing things you shouldn't. She's not doing drugs or getting drunk like you used to do. Remember those days, hm?"

Rainie responded, "If you're gonna be crappy to me, I'd rather you go somewhere else and be mean." The coolness stayed along with the mist. "What, Rand, you wanted me to get my life together, and I have, but is it not good enough? Sorry if you don't like me being happy."

In an almost growling tone, Rand spoke. "You know that's not it, Rainie. I can relate to Samantha."

Rainie asked, "Are you talking to her? Warning, it does freak people out when they see or hear ghosts. I don't freak out because I love you. We are part of each other."

"We were," came the cold response.

"We still are." The conversation ended when Rainie's phone rang.

"How's your day going?" Michael told her his last patient had canceled, and he was on his way home.

"Yay. Drive carefully."

WHAT'S NEXT

Marse looked up from his paperwork. His Russ-dar was spot on; he felt the nuisance approaching. "How's it hanging, Rick?"

"Same old same old, Russ. Is there something you need?" Marse's face of irritation spoke volumes. Even if Russ had something of importance to tell him, it would probably fall on deaf ears, as the man had worn every ounce of patience out of him with his cartel obsession. Russ pulled up a chair and leaned with his elbow on the desk, cupping his hand to his mouth like big secrets. The man took himself way too seriously. Marse all but rolled his eyes, thinking no one gave a shit about anything Russ did or thought.

"I know I've bugged you in the past, and I just wanted to let you know; you've been right all this time. I got a one-hundred percent confirmation that Mateo Moreno was assassinated. The stick on it was his best childhood friend, Javier Garcia—I think that's the last name— did the hit, and now he's number one in the Cartagena operation." Tobin nodded as though what he spoke was on the DL.

Rick rubbed his fingers on his temples, trying to ward off a headache from the incessant bullshit of Russ Tobin. "Good to know, Russ. Thank you. My concerns are not in Cartagena but on the rash of stolen cars and tainted drugs in our city. Whoever has dibs on NOLA and is in control has gone off the deep end. At least when Mateo was bossman, the drugs that flooded the city must've been good stuff, because it wasn't like it is now with kids that are overdosing left and right, not to mention the massive increase in car theft over the past year. For people that like to live in the dark and out of the spotlight, this new group of thugs are more daring and really don't give a shit. Car theft is going down all day, every day, and the boosters don't even have to lose any beauty sleep over it anymore—these punks are boosting the cars of people that have run into sandwich shops for five minutes. So, if you have any clues there, speak up, my brotha; if not, I got a shit-ton of open cases. We're patrolling pretty heavily, but with all the scandals of late, unless we see the crime in action, we can't profile and assume anything. The thugs have our nuts in a vice." Russ began to walk off but then did some hand gesture he must've thought cool—like some fraternity bullshit.

Marse looked back down at the new reports. The statistics were unfavorable for anyone owning a Jeep, Infiniti QX80, or a Dodge Challenger. On college campuses, trucks and Jeeps ranked as number one and two in stolen vehicles. Many of the students from Tulane and Loyola were from moneyed families who could afford expensive rides for their kids. Those were also a lot of the same people overdosing. The numbers were staggering, and all he could do was shake his head sadly.

❧

"Diego, we need to move on getting rid of my contact at NOPD," Delores said. "I know he's been in touch with dead Manny's people and had some conspiracy theory about Mat. The guy's name is Russ Tobin; he's a dirty cop to start with and has no loyalty to anyone. I guess it's whoever makes him feel important. As hard as the NOPD is looking at us, I thought he'd be a good one to have our backs, but he's a nothing, a nobody who thinks he's all that. Unnecessary baggage."

Diego watched her as she moved around the room. While he lusted for her, he also was beginning to despise her and her attitude. Delores was the one who was starting to feel like unnecessary baggage. She was calloused to life. She wanted power, and that was all that mattered—individuals no longer did. A life was a dime a dozen. His stomach twisted as disgusting slime came up the back of his throat. He left the room before he said something he wouldn't live to be able to regret.

Delores followed him. "You have no answer for me? Maybe you could say, 'yes, Delores; I'll handle this for you,' but you say nothing and walk out on me. Do you know what I am capable of, Diego?" He spun around, grabbed her by the neck, and pushed her against the wall. Her ebony eyes glared into his as she flung a knee toward his crotch while flailing her arms. With the other knee, she rammed his gut, but he persisted in squeezing her throat. Her petite body thrashed with an unimaginable strength for someone so tiny. He lifted her and threw her to the floor. She began choking, sputtering, and coughing, trying to draw in a full breath. With as much hate as she could muster, she wheezed out, "Fuck you."

Diego held her down and forced himself on her. She struggled but then became aroused by the display of strength, kissing him passionately. Tearing the shirt from his body, she grabbed him with savage hunger.

"I would do anything for you, but I am not your toy to order as you please, Delores. You must talk to me with the respect that is due a man, bonita." With each thrust, he expounded, "I. Am. Not. Your. Bitch. But, you, you Delores, are mine." The violent encounter changed their relationship right then and there.

From sheer exhaustion and emotional overload, they stayed on the floor. She now looked at Diego in a different light. She felt the corners of her mouth twitch into a smile that purred. He had always been like a weak puppy, nipping at her heels and fulfilling her every command. Now, he looked strong, like a man that would not take shit from anyone—a man that could meet her every need. He had earned her respect. While Javier had manhandled her with brutality, almost taking her life, he had not earned respect; instead, the actions were of betrayal, an unforgivable sin.

Michael reached into the glovebox and pressed the button. Slowly the gate opened, and out of the corner of his eye, he saw a pickup truck pull in closely behind him. He drove slowly down the driveway, long enough that the pickup made it through the gate before closing. Boldly and with attitude in his posture, Michael got out of his car and approached the truck. He saw both hands raise through the windshield. "Hey, pardner," Michael called out. "I think you've made a wrong turn." The closer he got to the vehicle, the more perplexed he became.

"How are you, Mike?" A hand waved from the window.

Michael took a few more steps closer as the man started to open his door. "Stay in your truck, sir." With a sudden awareness, Michael's eyes widened, and a broad smile crossed his face. "No, get over here." An older man with blond hair past his shoulders hopped out of the truck. "Oh my God, look at you." He embraced the man. "So good to see you, M—William. What brings you to the boondocks? Wait, follow me to the house. I know there's one particular redhead that's going to flip out." William nodded.

"And you, my friend, need to meet my wife, Noelle. I shall follow you, Mike. I would hate to be greeted with shotguns. Am I to understand your whole family is here? John, Wendy, Dave, and their boys?"

Michael shook his head. "Fuck! You know about my whole family, then? Wow, you will never cease to amaze me, friend. Follow me."

By this time, not only was Rainie impatiently waiting outside, but her mother-in-law and Wendy had joined her. Michael pulled up with the pickup right behind him. He could see the question on Rainie's face, so he quickly made his way to her. She welcomed his embrace. "Michael, who the hell is that?" she whispered as she hugged him. He took her hand and pulled her along.

The man and the woman were standing by their truck. "Rainie, this is my friend William LaSalle and his wife, Noelle." The young woman was obviously expecting. Fortunately, Noelle had a thick mane of black hair and eyes as dark as soot, so if the child were to be born brunette, there would be no room for question.

Rainie's face lit up, and her eyes darted between Michael and Mateo. Holy shit! Her heart rate picked up with an impending feeling of panic, and she felt certain she had a look of curiosity about her face. "William, I have heard so much about you from Michael; I feel as though I already know you." She approached him with a hug, which was out of character for a first encounter with someone, but she had to do something before she recklessly blurted out an inappropriate comment. Her actions took everyone, except the two newcomers, by surprise.

His eyes were alive with welcome. "And I, too, am delighted to meet you." Missy caught his French inflection. "This is my wife, Noelle." Noelle was clearly much younger than her husband, but from all appearances, full of affection for him. Her eyes danced when he spoke, and she held onto his words. From her slight fidget and longing looks at the man, her appearance screamed of a shy, submissive personality. Rainie couldn't help but think, shy? With this group of people? Lawd, have mercy.

Missy approached. "Francais?"

The girl answered softly, "Oui, but I do have English."

Missy continued, "Et je parle francais comme mes fils et ma fille. Bienvenue chez nous." (And I speak French, as do my sons and daughter. Welcome to our home.)

William took Missy by the shoulders and kissed each cheek. "Thank you, Mrs. Landry, Noelle is working on her English, but it is good to know you speak French in case she may need assistance."

"Y'all come on in, make yourselves at home. Can I get you something to drink? Hopefully you can stay for dinner. We rarely meet Michael, John, or Wendy's friends." Rolling around in Rainie's head was if you only knew.

"Knew what, Rainie? Are these bad people? They seem nice, and I doubt Mike has scumbag friends like—" Rand started in Rainie's head. Like what, Rand? Then clear as a bell, Missy's voice rang loud and clear—Enough! Rainie's head spun like on a swivel in Missy's direction, nodding in apology.

Everybody took a seat as Missy called Rainie in to help with refreshments. Rainie sheepishly entered the kitchen. Missy turned with her hand on her hip. "I don't know what the hell is going on with you and Rand, but it needs to stop. I have never known y'all to act like this before, and you're letting it get to you. If it were one of the boys, would you tolerate such talk? I think not. Make up with Rand. Something is hurting her, and I suspect you're dead-on correct in the maturity issue, but you need to level the playing field; after all, she is your twin."

Rainie pulled out the wine glasses and poured water into the remaining wine glasses as Missy prepared some snacky tidbits. "Honey, the French drink wine, pregnant or not. Their children even have wine with meals. I'm sure Noelle will appreciate a glass of wine. If she tells you otherwise, then get her water, but I doubt she will." Missy stopped a minute and kissed Rainie on the cheek. "It'll all be okay, my sweet. I don't want to come across as a bitchy mother-in-law, but I love you and see how much all this is tearing you apart. If I could talk to your sister, I would, but I don't have your gift. Sometimes I wish I did, but seeing what you're going through, maybe it's best I don't. God gives us the gifts He wants us to have." Rainie brought out what glasses she could carry, and Missy brought out the cheese and crackers. Michael jumped up to help. Rainie swooped into the kitchen. "Michael, hold me. How long are they staying? I have so many questions."

"Me too. I'm equally as shocked by our visitor. I don't know how long they're staying, but I bet at least through dinner. I'm sure he'll want to talk with me alone at some point." He held her tight, and the longer he held her, the more her tension eased. She could feel the muscles in her neck and shoulders releasing like tiny bubbles of anxiety bursting inside, her heartbeat slowed to a normal rhythm, and for one brief moment, all felt right in the world.

Rainie and Missy each carried two glasses of wine as they returned to the Hearth.

Before long, the kids came rushing in, sweaty and dirty. Closely following were John, Jack, and Dave. Sam brought Michaela down from Neverland, and preparations for dinner commenced. Missy had updated Dominique about the inclusion of two more for supper, and she delivered the food at the perfect time for dinner. The house was full of life and joy.

Following dinner, Michael and William stepped out by the pool, much to Rainie's bent feelings. "Why are you in town? I'm sorry, but I'm having a hard time calling you William. Please excuse me tripping over your name. Your wife probably thinks I have a stuttering problem, and who knows what my family thinks. I usually don't stumble on words." Both men chuckled. "I'm just curious. I didn't know if you had to tell me something, or—" Michael shrugged his shoulders, lifting the palms of his hands.

Mateo clasped his hands behind his head and stretched out. "No reason. When I heard your voice, I decided it was time to visit, just for a few minutes. Your family's hospitality is extraordinary. My wife is a quiet little woman, yet I see her opening up with such vigor to your wife, mother, and sister; perhaps, she misses female interaction." He closed his eyes with a look of contentment. "It is beautiful here, Mike. Like here, we live in the, what did you call it, boon-something." He smiled.

Feeling the urge to check his face more closely, Michael clenched his hands into fists and released them and the urge. "So, what really brings you to this part of the world? Not blowing smoke up your ass, but I thought I might come to Tadoussac around Mardi Gras, for real. Just Rainie and me. I want her to get to know you and you to know her. She's a rare woman, and I have been oh so blessed. Speak of the devil." Rainie appeared, walking up with John and Jack. The three of them joined the two men.

For the next hour, the five of them visited, talking about Canada and life, as Jack put it, life in the arctic. Jack extended an invitation for the new couple to stay in one of the guest houses for the night, but William declined with abundant thankfulness and said they needed to be on their way. The night wound down, William and Noelle left, the kids went down for the night, and the adults sat around chatting, warmed by the brilliant orange and blue flames from the fireplace, until bed. Rainie was tired and fell asleep quickly.

The sound of shuffling outside their bedroom door woke Rainie and Michael. They could hear Jack and John speaking in whispered voices, so Michael put on his jeans and joined them in the hall. Rainie peered out the door and saw the three of them huddled, Jack pointing toward the door at the back of the house. Both Michael and John went downstairs, and Jack headed with determined steps toward the back upstairs door. The grimace on all three of their faces was alarming, and the first thought she had was involving their earlier visitor. While she had been pleasantly surprised by his gentle nature, she knew Mateo, now William, had the potential to be ruthless, and it made her nervous, especially with strange nighttime activities taking place.

She felt a sudden chill as Rand's presence rushed into the room. Rainie pulled some jeans and a sweater on before grabbing her boots. The blood rushed with force through her body, and her fingertips tingled as though electrified. The fluff on her arms stood straight up, and her hair fanned out as though caught in the torrent of a windy day. "Rai, I didn't know she was going to do that. I didn't know, I swear." Taking a full breath, trying to de-escalate Rand's evident freak-out, Rainie calmly and softly responded, "Didn't know what, Rand?" Silence followed by a jittery answer. "Th-the boys." Rainie sat on the bed, pulling on socks before stepping into her boots. "What boys? My boys? Wendy's boys? What boys, Rand?"

"Oh God, no, Rainie, I'd never let anything happen to our boys. No, Sam's boyfriends. She's locked herself in Neverland and is doing all kinds of things with both boys. I swear I didn't know. She's not just making out with them anymore. She's doing things." Rainie thought, oh fuck. Rand, with a resounding follow-up, said, "Exactly!"

Rainie stopped putting on her boots, peeled off her socks, stripped down her jeans, removed her sweater, and put her nightgown back on. "I'm not losing sleep over some teenager sneaking boys in her room in the middle of the night. And, by God, if Sam's shenanigans wake up Michaela, there will not only be Jack's, John's, and Michael's hell to pay, there will be mine." Mostly quiet returned, but she could hear the men's voices and smaller male voices coming from down the stairs. "Rand, while we didn't do that as teenagers, a lot of girls do, and sneaking boys into their rooms in the middle of the night is not the end of the world. No need to worry yourself. Good night. I love you."

Michael tip-toed back into the room. "I'm not sleeping," Rainie said. He followed her comment with a chuckle. Rainie continued, "Rand told me what happened." Laying still with her eyes closed, tempting sleep, she tried to relax her mind. She turned over and looked him in the eye. "I'm nowhere near sleep. Gimme the scoop. Sam snuck two boys into her room and?"

"Let's just say there was a similar situation once upon a time in the hayloft." He couldn't hold back the laughter, and it spilled into the room. "Only problem, Mom's spidey senses were in tune, and Dad went to check things out. Sam's naked, both boys have their pants down, one manages to get by Dad and hops over the railing, not realizing the fall is substantial, and can't get up." By this time, Michael was laughing so hard he had trouble speaking. "Dad barks at Sam to put her clothes on, grabs the one boy by the scruff, and lands him with Mom, then sends John and me down to catch the kid if he tried to get up. That kid couldn't get up—his ankle's broken. Mom called the boys' parents, as Dad was too fucking pissed to talk to anyone. I'm glad it didn't wake up the kids because my dad was hot. F-bombs were flying. I'm not sure how long Sam will be punished, but let's just say she's not the sharpest knife in the drawer. She confessed to setting the whole thing up." With a prolonged laughing snort, he doubled up in laughter. "Fuck me, that was hysterical. I haven't seen my old man that pissed in a very long time." The prolonged snorting commenced again.

His laugh was contagious, but she managed to calm him down and herself as well. "Poor Rand is beside herself."

❧

Diego and Delores pulled out into traffic as they made their way to the warehouse. Delores dialed the familiar number. He answered, "Tobin."

"Hey, after thinking about our conversation, I might have some information about another group in town trying to edge in on our business. You could maybe get cred for the bust, and they'll be out my way, but we can take care of it if you're not interested. Just a thought." She gave him the address to her warehouse as though it was the made-up address of the new thugs, then abruptly ended the call. All of her guys were out looking for possible boosts and wouldn't be back for at least another hour at the earliest.

Russ jumped to the call and, in his cagey, up-to-no-good manner, headed out the office. Marse picked up on the sketchy vibes and tailed him. It didn't take long for him to figure out where he might be heading. While it wasn't the exact warehouse, it was only two blocks over and had the same feel, look, and nasty blacked-out windows. Whoever had taken over the operation definitely had shit for brains. Marse watched from half a block down. He saw Tobin get out of his vehicle, start stealth-walking along the side of the building, and then, to Rick's total disbelief, saw him bang his fist on the metal roll-up door. "What a fucking clown," Marse commented under his breath. He watched a dark vehicle coming up the wrong way on the street, rolling toward Tobin, who was unaware. While Marse had no love for the asshole, he couldn't watch as one of their own got mowed down.

Rick reached for the magnetic blue light to place on his roof when out of nowhere, a pickup truck tore around the corner, blazing automatic firepower into the dark vehicle, making a Swiss cheese mess of the car. Then, it tore off with no chance of capture. It was there one second and gone the next, poof. Marse called it in as he watched Tobin hit the ground defensively, looking like he was scared half to death. Not that Rick faulted him for it, because even at a distance, the whole thing had left him shaken. It all happened in a blink, so fast that he didn't get a clear look at the driver. He only noted that whoever it was had been alone. He called in the shooting and screeched to a stop near Russ, shouting as he rushed out of the car. "Tobin, you okay, you hit?"

"What the fuck just happened?" Russ Tobin seemed out of it, but then again, anyone in the same situation would be messed in the head. Once Marse sized up the situation, realizing Russ was severely shaken but not hurt, he waited for backup before approaching the dark car, all the while trying to reassure Russ all was well. From all appearances, there was no sign of life in the mangled car, but Rick wasn't about to take any chances. Circling his brain was a loop of questions—who was the person in the truck, where had they come from, and how had they known? It had all happened so fast, and Rick's attention had been on Russ. He knew the detective was playing with fire and that it was only a matter of time before he got burned. Still, Marse hadn't taken his eyes off the dark vehicle, which still gave no evidence of life. Several units descended upon the scene; some officers crouched behind their car doors with weapons drawn while a few honed in on the motionless, bullet-riddled car.

They slowly advanced towards the car, skirting close to the sides. Carefully, one officer opened the door to find two lifeless bloody bodies. The officer examining inside the vehicle looked over to Marse and swiped his unarmed hand beneath his chin, signaling all were dead.

Marse approached for a close look, and recognized Delores Moreno and Diego St. Marten, then called out to the other officers, "Another fucking cartel hit."

He walked up to Tobin. "Whoever was driving the truck saved your ass. Judging from the position of the bodies and the gun, St. Marten was about to pop you. Just a word of caution, be content to play on your side of the street, stop being a bitch for the cartel players, or I promise you'll end up dead, and it won't be an easy ending. They are merciless, Russ. Imagine the worst kind of death, and you haven't even scratched the surface of their capabilities and practices. They're fuckin' sick. Hear me out on this one."

In a shaky voice, Tobin responded, "Got that."

ॐॐ

New Year's Eve came—in all of its whistle and popping splendor. There was no doubt Jack and John relished the prepping and trial runs for the fireworks, and the boys were getting old enough that they could help, so Michael stayed back with Rainie and Michaela. Since the brouhaha with Sam and the boys, Rand had been distant, and Rainie could barely feel her presence. It had dwindled to silence. Missy had quite a few heart-to-heart discussions with Sam, explaining the full ramification of her actions and what was appropriate. It amazed Rainie how Missy could talk so openly without judgment or condemnation.

Michael listened intently, then reminded Rainie of how his mom had never cast judgment and had patiently accepted when he'd confided in her during the dark times. Curled in a ball on his lap, with Michaela in Rainie's, they sat by the fireplace, watching the flickering of the flames. "Why do y'all call this the Hearth when a hearth is a fireplace and not a room? Why not the family room? I've often wondered."

"It's from when John and I were young, very young, like three and four. Mom would say, 'Boys, don't go by the hearth,' so we would stay in the kitchen, and that became the name of the room for us, and it stuck." They sat quietly watching the flames. "You are too quiet; I feel like something might be brewing." His arm ran along her back, holding her close. He sniffed her hair, nuzzling her neck. "Mm, I love the smell of my wife. You have a distinct natural fragrance, almost like a hint of—"

"It's the red hair, Michael." He gave a slight chuckle. "Do you think your mom had any idea of the things you were doing in the dark times? She was so tender with Sam, but also letting her know at the same time that her behavior wasn't acceptable."

He answered. "She knew something, but maybe not exactly what. She knew I was sad and that was enough. He struggled to move his body. "Wonderful as this is, ladies; I need to stretch my legs." Like a Matryoshka doll with one wooden doll cupped inside the other, the little one popped off her lap, and then Rainie uncoiled from Michael's lap. He winced as he stood up. Michaela ran off to find Missy.

Michael loosened his shoulders, stretched each arm over his body, and pulled his knees up, one by one. He rolled his head in a circle; the pops of the vertebrae were audible to Rainie. Wow, I heard your neck from here. You need a massage, and I know just the woman to do it." She walked up behind him, and with a swift slap on the bottom, she let out a laugh. "Sorry, that was harder than intended." He turned abruptly and grabbed her, squeezing her tightly. In a throaty whisper, she responded, "Now get that fine ass of yours upstairs, and I want nothing but skin, Michael. Do you have any of that massage goop here? Or I'll have to use some olive oil and toss you like a salad."

Michael pushed away from her, laughing. "Rai, not a good, um, expression." She did a sideways glance with a perplexed look. His laughter caused him to gasp. "You have no idea of what you said, and it's sickly funny, partly because you said it with such innocence." For a moment, he stopped laughing, but his eyes were teared up. "There really is a similar expression used just like that, but it isn't what you meant."

John came in smelling of blasting powder and burnt hair. "What the fuck is wrong with him?" Rainie shrugged cluelessly.

"Rainie just offered to—" Michael started a long guttural snort sounding like a garbage disposal, then took in a deep breath, somewhat gained composure, and continued, "to toss the salad."

"Mikey, you are so wrong," John said, and he exploded in laughter. "Poor thing has no idea what that means, you bastard!" They were falling on each other, laughing.

Quickly Rainie picked up her phone and googled the expression. Her face looked like a cartoon character, mouth widely dropped and eyes as open as possible, then she turned to Michael, squinting her eyes. "Oh my God, that's disgusting. Michael Landry, here I was trying to be all sweet, offering a body massage for your creaky old ass, and you turn it into something nasty. I don't know if that massage is still an offer or just a mere blip from the past. What would even make your mind go there? Men!" She stood tapping her foot impatiently. "Now, if you can get your mind out of your twisted perversion and want that total body, I'm still willing. Time is ticking, buster, so you best get control of yourself, or you might just be sleeping with John tonight!"

Tears from laughter were streaming down his beet-red face. "I needed that. Nothing is better for the soul than busting a gut with laughter. Please, my lovely, can we go upstairs, and I'll take you up on your offer?"

Rainie pushed him from behind, "Get a move on; we don't have much time. I don't know how long your mom's gonna be up to running behind Michaela."

John chuckled. "Oh God, how I need a woman, one who'll toss— just kidding," he said, and headed toward the kitchen, where they heard him say, "Princess McKay."

Once in the bedroom, Michael stripped down to his boxers. "No sir, all off and lay on your stomach." Rainie looked in their bathroom cabinet and found some tea tree oil. "That'll work." She worked the oil into her hands, where it warmed and began tingling, and she started kneading his neck. "Michael, your muscles are like rocks. You need to start doing tai-chi again. Remember, you used to talk to me about how unhealthy it was for me to hold so much tension in my muscles? It's unhealthy for you, too." She moved down to his traps, to his gluts, then she started to laugh, thinking about the earlier conversation with Michael and John. "I don't think I'll ever be able to make a salad without conjuring up that picture." He chuckled quietly but was clearly getting into a zen frame of mind. After finishing his legs, Rainie told him to flip over. Straddling his body, she worked the sides of his neck briefly and then his pecs. Smiling down at him, Rainie pinched his nipples.

With a half-smile, he asked, "Why are these still on?" He tugged on her jeans. "They're stiff against my body."

"Oh, is that it? Well, the only thing I feel that's stiff belongs to you." She stood and peeled her jeans off. "I guess this finishes the massage, sir, now what do you want me to do?" She pulled her top over her head and dropped it by the puddle of clothing on the floor. Determined not to move, she stood as though waiting for instructions, with a slightly seductive coyness about her.

Michael propped up on his elbows, probing her body with his eyes. Slowly he moved to the side of the bed, still fixated on her hypnotic ice-blue eyes. Taking her hands, Michael pulled her between his knees, giving his full attention to her breasts. Softly he kissed each, arousing her nipples to perfect rosy beads—caressing them with gentle fondles, but gradually increasing the grip as the momentum climbed. With stuttered breaths, he whispered, "I want you, Rainie, all of you." She climbed into his lap, straddling his hips, took hold of his rock-hard, pulsing cock, guiding him into the warmth he desired. Gripping her ass, he flexed his hips, bringing their bodies into perfect unity. With guttural grunts, he grasped her hips tightly, moving her body with his in frenetic intensity. The anticipation of the moment of promise was immense and building as his body hit the pinnacle, roaring through her. Her body quivered with an involuntary shudder, then they both crumbled onto the bed, seeking rest from the magnitude.

Looking around in wonderment at the calamity, Tobin asked, "What were you doing here? I'm glad you were, but are you following me, and if so, why?" He held himself with his hands on his belt, head jutting forward with a grimaced look of how-dare-you. "What the fuck? We're on the same side, Rick."

Marse, still watching the chaos, glanced to his right, sarcastically retorting, "You sure about that? Because I'm not. I don't know who has you on a string, but obviously, somebody does, an' as I said, you better start sticking to your side of the street before I'm calling the lab to scrape what's left of you for forensic identification. I don't know what excuse you're going to give as to why you were here in the first place, but, regardless, I still have to cite it all in my report." No matter who took point on the incident, DEA, CIA, or Homeland, he was still going to have to report what he'd witnessed and would be dragged into countless interviews with whatever fed agency claimed this bullshit as theirs. The whole ordeal was above his pay grade. Unfortunately, he knew that he wouldn't be involved in the mess if he had kept his ass at his desk. He bit his bottom lip and slowly shook his head as the miserable thoughts ravaged his brain. "Oh well. What's done is done, dammit."

He climbed back in his car, wrote a few notes to keep it all fresh in his mind. Mike's face came to his mind thinking back on the strangeness of an incognito appointment from Delores—then, like a wild carnival ride, thoughts of the truck popped up—like, where did that truck come from? He knew he'd never get a straight, honest story from Tobin. He cruised back to the station but on the way called Mike.

Rainie picked up Michael's phone. "Detective Marse, it's Rainie. Michael will be right with you, or would you rather a call-back?" He said he'd hold, and the small talk continued. Michael quickly washed himself off and took the phone from Rainie. "It's just Rainie and me in the room; if it's okay, I'm gonna put you on speaker?" That way, both could hear and get dressed at the same time. They suspected a call upstairs to retrieve Michaela was imminent.

"Sure. Heads up on your latest weird patient, the one you called me about recently—she's dead. I thought that might be of interest to you. Can't discuss details, but I'm sure it'll be somewhere on the news. When I left the scene, I saw camera crews pulling up. That was it, Mike." They could hear John coming up the stairs.

Michael took the phone off speaker. "I look forward to hearing about the situation and will be on the lookout for the news. Thanks for the info. Happy New Year to you too." John rapped on the door.

He handed Michaela to Rainie. "I'm pooped, y'all. Princess McKay has had me running all over. Rainie, she's got your bombastic laugh. It's hilarious coming from a pint-size kid. Don't mean to rain on the massage, but I'm worn out. Mikey, we got everything set for the fireworks display, and it's gonna be the shit this year! Ya know why? Because I am the shit!" He turned and thundered down the stairs.

Michael called after him, "You're something, John, and it does involve shit, like full of—

Michaela looked at Rainie and said, "Daddy shit." Both she and
Michael looked at each other with panic in their eyes, trying to hold back
any laughter. Holding a solemn face, Rainie corrected the toddler, then
corrected Michael and said she would talk to Big J. "Mommy, J-dude
not Big J. No say shit, no!" Michaela tapped Rainie's arm and pulled the
perfect pout—jaw jutted out and bottom lip glistening with saliva.

"Downstairs, ladies, if you will." Michael led the way downstairs.

Rainie was going through the motions, but in the recesses of her
mind, she questioned if Mateo's visit had anything to do with his sister's
murder. The familiar knot in her stomach started tightening again, just
as it had when Michael had performed the surgeries. The holiday visit
had been a strange one. Sam's development started the whole thing off
with a bang, then the constant barrage of Rand's comments, Mateo's
visit with his expecting wife, Sam and the boy encounter, and now
the silence of Rand. She could deal with Michaela's ever-expanding
vocabulary; she had gone through it with both boys at about the same
three-year-old mark. It was scary to hear about the woman's murder,
but she figured people in cartel business knew they had a short life
expectancy, or if they didn't know, they sure as shit should have, but
the seemingly sweet man she'd met didn't fit the mold of someone who
would murder his one and only sister. His demeanor was not at all
what she had expected, and she could clearly see why Michael felt an
attachment to him, and it wasn't just because of the surgeries—the guy
was genuine. None of it computed. She put Michaela in a stroller and
brought her outside—maybe she might feel Rand's presence.

Michael had joined the guys by the firework staging area, leaving
Rainie to join the group or wander the property. "Michaela, want to
go see the horses or watch the ducks on the pond?" Not waiting for
a response, Rainie started toward the pond. They watched the ducks
bob in the water, submerging their heads with a quick dive to capture
an unsuspecting minnow or water bug. She looked up at the sky and
could see the brilliant constellations. Michael had taught her so much.
"Rand, I don't know where you are, but I want to talk to you. I'm
alone here right now; I know you freaked over Samantha's antics, and
I'm sorry Missy fussed. She can't hear you, but she sometimes hears my

thoughts, and I suppose she realized I was talking with you. I guess my face showed I was upset, and she put it together, or maybe I said your name, I don't know, and if I did, I'm sorry."

Rand's presence created a strange current in the atmosphere. It was different than usual; Rainie couldn't help but wonder if it was related to hanging around Samantha or if something was happening with the kinetic energy of her essence. Whatever the difference, it was noticeable.

"I know you're here; I can feel you. Do we need to talk?"

Almost in an echo, like she was talking in a tunnel, Rand responded, "You can't understand, and it's okay, Rainie. I'm fine, and yes, I've been mean to you. When you said I had a temper tantrum, you were balls-on accurate, to use one of your expressions. No more negative episodes. They won't happen anymore."

There was silence as Rainie tried to connect with Rand's feelings, but there was a void. She closed her eyes, tried to go to a peaceful place, totally relaxed, prepared to feel Rand's emotions. Nada. Was Rand blocking her feelings, or were they non-existent? Why would Rand say Rainie couldn't understand? Couldn't or wouldn't? Her chest felt restricted, like straps being pulled tighter. Her breathing all but stopped, making it hard even to swallow. It was alarming and scary, but as quickly as the sensation came, it left. Her natural breathing returned; her chest relaxed. Odd, she thought.

Rainie was ready to be back in her normal surroundings. Michael's parent's place was outstanding, but it was time to be home and settled— it was almost like the feeling of eating too much chocolate. So yummy, but one too many bites and yummy went directly to yucky and did not pass go or collect the $200. New Year's came and went, and John had been right. The display was something to marvel at, with the elaborate fountains of sparkles bursting in the sky. The oohs and ahhs from all were well-deserved.

While it had been an adventurous holiday, nothing felt as good as when they pulled into their driveway. Allie and Eric still had another two days on holiday, but the kids would be back in school on January third, and it was a brand-new year filled with hope and promise.

KNOCKIN' ON HEAVEN'S DOOR

The kids were back in school and getting into the normal swing of things; the vacation from dreaded homework fights had ended, and house rules were back in place. While, perhaps, humdrum and boring to some, it meant routine, sure and steady, reliable, no more unusual drama for Rainie, just the day in day out.

Dinner was just coming out of the oven when Michael pulled into the driveway. When he walked into the kitchen she had her back turned to the door, and was moving cautiously with a sizzling roasting pan, so he spoke softly so as not to startle her. "How's my sexy wife?" He waited until she had the hot food placed on the trivet, then grabbed her around the waist with a bouquet of gold-tipped white roses. He tickled her neck with soft, breathy kisses, giving rise to goosebumps and her deep rumbling laugh. "So tell me, my deliciously hot wife, where do you feel those kisses?"

In the midst of a laugh, she wiggled and turned in his arms. "Michael, what has gotten into you?" Looking down from lips to eyes, he leaned in for a passionate kiss. "The roses are gorgeous, and I love all this cuddly attention, but we need to have dinner." She caught herself, knowing damn well what his next comment would have been. He was playful, tickling, and gently fondling, which gave her the giggles and enticed her playfulness. Their eyes, locking, made promises for later.

A tiny voice rose from their knees. "Daddy, you pway wif Mommy? Me too!" Michael bent down and swooped the little princess into his arms, smothering her with kisses and tickles. Michaela had Rainie's laugh, no doubt about it—eliciting more laughter from the two of them.

Michael had a beaming smile. "Who would've ever guessed a laugh could be genetic, but she sounds just like you, Rai, just not as loud yet." He took Michaela off to get the boys for dinner and set the table as Rainie dished up the food.

Following dinner and baths, Thomas had Michaela on his lap as Rainie read a bedtime story. The boys didn't care about the story; they soaked in the love and attention. Kids tucked in beds; Michael started the shower while Rainie checked for messages. Suddenly her heart felt like it couldn't beat, and her breath was all but snuffed out. In seconds she started to struggle for breath, she started having weird vision changes, like she was looking at everything through a prism. As quickly as it set in, it stopped, and everything was normal. She freaked out. Her hands trembled, her stomach tightened, and the tears began trickling down her face.

Michael came out of the bathroom and, seeing her state, rushed over, embracing her. "What's wrong, Rai?" The tears turned into sobs. "Talk to me. You're shaking like a leaf." She clutched onto him, as if letting go was not an option. He stroked her hair. "Are you in pain?" She shook her head no. "I can't help if you won't talk to me." His eyes cast down, filling with tears that held on, refusing to tumble down his cheek. He felt a heart-wrenching fear.

She drew in a deep breath, trying to slow the sobbing so she could speak. "I think I need to see a doctor and get some tests run or something. It's like out of the blue, a boa-constrictor winds around me, and I can't breathe. It almost feels like my heart isn't beating, and then I get this tunnel vision thing. It scares the shit out of me, and there's nothing I can do, but as quickly as it comes on, I return to normal, as though nothing happened. It's weird. Sorry to put a damper on our sexcapades."

He took her pulse, checked her pupils, but was at a loss. "Do you want to go to the ER? Maybe we should. I don't like the sound of your symptoms, Rainie, and I don't want to wait until tomorrow to have you checked out. Give me your phone." Eric and Allie were due to have landed from their Colorado skiing trip an hour before, but he knew how travel could be. He called Eric, figuring if all had gone as scheduled, he and Allie would be on their way back from the airport. After a couple of rings, Eric picked up. "How close are y'all to being here?" They had just left baggage claim. "Let us know as soon as you get here." Michael briefly described Rainie's symptoms, concluding with her progressing to asymptomatic after the episode.

"I think you're overreacting, Michael," Rainie said. "I believe something is wrong, but I'm gonna see the quack tomorrow and move on from there. Just snuggle me to sleep." He laid next to her, spooning against her body. Gently passing his fingers over her arm, he kissed her neck. She could feel the wetness from his cheek. "Did you turn the shower off?" With an oh-shit moment, he sprinted from the bed into the bathroom, then returned to her. Sitting on the side of the bed, looking down at her, he stroked her hair. "Rai, are you feeling okay now? No more shortness of breath or chest pains?" She whispered she was okay. He went around the bed and climbed in next to her.

Unable to sleep, his mind began to run rampant with thoughts. The stream of unwelcome ideas caused his body to jump into fight-or-flight mode. Rainie rolled over, leaning against his shoulder. She could feel the tenseness of his body. "Michael, like you tell me, breathe. I promise I'm fine, and once I get everything checked, we'll find out whatever it is that's misfiring or too high or low."

Both of them had relaxed after a time, their fingers laced together, enjoying the restfulness of being close. They heard a slight tap on the door and told Allie and Eric it was okay to come in. Eric was full of questions and went into his E.R. mode without skipping a beat. "Is this recurrent, Rainie? Does it happen often? Describe the onset, what happens next, and so on, like a story—paint the picture for me." Quickly Rainie went through the episode in concise detail, and then mentioned it had happened one other time, during the holiday. They could tell Eric was perplexed from his facial expression and agreed Rainie needed to consult her doctor or get referred to a cardiologist. After the examination and interrogation from Eric, Rainie wanted to hear all about their trip. Allie held out her left hand, presenting a sparkling diamond engagement ring.

Rainie remembered all too well the feeling she'd had when Michael proposed. She swallowed down a lump that was forming tears of excitement. "Do I need to start looking for a nanny?" Allie responded that a new nanny was premature.

The following morning, Rainie called her doctor, who arranged for a morning appointment. Michael had Beth move his patients to another day, at least the ones Zeke couldn't take, to be with Rainie. Through the influence of Michael and Eric, Rainie was able to see a cardiologist, which was usually a two to three-month wait, unless in case of an emergency at the hospital, and then it was whoever was on call at the time.

When all the test results came back and scans had been read, the doctors concluded Rainie was as healthy as could be, and there was nothing abnormal physically, but maybe the feelings had been stress-induced. Her GP prescribed a mild tranquilizer as needed.

"Michael, I don't think this was stress, at least not the other night. Maybe the episode at your parents was, but I sure as hell am not taking any happy pills. Whatever, let's call it a fluke."

And quick as a snap, life was back to normal.

❧☙

Mardi Gras was fast approaching, and Michael still had not given Rainie any clue about their getaway. Their last surprise trip had been the honeymoon, and it had been like nothing she had ever experienced. So, in a grand Michael gesture, she trusted without question.

Michael cut his office hours to four days a week, which in turn made his day a smidge longer. As Rainie had pointed out, adding an hour to each day was counterintuitive to the plan. His third patient of the morning was running late, only by a few minutes, so Beth messaged Michael that a Mr. LaSalle was on hold. Grinning, he picked up the phone. "Bonjour, my friend. How are you?"

"Bonjour, Mike. I am fine, and you and your family?" Mateo inquired.

"If you're wondering, I have made all the arrangements for our visit. I'm surprising Rainie. From everything I've seen, it looks beautiful."

"It is magnificent. Still rustic and backward, but heartily embracing the beauty of Mother Nature. I wish you and your bride would be guests in our home. There's no need for other accommodations, but the Hotel Tadoussac is nice if that is what you prefer. Our home is lovely, and we do have a guest cottage for privacy. We are in the middle of the woods, and it is very beautiful. Please reconsider being our guests."

Michael's mind churned the thought over. He didn't want to take Rainie anywhere that wasn't spectacular, but he wasn't sure how she would feel about staying with William and Noelle, even in a guest house. Their last two nights would be glamourous and sophisticated as their reservations were at Chateau Frontenac, a historic property owned by Fairmont hotels in Quebec City. Although Rainie didn't speak French, many of the hotel employees would speak English; besides, she would never be away from him, not even for one minute.

"I'll take you up on the offer. I want this to be an exceptional experience and staying with you and Noelle will be an adventure. We'll arrive the Thursday night before Mardi Gras, travel to you on Friday, be with y'all until Monday, and then head out early to Quebec City for a couple of days." The small talk continued for another five minutes when Beth poked her head in, saying his patient had arrived.

☙☞

It had been a long few weeks since Rainie's health episode, leaving only a diffused memory of that night. The next day they were scheduled to fly out on a six-day holiday. Between Allie, Rainie's parents, and Michael's parents, the kids would be well-spoiled. All Michael had told her was to pack like she was going to be freezing her ass off, but not ski clothes. True to his feelings, Michael had booked the same private jet they used for their honeymoon. The only thing he hadn't shared with her was their destination.

"I'm all packed, Michael, complete with lots of warm sweaters, mufflers, caps, and gloves. And are you packed? I don't think so," Rainie chimed in a sassy tone, then climbed into bed dressed in her favorite flannel nightshirt. He smiled at her as he walked into the closet and came out with a packed suitcase. "When did you do that?"

"I've been packed since I made our reservations. I knew it might

get crazy with parade nights, dinner on the fly, and patient accidents."
Holding his thumb to his lips, he tipped his hand up as though drinking
from a bottle. "So far, everyone must be staying sober or at least on
their feet. We've had not one broken nose from kissing the curb."
He climbed in next to her. "It's chilly in here, don't you think?" The
temperature outside was in the low-forties, but their bedroom, instead
of being warm, equaled the air outside minus the cutting wind. Michael
reached over and pulled her close. "Much better. We'll be like birds on
the wires, keeping each other warm." He snuggled as close as he could.
She could feel his body shivering next to her.

"I'm cold, but you must be freezing. The mattress is shaking from
your shivering." She turned and put her hand to his forehead. "Thank
God, your temp feels normal. I've never seen you so cold, Michael.
Your teeth are even chattering—

He interrupted, "What part of I'm freezing didn't you get? What I
don't understand is why you're not; you're the one who's always cold.
Damn, I hope the heater isn't on the fritz. God, the thought of getting
out of bed to check it sucks, but there's no time like the present. Keep
my spot warm!" He quickly jumped out of bed, grabbed a sweatshirt,
and flew into the hallway, where he stopped on a dime. He had a most
puzzled look on his face as he looked back in their room to Rainie.
Then he proceeded back to their room. "It's almost too warm in the
house. I don't get it. Did Stella pull a funny and block the vents in
here?" The room seemed a little warmer than when he had just walked
out a minute ago, if that. "Strange. It feels better now."

"Maybe you should've had the sweatshirt on the whole time. I
know you say you can't sleep with a shirt on, but you can't sleep if
you're shaking from head to toe." When he closed the door, it was
like a gust of arctic air swept into the room, so he quickly opened
it back up, and the sudden freeze vanished. He pulled a chair up to
check the vents, only to find nothing was wrong with them. Michael
put the chair back, left the door open, hurriedly peeled his sweatshirt
off, and slid into bed. "Well, I guess that means we won't have a
before-the-holiday romp."

She sighed and rolled over. "But we will have six days where I
expect you to service my desires." Her tone was playful and tempting

at the same time, but the door was open, meaning the playground was closed for the night.

☙☙

Michael's alarm went off, and when he reached for Rainie, he found her missing. "Rai?" No answer, but then he heard activity from downstairs. For that one brief moment when he wasn't sure where she was, he noticed his stomach clench, heart pound, and realized he was having a Rainie moment. "No fucking way. I'm developing a panic disorder like my smokin' wife." He felt something behind him, and when he turned, Rainie was standing in the doorway, arms crossed with a huge grin. "You always talk to yourself like that?" She grinned. "I swear, Michael, the more we're together, the more you're becoming me, and I'm becoming you. I'm waiting for the talking with your hands to begin any day now." She slowly walked up to him in a sultry manner. "What you need, Michael is—"

The blood-curdling scream rang up the stairwell. "Mommyyyy!" They both rolled their eyes. Rainie called down that she was on her way.

"I need to scat, and you need to get dressed. The car will be here in half an hour. I brought the bags down already. So move it, stud." She gave him a quick good-morning peck and was on her way to the wee one before another war cry was released. Already dressed and more than ready to depart, she looked great, and he could tell, oh-so-ready to be out of there. It was perfect timing; he washed, dressed, and was in the kitchen for a fifteen-minute bon voyage from the kids and Allie. Everyone heard as the car pulled up. Before the driver even knocked on the door, Michael had both bags, and the front door opened.

They blew kisses as the car pulled off. "I'm a horrible dad; I couldn't wait to get out of the mayhem, while you seem together, without a pensive bone in your body. After the heater shit last night, with interrupted sleep and the absolute chaos in the kitchen, I couldn't get out of the door fast enough. Rai, I love our kids more than anything in the world, but sometimes, it's way overboard. The thing is, it's not the boys; it's the knee-high terrorist. Tell me this isn't her personality, and it will pass at some point in time." He looked perplexed, and all she could do was laugh. "You think this is funny? What parent is chomping at the bit to leave their kids?"

With a deadpan face, she answered, "All parents, Michael, but by tomorrow you'll be pining for them." The edges of her lips turned up slightly as she patted his hand. "They get wound up even more when they know we're leaving for a few days. It's like when a parent gets sick; usually, kiddos become more demanding; they don't like Mom or Dad being ill. It scares them, somewhere inside." She stroked the side of his face, giving him a meaningful kiss and looking him closely in the eyes. "You're a fabulous dad, and it's perfectly normal to want to bolt sometimes, especially with a three-almost-four-year-old child, but she is a tad spoiled with two big brothers to chase her every command. I wouldn't have it any other way."

Traffic wasn't too bad, and they made it to the airport with time to spare. While waiting in line at security, Rainie began the barrage of questions about their destination. Even though Michael was comfortable staying at Mateo's for a couple of days, he worried about Rainie's reaction. Would she be okay with it and not bothered, or would she be uncomfortable? She wasn't much of a mystery. Her every thought was revealed on her face, and if she was displeased, everyone would know it without her saying a word. Time would tell, and he hoped she would be okay with his decision.

The flight was exceptional, and while they didn't revisit the mile-high club, they had time to chill, talk, and reconnect, and it was bliss. With each passing hour, a layer of stress sluffed off, and by touchdown, they were like two young newlyweds, all over each other without a care in the world.

As soon as the hotel door room closed, they were disrobing, leaving clothes where they fell. Between passionate kisses, Michael, through breathy words, groaned, "Oh, God, I wanted you last night." In the midst of kisses, he backed her to the bed, where they drew together with magnetic force. His kisses flowed from her lips to her neck and shoulders as his body arched over hers, giving and taking pleasure with each thrust. She held onto his body, moving with him. While not a marathon, their mission was accomplished with tenacious power, and they lay there, bodies entangled in reprieve. Not even rousing for dinner, they instead ordered a selection of appetizers and desserts from room service, finally giving way to a restful and peaceful night's sleep a few hours later.

Quebec was cold, a kind of cold that struck straight to the bone. "Michael, spill the beans," Rainie commanded through chattering teeth. "Not that I don't appreciate this surprise trip to Quebec, but it's hardly a place I would've thought you'd have chosen, especially this time of year. Something I'm not getting?"

Michael's expression screamed with a thousand unsaid words, and there was far more to the story than a getaway trip to Quebec. With a bright smile, glistening white teeth, gorgeous dimples, and sexy sparkling eyes, it was a face she could look at forever. In typical Rainie style, she continued with the questions.

Michael looked ahead, casually glancing at her as she expounded. He pulled onto Route 167 with a gleam of satisfaction in his eyes as to her expressive surprise and curiosity. "Rai, we're not staying in Quebec City for the next couple of nights, but in private secluded accommodations, and I have plans for you, my nymph. Clue one: You'll see sights you've never seen before. Clue two, and lastly, you'll feel sensations unparalleled by prior experiences." A spark lit his face as he watched her ponder his comments. "It's nowhere on your radar. Just sit back, enjoy the sights, and relish the quiet time. I feel those wheels of yours turning, but let it go, my love. Just think, no kids, no fighting for our attention, and the terrorist is terrorizing somebody besides us." He punctuated it all with a light chuckle filled with love. "Breathe, Rainie. No worries, okay?"

The mere purr of his voice released the heaviness of her questions, literally dropping her shoulders, slowing her breathing, and the once-rapid beat of uncertainty in her chest settled. Her body had absorbed every word he'd uttered and responded in kind. Everything about her apprehension changed, including her posture and body language.

After two hours, they stopped for a quiet lunch in a sparsely populated town. The roadside café was charming. They sat across from one another, captured in each other's eyes. Their souls interlinking. A delightfully chatty young woman placed a plate of cheeses and assorted breads before them, paired with glasses of hearty red wine. Rainie gave him an inquiring look. "Wine? Midday? Us?"

Michael clasped her hands, softly twining their fingers. "It's perfect for the cheese and bread. Enjoy. We're on holiday, and I imagine we'll be raising a few more glasses. It's been long enough that I'm not worried about cross addiction from your past. I think for you, it was more of headspace and lack of self-assurance than addiction. No worries, if I believe we're venturing down a slippery slope, I'll drag the anchor." She slowly grinned, raising her glass and peering over the top; she drew in a deep breath, the bouquet teasing her senses. "Salute!" he said, and they touched glasses with a tiny melodic chime.

The young woman, while somewhat fluent in English, was obviously making an effort for Rainie. Michael kept his want of Français under wraps, being that this was a holiday for the two of them completely and totally together from every aspect, and his French would have created, intentional or not, a wedge. Because he and Mateo were already close, Rainie might feel like a third wheel, even though Noelle would be there. Mateo's wife came across as more docile, perhaps more submissive than Rainie, and would be content to be on the outside looking in. Michael planned on keeping conversation strictly between the four of them, including Rainie in everything. No secrets, no clandestine conversation—nope, not for anything—even the odd timing of his visit and Mateo's sister's murder. Between the cheese and bread, a cup of soup, and a tasty homemade dessert for two, they were refueled and ready to continue. After only a few hours had passed, a feeling of reconnection filled the air with coughs of laughter, flirty touches, and a co-mingling of thoughts and words. While exceptionally close, they both, at times, missed their private bubble of intimacy amid the constant demand of parenthood.

Michael veered off the main road, and for the next twenty minutes, Rainie sat in silence, absorbing the beauty of the passing countryside. The woods were dense. Michael came to a slow crawl and turned onto a narrow, rugged road. He navigated the hairpin turns and sudden slopes with precision, Rainie continually slamming on the imaginary brake on the passenger side.

"Calm down; we're fine." He glanced over at her, glimmering confidence in his smile.

"Eyes on the road, eyes on the road, Michael. Where the hell are we?" The density broke to a clearing. Ahead was a large stone home with a welcoming veranda. A man and a woman stood waiting. The closer they got, the easier it was to recognize the people. "Michael, why are we at M—William and Noelle's? I thought we were going to be alone, isolated, just the two of us, to relax. Waiting for an execution hardly constitutes relaxing." She was talking through her teeth with a glued-on smile, in case, by chance, someone had binoculars on them and could read lips.

Their host walked up to Michael's side window with a warm smile. "Good to see you two. Follow the road around, and it will lead you to the guest house. Please join us once you get settled." He stood back, sweeping his arms toward the right side of the house. The property was beautiful, and the view breathtaking as it overlooked a pristine body of water. They pulled up to a quaint guest house facing the magnificent view.

The cottage was equipped with everything one could want. The living room and kitchen were an open space with windows facing the water. The bedroom, off the living room, had an equally exquisite view. They bundled up and walked back to the house, where they were greeted by Noelle. By the looks of it, she hadn't much longer before the birth of the baby. "Please come in and get out of the cold. Will is preparing dinner; I hope you are hungry." She walked them into the kitchen.

"Tell me, were your travels good? How was the stay in Quebec City? Nice, yes?" Rainie and Michael sat on stools at the kitchen bar. William had his hair pulled back into a ponytail, and his demeanor, like when he'd visited Michael's parents, was laid back and calmly pleasant. His eyes were a golden color, which Rainie hadn't remembered. Like Michael, when he spoke, he looked the person directly in the eyes, rarely breaking the connection.

From the kitchen bar, they moved to the table, and feasting commenced. William said grace, thanking God for family, good friends, and the bounty before them. Rainie was touched, but then, her thoughts diverted to family. What an odd thing for him to say? She couldn't fathom what family he was referencing. It was like a multiple-choice test—a. his first wife and children, b. his new wife and baby on the way c. his sister, or d. all of the above. She pondered the thought but could feel eyes piercing her thoughts.

After filling their plates, Michael was the first to speak. "You are full of surprises, my friend. I had no idea you were so into cooking." Michael gently shook his head. "I guess, learn something new every day. I, too, like to dabble in the kitchen, but this is excellent—a combination of fresh fish and bananas. I would've never put the two together, and besides, in this freaking climate, where the hell would you get bananas?"

Over a few glasses of wine, the four of them spent the next few hours talking about mundane things such as fruits and vegetables, newborn babies, prices of gas in Tadoussac versus New Orleans, and the general state of the world. In all the worldly controversies, never once were cartels, drugs, or U.S. border concerns a topic of discussion.

Feeling a light buzz from the wine, Michael called the night, knowing Rainie had to be more than buzzed. While she hadn't been overly talkative, all her mechanisms of defense were down. Sitting close to him, she ran her hand up along his thigh, gently and lovingly massaging.

"Y'all, we're calling it a night," Michael said. "I guess this Canadian air has me worn out." He stood in front of Rainie, taking both her hands; he pulled her to standing and led her to the door, bidding all a good night.

Once inside the guest house, Rainie, trying to take off her jeans, tripped and fell into Michael's arms. With a slight slur, she flirted, "You're always there to catch me. Kiss me, Michael. Take me in your arms, and remember, there's no one around to hear my squeals of rapture, so just take me. Make me yours."

He started to help her with her sweater and hold her arms at the same time. Perhaps they should've stopped at a glass or two, because she was more than buzzed; she was trashed. His first hint was her dirty talk rumbling out her mouth. He carried her to the bed. "C'mon you. I think it's time to get into bed before someone falls." He smiled at her coyly.

Tapping her finger to the tip of his nose, Rainie said, "By all means,

Michael, I don't want you to fall. Come to bed with me. You know what went through my mind after grace?" Michael locked his mouth to hers; he knew where the conversation was going, and even though he didn't think the guest quarter was bugged, he wasn't chancing Rainie expounding on the mystery murder.

"Come on, Michael, bring out your mighty soldier to play. I need ransacking and ravaging." She reached for him, but he turned quickly, telling her he promised not to disappoint, but he needed to get his shoes off and get himself ready for bed. "Fuck that, just whip it out. Give me what I want, now." She put on a well-overdone pout. She writhed on the bed in all her nakedness, making a mess of the bed linens. Rainie put a finger to her lips in a most seductive manner and grasped her breast with the other hand. "You're gonna miss the party, Michael. I've just gotten started revving this engine." She moved the hand from her breast to the delicate strip of ginger tufts leading between her legs. "Ooh, Michael. I'm so hot for you."

He chuckled. "You, my woman, are a hot mess, but you're mine and ravage you, I will." He crept into the bed, with force, he quickly slid her body toward him. "I think you're completely shit-faced, but I'm going to make sure you remember getting nailed come morning. You'll know I pleasured you to insanity." With a half-crooked smile, he raised her leg, lightly biting the inside of her thigh while attending to her wet and begging lush bits. He was a commander of his prowess, bringing her to revelry time and time again. He knew her desires and her body well and that soon he'd hear her cry, "No more," and then he'd take his need and desire, fulfilling her expectation with deep, crushing thrusts followed by a robust release flooding her sated body. Their intimacy was beyond description, and drunk or not; she was the most sensual being he had ever encountered. As she snuggled next to him, he lightly ran his fingers along the side of her face. "Your skin is like petals of a flower, so soft and almost satiny. You bring out my fiercest desire just by being you. It's nothing you say, it's just you and your natural, raw sensuality." He kissed her fingertips. He turned out the sidelight.

The room was pitch black. Rainie whispered, "Michael?"

"Yes, Rai. What's up?"

"I haven't heard or felt Rand in a long time. It's weird, and I miss her, even though she was bitchy as all hell. I thought we patched it up. Oh, and I didn't remember your friend's eyes being golden."

"Contacts, my love; otherwise, they'd be dark as soot. Regarding Rand, I wouldn't worry. She loves you and isn't far from you ever. Trust in that. Good night, my love."

"Good night, Michael. I love you, and I hope you're right about Rand." She snuggled closer to him.

The following morning was beautiful, with bright blue skies. A few billowy white clouds floated high in the sky. After bundling up, they stood at the edge of the property, looking down a hundred or more feet to the water directly below, which was beautiful but terrifying at the same time. The view was spectacular, and Rainie pulled out her phone for a few pics and a selfie with Michael.

From a distance, they heard a bellowed "Good morning, friends." Mateo had even changed his gait, Michael noticed. He had more of a spring in his step, whereas, before, his gait had been more fluid, as though he'd glided across the floor; now, he was like a plain guy from a backwoods country town. "What an adventure I have for you today. Unfortunately, Noelle will not be joining us because the baby is due very soon. Too bad it is not whale watching season or hiking in the Canyon Sainte-Anne. Truly, you must visit sometime in May through the summer, even into September and October. Mike, make a point of bringing the family during those times. What an education, but today we will go hiking if you two are up for it. They walked up to the house as Noelle was heading down.

Noelle was dressed warmly in a heavy coat with a woolen cap and muffler to match. Even with the hat, her long dark hair whipped around her face, catching in her eyelashes. Rainie couldn't help but notice how young she appeared. She figured Mateo had to be near fifty, if not in his fifties. He lovingly greeted her with a sweet kiss and took her hand. Through a bright smile and thick French accent, she spoke. "Will is taking us to the best breakfast around. Then you go on adventure. This time of year, most closed." Breakfast, indeed, was delicious and full of lively conversation and was one of the few places open year-round. Mateo was doting over Noelle, perhaps making up for all he'd missed in his first marriage, and enjoying every minute of his freedom and new unencumbered life.

As they parted company with Noelle, Rainie offered to go back to the house with her. Inside she was screaming "no" to hiking in what felt like sub-zero temperatures. She was more than delighted at the thought of a warm fire.

"C'mon, where's your sense of adventure, Rai? We will only go a short distance." Michael took her hand, pulling her to him.

Mateo said he understood, and that it had taken him some time to adjust to the different climate. It was such a contrast to where he'd lived before. Reluctantly, she agreed to go. While she had to admit to the beauty and that she had warmed up with the hiking, after two hours, all bets were off, and she was ready to head back to the house. "Rainie, we have a hot spa connected to the house. You will warm up quickly. Poor Noelle is at the point where she can do nothing but wait for the little one, enjoy a good meal, read, and watch her programs on the television. I have acclimatized to the coldness, and it makes me feel robust and alive." Mateo balled up his fists, as though taking a muscle-man flex pose. Then burst into laughter. The two men chatted during the hike about nothing in particular and yet everything. Subjects varied from Louisiana politics to American politics to the thought of being a father at Mateo's age. Rainie wanted desperately to ask him about his previous wife and children, but knew he had chosen to close the door there, and who was she to try and pry it open?

When they got back to the house, Mateo brought them into what he called the spa room. It was like a hothouse, with steam rising from the whirlpool. To Michael's and Rainie's surprise, their host discarded all his clothing and sunk into the water, letting out a peaceful sigh. Michael, while a bit timid initially, started taking off his clothes. She looked at him with an expression saying, not gonna happen.

What the fuck? Just how friendly does he want to get?

Michael saw her reaction and asked if Noelle might have a swimsuit or shorts and tee shirt for Rainie to wear. She was easy to read—her eyes opened wide, and she got an unpleasant smirk on her face, and he knew her stomach was twisting in knots.

"I am sorry, my dear, if I made you uncomfortable," Mateo said.

"It is usually only Noelle and myself, so I did not give it any thought. Please accept my apology." He called to Noelle, who beckoned Rainie inside. The young girl grinned and handed her a bathing suit that was more like butt floss and two minuscule fabric triangles, barely enough to cover her nipples, attached by thin cords to tie the material in place. Rainie donned the suit, grabbed some towels, and, along with Noelle, joined them in the hothouse; although Noelle could not enjoy the water, she seemed delighted with the company. Rainie giggled to herself, wondering how Michael would feel being in the buff with Mateo's young wife sitting by watching, perhaps even enjoying the view. Michael was a most handsome specimen of a man.

After twenty minutes, Noelle went inside to start preparing a meal. Michael took the opportunity, jumped out in all his nakedness, toweled off, and had his clothes back on in minutes. Mateo took his time, threw his clothes over his shoulder, and padded into the house naked as a jaybird. Rainie, whispering under her breath to Michael, said, "I hope he puts something on for dinner, or I don't think I can sit at the table with a naked man." She'd had enough of people, they were weird, and all she wanted was Michael.

Finally, walking to their dwelling, she added, "I don't want to offend you, but this has been a strange experience. Mateo, Will, whatever, all I want is you. He's a nice guy, and if I didn't know the whole story, I'd think he was a throwback to the hippie days, our parents' time. He has literally let it all hang loose. The only cock I care about is yours, and, boy, it was a show I didn't want to see. Now, because you made me go on the hike, my calves are still tight, and I could use a massage. Hint! Hint!" Michael pulled her in closer as they walked arm in arm.

Once inside, off came the clothes, the massage began, and like with most of their massages, the body heat kicked in, and they were off to the races. Not missing a beat, they were all over each other—caressing, fondling, exploring, and gratifying. Michael's prowess had not diminished over time, and his goal continued to be all about her pleasure. He had a plethora of sexual innovations, and never ceased to amaze her.

The following day flew as they drove back to the city after bidding farewell to Will and Noelle. Once in Quebec City, they spent two nights at Fairmont Le Chateau Frontenac. It was the crème de la crème, and even though they basked in spectacular accommodations, dined on gourmet meals, Rainie was ready to be back home.

☙

There was nothing like being home. The squeals of the kids upon their return were nothing short of legendary rock star material. The children's effervescence was contagious. While it was a most active night and all the tales of excitement during their absence were regaled, eventually things began to settle, and bedtime finally arrived.

"C'mere you," Michael said and drew her into his arms. "I love you, and while it wasn't a typical what-one-might-expect kind of getaway, being with you is all that matters." The closeness between them was undeniable. With a fist full of hair, he pulled down, tipping her head back slightly, exposing the entire length of her neck, one of his favorite canvases to paint with kisses—only surpassed by her tempting lips. He kissed her deeply with every ounce of passion he had, but after a minute, her body suddenly went limp. She completely collapsed in his arms. He laid her on the floor. She wasn't breathing, so he dialed 911, then proceeded to perform CPR, all the while begging for her to wake up, to breathe, not to leave him. Tears flowed down his cheeks, but he tried to stay strong and in control as he compressed her chest and blew what he hoped was life breath into her lungs, but her chest wasn't rising, her heart wasn't beating. "God no, no." He shook her harder, calling out to her, begging her to breathe. Her pulse was absent, and no matter what he did, he couldn't start her heart. At the top of his lungs, he yelled, "Rand!" And with this plea, Rainie drew a deep, rattled, and gasping breath. He felt her carotid artery, and her pulse had returned, however, unnaturally bounding, but she remained unresponsive to his cry. "Rainie, wake up. Oh, God, help us."

The EMTs arrived, starting oxygen and an IV. Michael tried to explain what had happened, but it didn't make any sense, and they didn't understand. They heard he kissed his perfectly healthy wife, and she crumbled. They quickly transported her to the hospital. The nightmare was a blur of incomplete thoughts and unanswered questions. They ran every test imaginable, to no avail. No one could come up with a viable explanation. Without cause or reason, one of the techs noticed what looked like necrotic tissue in one of her lungs, not that something so small would've caused her breathing to stop. Michael held her hand and prayed. Her parents were inconsolable, but through their sobs, they prayed with him.

Eventually Rainie's pulse began to return to normal, as did her breathing, but nothing pulled her back from the abyss. After talking with the cardiologist, Michael remembered the two episodes Rainie had told him about. While all the tests, at the time, came back as "within normal range," Michael believed in his heart that it was a spiritual matter. He had called his parents, and they started heading his way immediately. After what seemed like an eternity, he heard them coming down the hall. He fell into their arms.

His mom had a determined look on her face, with none of her usual warmth. "Michael, you need to get a grip. Rainie is going to be alright, do you hear me? Draw on your faith. I want to spend a moment with her without any other buzz going on. I think I can get her to respond. Do you trust me?" How many times had he said those exact words to Rainie? And all of those times, he had always been correct. He nodded.

Missy went to the bedside, held Rainie's hand, and closed her eyes. She stayed by Rainie, silent for over half an hour, and then a look of peace came upon Missy's face as a single tear rolled down from her eyes. Missy left Rainie's side and moved next to Michael, encouraging him to step away from everyone else. She whispered to him, making sure no one else could hear. "It's between the sisters, sweetheart. The best way to explain my understanding is they are saying goodbye. Rainie doesn't want to let Rand go; you must talk to her, Michael." She held his hand.

Everybody stepped out of the room to give him a moment alone. According to the doctor, there was no telling how long she would be unresponsive. Michael pulled up a rolling stool and spoke in a whisper. "Rainie, I know you can hear me. Mom says this has to do with you and Rand, and if that's so, you need to come back to us—to me, the kids, and your parents. It's not your time to check out, and if Rand is ready to go, you need to give her permission. Tell her it's okay and that you will be okay, because you will. Rainie, do you trust me? Everything will be okay, and one day, not this day, but one day y'all will be together again. You have to let her go, and you, my love, need to live." Tears trickled from the corners of her eyes, wetting the pillow beneath her head, yet she remained unresponsive.

Hours passed, and it was a constant stream of Rainie's parents, then Michael's, but he wouldn't leave her side. He held her hand and rested his head next to her. His eyes were swollen and red, and he was exhausted. His heart literally ached as though crushed, and his breathing would hitch as he tried to retain control. What good would he be if he fell apart? He'd be of no use to the kids, and he had to stay strong. His mom had said Rainie would be okay, and she had never let him down before. Why did he think this would be any different? It wouldn't. He didn't get the gift, as she called it, but he knew it was real.

☜☞

"What's happening to me?" Rainie asked Rand in a hollowed echo of a voice.

They stood facing each other, with their hands pressed against each other. "It's my fault, Rainie, and I'm sorry." They laced their fingers. "After watching Samantha and her fooling around with the boys, I got angry. I didn't get the chance to be a teenager and watching Sam just reminded me of that. For years, hanging in the corners of your mind was enough. To hear you laugh, cut up with Mer, and be a crazy teenager. I felt like the three musketeers, and my being there never felt wrong; it felt right and okay."

Rainie shook Rand's hands, so they both swayed. "It felt right because it was okay. I'm scared Rand, I feel hollow and empty, and I miss my husband and kids. Am I dying? Please tell me no. I'm not ready."

Rand looked down, taking her gaze off of Rainie. "No, but almost." Rainie reached out to Rand lifting her chin. "I almost killed you; I didn't mean to, Rainie; I just wanted to have a real kiss like the kind you get from Mike. I practiced a couple of times to dwell in you, ya know, to feel again, but it doesn't work that way. Rainie, I don't want to leave you, but it's time for me to go to Heaven for good. I know we'll be together again. You have to live, raise your family, be there for Momma and Daddy, and grow old with Mike. Just dream of me sometimes and tell your kids about me. I love them, and I love you, but I can't do this anymore. I need to be with God. Wake up, now; your family needs you. Let go, Rainie. Please let me go."

Rainie squeezed Rand's hands. "Are you saying it's my fault you are here? Because I've held on and not let you go?"

Rand shook her head. "No, not always. At first, I wanted to comfort you, get you straight, and stop you hurting Momma and Daddy, but then I loved being with you and Mer. Then when you started doing bad things, I felt I had to stop you, but now, right now, it's you not letting go. Please let me go and wake up."

"I'm sorry, Rand. I didn't realize. Go to Heaven and be with God. I'll miss you, but I'm okay, besides, it's not like it's forever. I will be with you again." The vision of Rand and the feeling of her hands slowly drifted. All Rainie could hear was the most beautiful music, but it was different; it was beyond comprehension. Rand turned toward the heavenly sound, and Rainie watched as the vision of her sister walked away, and then in a blink, Rand was gone.

෨෩

He heard a faint whisper. "Michael." With a flutter of excitement, relief, love, and a whole jumbled mess of emotions, he raised his head, looking toward her face. Her dramatic ice-blue eyes smiled at him with a look of hope and promise. "I've missed you. Rand and I said goodbye; I had to let her go. She will finally rest in peace."

EPILOGUE

Not a day goes by that I don't think of Rand. When I look back on how she chose to stay amidst the hell of my impertinence and recklessness, constantly trying to lead me along the straight and narrow, I'm overwhelmed by her love. I must confess, I find myself studying the mirrors, still in anticipation of seeing that something extra, but she is truly gone. Had Michael not experienced many of the Rand moments, I would have thought myself crazy and willfully living in delusion, but she had been there trying to coax and guide me...a job I wouldn't wish on my worst enemy. I am and will be forever grateful.

And in keeping with truths...life goes on...and it did in a big kind of way, with blessings of abundance. Michael and I grow closer every day, and with each passing moment, I feel more and more blessed. Our numbers have increased, and all told, Michael and I have another two children, giving us a whopping five-child family...never in my wildest dreams, but wow, they are amazing little people. We figured out the dilemma and put a television in our bedroom! While Michael recently turned fifty and I (his much younger wife, ha, a mere forty-four) have never lost the insane chemistry that draws us into passionate oblivion—and may that continue until we draw our last breath.

Our love transcends well beyond my dreams. Michael, handsome as ever, looks even more sophisticated as his hair has silvered slightly at the temples, and perhaps mine would have changed with time, but with state-of-the-art products, my colorist makes sure my hair stays the deep auburn of my youth. And while Michael continues to boast about plans for retirement, those plans have yet come to fruition, although we manage to globe-trot on many occasions with our small tribe. Thank God for Zeke, Charles, and Jonathon...did I mention the practice is growing exponentially?

Momma and Daddy, the epitome of love, continue with their Friday-night dates and a full social calendar, although I've noticed Momma starting to show her age. Daddy's sharp mind prevails as his body slowly consumes his strength, but when their time comes, I know I'll be good and handle it with grace. Sadly, we've lost Jack from a massive heart attack. To this day, I can hear him calling me his Rainie-girl. He was a fabulous man.

John, his wife, and their two boys live on the plantation. Michael and I giggle, knowing full-well John will get his comeuppance as both kids are John-esque. Time will tell, but I'm looking forward to the show. Oh, I forgot to mention he married Dominique, and they keep watch over Missy; however, there's no mistaking Missy rules the roost, which John and Dominque accept. Missy doesn't age, period. Jack's death hit Michael hard, but the main concern they had was whether Missy would be able to move on from the heartbreak, but she's maintained her strong resolve.

My sweet Mer is a great mom, and Paul, while surrounded with nothing but females, rolls with it. He's adept at tying the perfect hair bow and creating ponies without lumps and bumps. While feistier than Mer ever was, at least openly, her girls are great friends to McKay, and I see many years of besties ahead. Oh jeez, that spells trouble. McKay, being the only girl, is surrounded by brothers. The two older keep a protective watch over her, but she manages to harass her two younger brothers, driving them to distraction, but that's our devilish daughter. Oh, and yes, she most definitely has my laugh. I had no idea how loud and obnoxious it was...but it is what it is, right? Thomas is strikingly handsome, and still God's gift to the sporting world. Henry, my gentle, loving soul, is wicked smart and the observer of the family. Chase is much like Henry, smart and demure, and then there's Jack, big, broad, with a personality and manner reminiscent of his namesake.

As predicted, we've grown away from Pandora, and piece by piece, the once studio of delight has turned into lovely sleeping accommodations for our incognito friend from the frosty north. At first, it felt daring, but William LaSalle has become a frequent visitor and known to some of the residents of the French Quarter as the friendly old French hippie. With a yellowy gray braid down his back and faded low-slung jeans complete with worn holes, he looks the part. He strolls the streets in his Birkenstocks, no matter the weather. One would never link the once formidable cartel boss with this eccentric older man. Occasionally, if we catch him early enough, he has yet to put in the colored contacts, and his ebony eyes glitter with mischief. Sometimes Noelle and Francois come in tow, but usually not. I often wonder if, by chance, he's up to something, but that's not my business.

I remember well the day the newest television reporter graced the screen. Ryan, my once-upon-a-time-way-too-young love interest is still precious and has grown into a most handsome man. His face will achieve greatness in the television news world; I have no doubt. I can't help but wonder if he still jams to the Stones doing the horizontal mambo while toking on a doobie.

Detective Marse did indeed retire and move to Covington, away from the madness of the city, just a mere forty-five minutes from our home. He is very much our friend and comes to many of our family barbeques and get-togethers. Yes, our lives are blessed and beyond. And, well, that's about it...life has marched on, and I'm happy and grateful.

Hey, y'all, thanks for listening to my story, for loving Michael and all the people that have graced my life, and yeah, I'm still out there a bit, but, trust me, Michael reels me in when necessary. I'll think of you, and don't ever forget that I wish you love above and beyond. It's been real, y'all!

Many thanks...

To God for granting me the Serenity to accept the things I cannot change, Courage to change the things I can, and the Wisdom to know the difference.

To my husband, Doug, who has stood by my side, giving me the inspiration to press on and for loving me beyond all measure, thanks are not enough. You, my love, inspire me.

To my kids, for being loyal supporters and venturing to read the books separating Mom from Author. I know it had to be harrowing at times. Y'all are the best fan club ever!

To my readers for following the story, loving Rainie and Michael, and spreading the word building a broader readership, thank you, thank you.

To Mark Malatesta who encouraged me and taught me some of the ropes of the publishing industry.

To the fabulous editors who have kept me in line and the story in sync. Julie Mianecki, a compassionate touch and an eye for detail. I still think she's Editor Extraordinaire. Where would I be without Paige Brannon Gunter? She has walked with me through the entire trilogy, loved my Rainie, helped me with adolescent Rand, and explained to me that not everyone likes chocolate ice cream.

To Gene Mollica, who designed the perfect covers for the trilogy and listened to my every wish. Just for the record, his specialty is urban Fantasy and sci-fi, and he has designed the cover art for several New York Times bestsellers. Hence, it was out of his wheelhouse for my happily-ever-afters, and he excelled beyond measure.

To Cyrus Wraith Walker, patience with a capital P—thank you for all the hand-holding, and as before in the other two books of the trilogy, the interior formatting came out perfect.

Leaving a review is always appreciated, thank you.

About the Author

Born and raised in the enchanting city of New Orleans, the author lends a flavor of authenticity to her story and the characters that come to life in the drama of love, lust, and murder. Her vivid style of storytelling transports the reader to the very streets of New Orleans with its unique sights, smells, and intoxicating culture. Once masterful event planner, now retired, she has unleashed her creative wiles in the steamy story... *Half Past Hate.*

CPSIA information can be obtained
at www.ICGtesting.com
Printed in the USA
FSHW011003011221
86556FS